I0611202

The Wicked Earl

MJ Coyne

First published in Great Britain as a softback original in 2020

Copyright © MJ Coyne

The moral right of this author has been asserted.

All characters and events in this publication, other than those clearly in the public domain, are fictitious and any resemblance to real persons, living or dead, is purely coincidental.

All rights reserved.

No part of this publication may be reproduced, stored in a retrieval system, or transmitted, in any form or by any means, without the prior permission in writing of the publisher, nor be otherwise circulated in any form of binding or cover other than that in which it is published and without a similar condition including this condition being imposed on the subsequent purchaser.

Typeset in Dante MT Std

Editing, design, typesetting and publishing by UK Book Publishing

www.ukbookpublishing.com

ISBN: 978-1-913179-86-1

Cover photos:

Jesalous Wall © Jonjames1986 – creativecommons.org/licenses/by/2.0/deed.en

Duel © Mike H – shutterstock.com

The Wicked Earl

To my wife and best friend *Angela*, a big thank you for all your encouragement at a time when you were battling serious illness and continue to do so. Your strength is my strength. I love you Xx.

References

The Belvedere story
Belvedere house and gardens
From wicked to wonderful – The Irish Times.
The Earl of Belvedere by Denis O' Neill.

Introduction

In 18th century Ireland a beautiful young woman is accused of adultery and is incarcerated for 31 years by her obsessively jealous aristocratic husband, The Earl of Belvedere. When the full extent of his cruelty reached the public domain, he became better known as *The wicked Earl.*

Robert the Earl of Belvedere accused his wife Mary of being unfaithful to him, naming his youngest brother Arthur as her suitor. The evidence having been supplied by Robert's other brother George one year his junior, the reason for his treachery shall become apparent, but the bitter family feud that followed can only be described as dark and disturbing.

This interpretation is a combination of historical data, innuendo, rumour and a generous dollop of fiction. All anyone can say for certain is, Robert Rochfort did not inherit the title of the Wicked Earl: he earned it.

The first mention of the Rochfort family is the year 1216 when a family of French nobility named "de Rupe-Forti" settled in Ireland. The family name was hyphenated at the time as it represented the joining of two wealthy aristocratic families. The house of de Rupe now Roche and the house of Forti now fort. So was born the family name Rochfort.

The Rochfort family were given the Gaulstown estate by royal decree in the year 1216. This was the year after the signing of the magna carta Libertatum, also known as the charter of the liberties. This was a charter agreed by King John of England, at Runnymede near Windsor on the 15th June 1215. The document was first drafted by the Archbishop of Canterbury, the intention being to make peace with the unpopular King John and a group of disgruntled Barons. It promised the protection of Church rights, also protection for the Barons from illegal imprisonment, access to swift justice and limitations on the amount of tax taken by the King.

The charter was to be implemented by a council of 25 Barons but neither side upheld their commitments and the charter was annulled by Pope Innocent the 3rd leading to the first Barons war. Nobody wanted this war and soon members of the nobility were trying to negotiate between the warring parties. One such man was Peter de Roche, the Bishop of Winchester and for his part in the negotiations that eventually brought King John's son and heir Henry the 3rd to the throne was awarded a large swathe of land in the County of Meath in the heartland of Ireland. After the partition of Meath in the 16th century and the boundary changes that followed, the Rochfort family lost part of their Gaulstown estate but gained the magnificent Belvedere estate on the shores of Lough Ennell now situated in the County of Westmeath.

Chapter 1

Robert Rochfort as a young boy instinctively knew he would inherit the lands from his father George the First Baron of the exchequer and sitting member of parliament for the County of Westmeath. If Robert were alive today the sudden deaths in his family would without doubt have been investigated. The Rochfort family home, Gaulstown Hall, was a magnificent manor house guarded by a moat that had long since relinquished its relevance, no longer fortified as the need to defend itself against marauding bands of thieves was long gone. Now grass grew where water once offered protection. The gate lodge at the entrance to the estate stood behind two large black iron gates; high on those gates the words "In Deo Speramus", in god we trust. The lodge came with the much sought after position of gatekeeper but a more accurate job description would have been general handyman; however, the fact that a home came with the job made it one of the more attractive positions at Gaulstown. For now, the lucky holder of the coveted position was Fergus Kane, a tall, slightly built man with large green eyes that seemed to look through you. He was married to Shona, a local girl, and they had two young daughters, Clare, three and Jane, two, both too young to take up employment at the big house thus fulfilling their destinies. Fergus' duties were many fold; guarding the gates was by far his most important duty but he was also required to work in the grounds of the walled gardens at busy times throughout the year. On such occasions his wife Shona would stay close to the gates while maintaining the many flower beds that welcomed all to Gaulstown.

The long avenue weaved its way to the main hall, a well-worn track with furrows that bore witness to the legions of traffic over the centuries. Every now and again through gaps in the trees, the visitor was teased with a tantalizing glimpse of Gaulstown Hall in the distance. The last one hundred yards of avenue leading to the entrance was surfaced with gravel and loose stone, all sourced from active quarry works on the Gaulstown estate. The avenue was lined on both sides with a variety of evergreens, from pine Montereys that can grow up to one hundred feet tall to the smaller pinion pine interspersed with spruce and the classic Cyprus twist.

The Baron loved this time of year; he would often take one of the bay mares for a trot along the avenue especially in early spring and summer when the warm sun encouraged the sap to rise, blending the scent of spruce pine with freshly cut meadow the resulting perfume intoxicating his lordship's senses; on such occasions he was often heard to say: "Ah! nature at its most beautiful."

Gaulstown Hall was rectangular in shape with a concealed inner space that served as the family's private garden. Built in classic English style, a castle in all but name. Two turrets, one on the east wing, one on the west, where flags emblazoned with both family crests gently fluttered on a soft summer breeze most distinctive against the bright blue sky. In front of the main entrance was a large circular island covered in seasonal plants; in the middle stood a large statue of Kratos, the Greek god of strength, power and sovereign rule.

Sixteen bedrooms were situated on the two upper floors, eight on the west wing and eight on the east wing, plus a ground floor and basement. The top of the house mainly comprised small attic rooms; most were empty, used only on very rare occasions. The entire household believed the top of the house to be haunted – there were numerous reported sightings of ghosts fitting the descriptions of long dead ancestors still prowling the empty halls; a good reason not to venture up those narrow stairwells.

The first floor consisted of eight large bedrooms lavishly furnished with the latest French imported fashion ideas; these rooms were used by members of the family and those closely related. Each wing had a large suite reserved exclusively for visiting dignitaries. The ground floor had the usual array of rooms, all sumptuously decorated. From the drawing room situated on the west wing one could walk along a narrow corridor with high ceilings past the study then on to the library. From there through a low narrow passageway that can only be described as a tunnel, no more than six feet high and eight feet long – everyone ducked on entering, even Mrs Doolin, the cook, and she was only five feet two inches in height. This led to a larger hallway that took you past the music room and on to the large parlour. The entire household referred to the parlour as the "family room". Past the parlour was a large single oak door leading to the vestibule which in turn introduced you to the vast half-moon shaped entrance hall.

This space was a semi external space, the walls were painted a silver grey with the explicit intent to discourage anyone from loitering there too long. The seating was intentionally sparse without any soft furnishings, and in the centre of this vast area hung a candelabra chandelier fashioned from deer antlers and held in position by a gold braided rope threaded through a series of hooks imbedded in the ceiling and down the wall to a point where a male member of staff could release the rope and lower it for cleaning. The imperial oak staircase consumed the entire central area, the first flight rising to a half landing then dividing into two symmetrical flights both rising with an equal number of steps with turns leading to the next landing.

Behind the staircase and recessed in the back wall were three sets of double oak doors, two of which led to the veranda that overlooked the inner garden. This was an immense space filled with various plants and shrubs protected from the worst of the elements but still allowing access to sunlight for the more discerning plants. The double doors furthest to the right led to the main hall where in medieval times the entire household would sleep while the master and his family slept in the dais; today it was used mainly for functions like weddings, balls and the odd recital.

On very rare occasions like Christmas, especially when the boys were young, the family would take dinner there, although that tradition stopped a long time ago partly because the family could not stay in the confines of each other's company for very long and the fact it was bloody cold even in summer.

The main hall was a large rectangular open space; in the middle of the long wall to the right-hand side was a very small oak door, five feet six inches from the cold stone floor to the top of the arch. The fairy door the boys called it for as long as they could remember. Above was a row of high, narrow stained glass windows depicting scenes from the First Barons' War and when observed from the high table the scene can only be described as magnificent. The first window contained predominantly yellow and red glass, on one side the Barons with swords drawn, on the other the Crown forces. The second window in green and orange depicted Pope Innocent the 3rd wearing the Pope's Mitre and holding the warring parties apart, the third in shades of blue and yellow depicting two hands clasped together in friendship, the fourth in greens and yellows depicted the classic sign of peace – two white doves with olive twigs in their beaks. Then to the gable wall. The largest stained-glass window in Westmeath, bigger than all the other windows put together, incorporating most if not all the colours of the rainbow, the scene portrayed the young King Henry kneeling to receive the crown from Robert Rochfort's ancestor, Peter de Roche. This was a display of status in brilliant technicolour there for all to see and admire.

Through the fairy door one entered the small chapel with just enough room to hold a large family and no more. The minister would only turn up for service when requested as a regular service would not suit the Baron's busy schedule.

Below stairs and directly beneath the great hall was the kitchen; Mrs Doolin the head cook/housekeeper and matriarch liked to call it "The heart". At each end of the kitchen was a cupboard with ropes and pulleys that allowed the kitchen staff to serve both the great hall and the dining room at the same time if required. Attached to the large kitchen was the pantry, accessible through a small oak door like the fairy door but with one crucial difference: it was designed to keep pilfering to a minimum. It was reinforced with iron cross members plus a combination of locks that were meant to keep everyone out; the only other member of the household allowed to have a key was the head butler, James Clarke.

Mrs Doolin was in her late thirties now, but when she had taken up employment as a kitchen maid, she was only fourteen years old. Over the years Aideen Doolin was transformed from a wee slip of a girl into everyone's trusted agony aunt, 'wedded to the dammed place' she often sighed. On rare occasions she would pay a cursory visit to her only living relative, a brother who lived in the village; it was the only time she would part with her beloved pantry keys saying, "I can't be in two places at the one time".

Leaving the kitchen pantry, one entered a corridor that mirrored the one upstairs. The most important room on this corridor was a large anteroom used by members of staff, but there was a strict protocol as Mrs Doolin always sat nearest the potbellied stove in winter and the large open window in summer and woe betide the poor soul that fell foul. Along the corridor past four large staff bedrooms, one for the female staff and one for the men, each with six cast iron beds, another smaller room for Mr Clarke's sole use and one for the staff of visiting dignitaries; each of the larger rooms could sleep up to eight. Most of the household lived in on weekdays, some in turn acquired permission to visit family members in the village of Rochfortbridge at weekends.

Past the bedrooms was an array of smaller rooms mostly used for storage, then on to the corridor's end and the last remaining room that everyone tiptoed by, Mrs Doolin's bedroom. Her room was situated at the end of the hallway by design, next to a large solid oak door with two large slap bolts and one dead lock. The door led onto the courtyard and was for the explicit use of domestic staff, but this door had a dual purpose depending on Mrs Doolin's mood. Lock em in or lock em out.

The village of Rochfortbridge derived its name using a simple formula. First there was Gaulstown Hall on one side of the river Derry, home to the influential Rochfort family planted by the English and barely tolerated by the native Irish. On the opposite side was the village, a simple row of artisan cottages plus the obligatory ale house, accessible only by bridge. Its very survival in the beginning depended on the estate – most if not all its residents worked at the hall in one capacity or another, at one time or another, not that they loved the Rochforts but because they needed the Rochforts to survive.

1727 Robert Rochfort at the tender age of twenty was on the cusp of a great adventure and as he stood at the entrance to Gaulstown Hall he surveyed the mature rolling countryside that seemed to blend with the horizon and thought, 'all of this will soon be mine' and as the entire household assembled on the entrance porch a warm sun bathed all. The reflected sunlight on the tree-lined avenue seemed to dance from leaf to leaf, tree to tree, instilling a feeling of wellbeing especially in the Baron – after all, he was killing two birds with one stone for the separation of mother and son would be a relief to all at Gaulstown.

"Robert, your carriage is ready," announced the Baron.

"Yes, Father," replied Robert as he made his entrance onto the porch. He gave a cursory glance in the direction of the servants then fixed his gaze firmly on his father George, took two steps forward, shook his hand and said:

"Goodbye Father, I shall do my utmost to enhance the Rochfort family name," then bowed his head. He then turned his attention to his mother, Lady Elizabeth Moore as she insisted on being called. Robert proceeded to kiss the back of her hand and whispered, "goodbye Mother" but in his mind added the proviso 'good riddance'. He then turned to his younger brother George, took his hand and found the response to his manly handshake weak, more in line with the Judas he was destined to become. Disappointed, he turned to his youngest sibling Arthur and found his grip to be somewhat more sincere.

With formalities over, Robert made his way to the waiting carriage where Rose and Thorn, the two bay mares, were getting a little impatient in what was a warm sun, unusual for early-May. Robert placed his left foot on the small stirrup step, causing a slight ripple effect, a sway of the carriage, in turn a swish of tails and a flash of black mane from Thorn. This created tension on the leather reins reminding the driver, Patrick Cleary, of his duty to keep the situation under control. 'No need to worry' thought Ned Flanagan, the footman, for downstairs had a pet name for Patrick and that was safe hands.

"Woo girls," commanded Patrick in a low confident voice, enough to calm the situation.

Robert settled, facing both the driver and his destiny with reserved excitement while Ned Flanagan made sure the door of the carriage was firmly shut – as far as he was concerned Robert Rochfort would not be getting out again, at least not here and not today. 'Good riddance, ya dangerous little bollocks,' thought Ned.

"Giddy up," commanded Patrick Cleary as a couple of blackbirds sang their sweet song only to be interrupted by the ugly squawk of a single crow watching proceedings from the turret on the east wing. "Must be an omen," muttered Ned under his breath and as the carriage wheels started to gain some traction the sound of loose stone bereft of solid foundations appeared in some small way to foretell the fragility of Robert's future, including the unknown dark events that would in the end consume the Rochfort dynasty.

As Robert's carriage made its way along the tree-lined avenue, the same trees that for centuries stood like sentinels, a soft breeze encouraged the herbaceous perennials among the pines to gently sway, as if presenting a guard of honour for Robert as he left the confines of the Gaulstown estate. As his carriage meandered along the avenue it resembled a snake seeking out its prey, the kind of prey that would feed Robert's intense hunger for power.

When almost at the gate lodge Robert could not resist the urge to glance over his shoulder and gaze one last time at the magnificent splendour that was Gaulstown Hall. He noticed that everyone had left the stage except for the still squawking crow.

It was now Patrick Cleary's responsibility over the next four hours to deliver Robert to his Majesty's port of Waterford where the steamer Athlone would ferry Robert across the Irish Sea and join the maritime route up the river Avon and on to the infamous slave port of Bristol. The journey from Bristol to London was a precarious one – almost the entire Gaulstown household secretly harboured dark thoughts of highwaymen ready to end the life of the future Earl. That was not to be, as two gruelling days later punctuated with a stopover in Winchester at a coach inn called the Bulls Head, Robert arrived safely at his destination. The significance of Robert's stopover was not lost on him for the name Winchester was branded on his soul for it was here in Winchester that Robert Rochfort's ancestor Peter de Roche presided over his flock and from Winchester etched the name Rochfort in both Irish and British history.

It was almost dusk as Robert's carriage came to a halt outside the lodgings Baron George Rochfort had arranged in advance. The same rooms he himself used on official visits to London in his capacity as Baron of the exchequer and sitting MP for the county of Westmeath.

The five-storey townhouse was indeed a mansion, situated just a stone's throw from the heart of the British empire and the seat of real power, the Monarchy. Great Collage Street boasted a row of red-bricked terraced houses with large leaded windows, some of which seemed to trace an angle of forty-five degrees. Robert deduced the reason for this visual imbalance was a stairwell, as it was repeated three or four times over the entire row of houses.

The surrounding stucco work portrayed a level of craftsmanship you would come to expect in such a distinguished part of Westminster and as a gentle mist began to fall, Robert stood for a moment surveying the impressive scene that was blossoming before his eyes. With no manservant to take his trunk, Robert enlisted the help of the young coach driver who had safely negotiated the journey from Bristol to London. With his belongings stacked on the entrance porch, Robert thanked the coach driver; he in turn tipped his cap in receipt of the few copper coins and said "good night, sir", while under his breath muttered "miserly bastard".

Robert slowly raised his cane to eye level, the serpent-shaped handle with its split tongue glinted in the dim light as Robert delivered a couple of robust knocks to the large brass plate, then waited for what seemed like an eternity.

The descending mist was getting heavier and began to reflect a strange almost surreal light that seemed to bounce off the worn street cobbles below. Robert was in no mood to wait any longer than necessary and just as he raised the snake's head for the second time intending to strike hard, he heard the rattle of keys on the other side of the door and as it slowly opened, a warm orange glow from the candelabra flooded the entrance, adding an air of melancholy to an already dream like scene.

"Good evening, sir, Robert Rochfort I presume, glad to see you have arrived safe, welcome, my name is Charles, I shall be at your service for the duration of your stay," at the same time pulling on the servant's bell cord. Almost at once two young footmen appeared from the direction of what was the entrance to the basement and the servants' quarters. Charles instructed the footmen to take Robert's trunk to his lodgings.

"This way, sir."

And after three flights of stairs Robert sighed, "At last for my energy has deserted me."

One of the footmen enquired, "Have you a specific time for your morning call, sir?" to which there was no reply.

"Good night then, sir."

Still no reply. Robert was already walking toward the window. He seemed transfixed; probably the reason he did not notice the servants take their leave, or maybe it was plain old arrogance. Robert suddenly felt energized; sleep was now on hold as he strained to gaze through a small pane of uneven glass, one of many individual panes supported by lead cames.

When he got close enough to touch the glass with his nose, all he could see was his own reflection staring back at him, and as his eyes began to adjust a faint outline was beginning to form. Slowly he began to recognize the unmistakable outline that was the Palace of Westminster shrouded by a ghostly light emanating from the many oil lamps that surrounded the cradle of democracy. Robert now in a dream-like state suddenly realized he was talking to himself mumbling the words "democracy"; 'it's absurd,' he thought, 'how any two incompetent illiterate fools could outvote a genius'. He began to imagine the mist as a fog, shimmering as it crawled through the streets of London, caressing the cobbles like some sort of medieval plague intent on bringing death and misery to all in its path. 'Maybe this is what it was like for my ancestor Peter de Roches all those years ago around the time of the black death,' he thought. Robert poured himself a brandy from the cut-glass decanter, took a large cigar from the box provided and slowly raised it to his nose, inhaling the sweet aroma. Striking a match created a rather odd reflection of himself in the uneven glass that now separated him from the cool night air. 'How appropriate,' he thought, 'a ghostly image to match a ghostly view' and between sips of brandy tinged with the taste of the excellent cigar, Robert gazed across London as far as the mist would allow. After some time, he raised his glass and gave thanks to his beloved ancestor Peter de Roches.

Chapter 2

The Baron George Rochfort stood looking into the mirror not recognizing the older man staring back at him. Chuckling, he thought, 'I may not be the most handsome man in Ireland but I am one of the wealthiest' as he held his midriff in with a firm hand, then smiling he dismissed his reflection with a wave of his hand. Just then Lady Elizabeth entered his quarters and he wondered if she had heard his comment or noticed his dismissive wave. He quickly engaged his wife in conversation.

"Elizabeth, have you finalized arrangements for the visit of our good friend Jonathan Swift?"

"Not quite, George, it's on my list of things to do, but first we must arrange George Junior's place at agricultural college, plus Arthur's registration at Trinity; only then will I have time to accommodate your request. What about you?" snapped Lady Elizabeth. "Why can't you arrange Jonathan's visit?"

"I must be in Dublin for a parliamentary meeting, Elizabeth. It could take some time; I have commitments."

"You have excuses, George; I did not literally mean tonight; never mind I shall take care of it as I always do."

Changing the subject, the Baron continued. "You mentioned George, may I suggest Multyfarnham College, it being so close to Gaulstown, George could blend the theory of estate management with the practicalities without having to travel."

"Yes that was my thinking also, you are not completely useless after all," groaned Elizabeth.

'Roll on Dublin,' thought the Baron, 'peace for a few days' then continued the conversation. "Arthur will start his business studies in September I assume," hoping for a more civilized answer.

"Yes, Trinity, it's in the process of being arranged" was the curt reply. Maybe it was the fact that Lady Elizabeth Moore was in her own right a member of the nobility – she was, after all, the daughter of Henry Moor, 3rd Earl of Drogheda, who had encouraged Lady Elizabeth to feel superior to most and inferior to none. The fact that her father, the 3rd Earl, was a drunk, a womanizer and a compulsive gambler were of little importance in aristocratic circles. Elizabeth was almost six feet tall and seemed to tower over her husband, giving the aesthetic impression of a mismatch whenever they happened to pose together mostly at official functions the Baron always felt inferior. Did they ever love each other? Maybe, they were not particularly attracted to each other at the beginning although Elizabeth was considered to have a pleasant face but undeniably no beauty. Their marriage was arranged, of course, as were most if not all aristocratic marriages of the time and for the usual reasons: wealth, status and prestige. But all those years ago when they were both young, in their prime, a more powerful natural force assisted Elizabeth to conceive, the omnipresent lustful desire.

After the birth of their fourth child in as many years it started to diminish with fervour and in time was replaced by inertia, first manifesting itself with separate beds then separate bedrooms and now almost separate lives – except for the interaction with their children or household staff they may never have spoken again.

She loves me she loves me not
He cares for me does he not
In separate rooms we lie awake
To ponder in darkness
Our greatest mistake

Lady Elizabeth did not take alcohol very often and for good reason: it simply did not agree with her. Every now and again Elizabeth would forget her many promises to the Baron and drink a little too much; every time that happened the same old stories resurfaced and tonight was one of those nights. Elizabeth knew she was breaking the rules but could not help herself – the frustration seemed to build up over time when that happened, she just had to let off steam.

"George! Remember the time when Robert was twelve years?"

Not allowing her to finish, the Baron raised his voice: "Stop this instant, Elizabeth. I thought we agreed never to speak of it again for pity's sake," as he instructed James Clarke to take the remaining alcohol from the room. She did not even notice James take what remained of the brandy – now bolstered with alcohol she was determined to recall once more the time Robert took a six-inch bradawl from Patrick Cleary's toolbox and set about exacting some form of retribution for the family's cat's perceived lack of respect.

"I will rip your heart out," cried Master Robert as the cat began the long climb up the narrow stairwell on the west wing, with Robert close on his heels, shouting profanities all the way to the top of the house then along the empty corridors.

"Come here, you vicious creature, you will never scratch me again, I promise you that, come here, you vicious creature." Loud echoes bounced off the naked walls and combined with the scratching sound of extended claws trying in vain to gain traction on the bare hardwood floor. The commotion made such a racket even the servants in the basement heard the disturbance.

As the commotion was emanating from the top of the house some thought the evil spirits had found a way to cast off their eternal chains; in a way, they were right. Pursued by Robert, the terrified cat made a fatal mistake: seeing an open door it turned into one of the small empty rooms just under the turret on the east wing. With no escape Robert slammed the door shut with force shouting, "got you". Out of breath and out of patience, Robert stood and stared with eyes that lacked compassion. The feline sensing the mood, took up the classic defensive pose, arched back, claws extended and hissing loudly. Robert stared directly at the cat as he took up the classic attacking pose, but before the cat could strike in its defence and run, Robert lunged forward, driving the bradawl through the top of the cat's head with such force, he pinned it to the floor.

Lady Elizabeth did not even notice the Baron take his leave – he had heard it all before and did not want to relive it all again. Later that night when they were both worse for wear the Baron and her Ladyship had a massive row.

"Why would you want to recall that story again, Elizabeth? I will never understand. We agreed never to speak of that episode again," added the Baron.

"Yes, George, but we also agreed never to discuss the rape or his attempt to drown his own brother. I could go on."

"Elizabeth please, why do you insist?"

"I cannot answer your question, George, for I feel bad enough as it is; maybe I needed some support – god knows I get little enough from you," she shouted.

The memories of such evil acts perpetrated by her eldest son were constantly playing on her mind and every now and again she just had to vent her anger. She felt truly alone in her torment for she now looked on her son Robert with suspicion and at times even fear; it left her promising herself never to touch a single drop of alcohol ever again. The rape was too dangerous to discuss under any circumstance, alcohol or no alcohol; that was one story her Ladyship never dared discuss and her Ladyship was not the only member of the household to feel this way – just ask Edward Flanagan, better known as Ned below stairs. He had begun his service at Gaulstown when he was just nine years old; his mother had had no choice but to offer him and his sister Bridie into service up at the big house – it was their only chance to stave off hunger and desolation after their father died at the age of thirty-two.

He had laboured on the land all his life including the Gaulstown estate so their fate was sealed. Over the coming years both Ned and his sister applied themselves to their work with diligence for there was always someone waiting in the wings ready to take up any position that became available up at the big house. When Bridie turned eighteen, she left the service of Gaulstown to take up similar employment at nearby Middleton Park House. Ned, on the other hand, was content to continue in service at Gaulstown. He had completed his apprenticeship and was quite happy to cement his position as footman on the Gaulstown estate. Bridie was in love with one of the young gardeners at Middleton Park – the reason she had taken up service there in the first place. She went on to marry Sean, her first love, and had one child, a daughter they called Sarah, but tragedy struck when her young husband died of consumption one year after they married.

With a newborn, Bridie was surplus to requirements at Middleton and was forced to return to her home village of Rochfortbridge where she lived with Ned in his small artisan cottage. Ned decided that it was best for all if he took on the responsibilities of this ready-made family and decided never to marry but instead to devote his entire life to looking after his sister and her beautiful daughter Sarah.

As the years passed, they looked like any other family trying to make ends meet under the harsh conditions that prevailed at that time. After years of meagre existence things again took a turn for the worst – the one-story Lady Elizabeth was determined not to discuss, the rape. At the time it begged the question: how far should a parent go to protect their offspring? They were sorely tested on that very point after Robert cornered the young chambermaid, a twelve-year-old girl from the village, while she carried out her duties in one of the bedrooms. To make matters infinitely more serious, the young girl's name was Sarah Flanagan, Ned's niece. When the news of the rape leaked out, it took the combined physical strength of both Patrick Cleary and James Clarke to physically restrain Ned, preventing him from doing something he would certainly regret.

But now six years had passed and some memories were beginning to fade; however, for Ned the events of that fateful day were as vivid as if it happened yesterday. Not only did he lose his sister to melancholy he also lost his only niece who Ned considered his own flesh and blood – in his world he was Sarah's father in all but name and over the next few weeks he had had to suffer in abject silence while her Ladyship and the Baron planned to have Sarah and her bastard child banished to the colonies, some say Van Diemen's Land.

The entire domestic household were left in no doubt that if any one of them were heard discussing the incident as it was widely referred to, instant dismissal was the price they would have to pay. To this day it hung over Gaulstown like a black veil.

Chapter 3

The day after their argument

"I want to apologize for my behaviour last evening, George. I intend to curtail the amount of alcohol I consume in future."

"Where have I heard that before? Let's not speak of it again, agreed?"

"Agreed," answered Elizabeth. In the cold light of day and sober, she was quite happy to discuss anything other than her son's potential for both violence and depravity.

"What time do you intend to leave for Dublin?" enquired Elizabeth.

"Five pm, the carriage journey takes four hours approximately, but the clouds look heavy. I fear we may have some rain."

"Will you stay in Dublin tonight?"

"No, I intend to stay in Swords."

"Perfect opportunity to invite the Viscount – he and Jonathan could keep each other company on the carriage ride down to Belvedere."

"I shall make the necessary arrangements this very night – you can cross that one off your famous to-do list, my dear." Then he scurried for the door before Elizabeth had time to formulate one of her acidic replies.

Five pm. The Baron greeted Rose and Thorn with a juicy red apple each; his lordship always performed the same ceremony before every journey for as long as he could remember.

"Be good girls and let's make this journey a safe one," as he stroked Thorn's long black mane. "Patrick, let's make good time. I would like to arrive at Viscount Molesworth's home by nine pm if possible."

"Yes, my lord," replied Patrick as he wrapped the woollen blanket around his legs, the one Mrs Doolin had instructed Ned to place on the hard-wooden bench seat that Patrick would have to endure for at least four hours with just one scheduled rest stop in the village of Maynooth on the way; it promised to be a tiring journey as light rain began to fall. The Baron's carriage arrived at the entrance to Brackenstown House, the Viscount's country residence in Swords, a suburb of north County Dublin. The manor house was situated on a demesne and considered to be one of the finest houses in Ireland. It was almost dark as Patrick exhaled his usual command to stop "woo girls", then climbed down from his soggy perch and stretched his legs to encourage the blood to flow more freely, then knocked softly on the carriage door.

"You awake, my lord?"

"Yes, I presume we have arrived at Brackenstown," as he flipped the lid on his newly acquired toy, one of only a handful in Ireland, his Abbe de Hautefeuille timepiece saying, "perfect timing".

"Yes, my lord, we made very good time."

Just then the entrance door opened and the Viscount greeted his friend.

"Welcome, George, you must be famished after your journey; refreshments await in the parlour."

"Thank you, Robert, that would be most welcome."

"Don't worry about Rose and Thorn; Thomas will see to it they are watered and fed."

"Thomas, before you see to the horses please take Patrick to the servants' quarters for refreshments," added the Baron.

'Thank god,' thought Patrick.

"Come, George, time for that brandy, how long has it been?"

"Almost two years, Robert."

"Let's not leave it so long next time."

"I mean to discuss that very issue with you, Robert. I have a proposal you might be partial to," answered the Baron.

Viscount Molesworth proceeded to usher the Baron to the parlour, a magnificent room fifty foot by twenty-five foot, large enough to accommodate a grand piano, four leather chairs, two four-seater leather couches and a selection of baroque furniture including three half-moon tables. Along one wall stood an ornate hardwood cabinet, probably oak, in classic French style, displaying two expensive vases and a candelabra. The African oak floor, what you could see of it, was polished to a high sheen and on top lay a hand-woven Turkish carpet fused with the brilliant vibrancy of what appeared to be the entire range of primary colours, unveiling a floral pattern that would please even the most discerning eye. The ceiling was high, approximately twelve foot and covered in ornate stucco work; the craftsmanship was exquisite. The ceiling flat beds were painted a soft olive green that was complemented by the brilliant white of the stucco work. Gold leaf adorned the egg patterned cornice and in the centre was a large chandelier fashioned from rough steel that was pummelled into shape by the village blacksmith and painted black; it resembled an upside-down bluebell.

The walls were covered in hand printed wallpaper incorporating subtle shades of green foliage to match the ceiling beds. Strategically placed works of art added a depth of warmth and sophistication. The eyes were then drawn to two high recessed windows with wood panelled shutters from ceiling to floor enveloping most of the wall facing the demesne.

The pelmets were big and bold, covered in a soft primrose yellow material, probably silk; the design on the drapes mimicked the design on the Anatolian carpet and stopped just two inches from the floor. In the centre of one wall was a large half-moon mahogany table with four half-moon drawers expertly inlaid with a brass thread that weaved its intricate pattern throughout, giving the impression it was seeking a place of refuge. On top stood a bronze bust bearing the likeness of Robert Hooke, the English Philosopher; on either side stood matching Chinese vases on plinths of Grecian marble, again with a soft green floral pattern in keeping with the general theme. But wait a minute.

"Who is this?" enquired the Baron. "This can't be Mary."

"Yes," replied the Viscount, "don't they grow up quickly?"

"How old are you now, Mary?" enquired the Baron. Mary was sitting at the family piano playing a classical piece by the Russian composer to the Empress Elizabeth Grigori Nikolayevich Teplov. Mary interrupted her practice as she stood and offered her hand.

"Twelve, my lord."

"My my, how you've grown in two years and so accomplished for such a young lady," added the Baron.

"Oh! Please, your Lordship is far too kind," answered Mary.

"Your brandy," interrupted the Viscount.

"Thank you, Robert." Then turning to Mary once more. "Please Mary, play some more, that was quite wonderful," encouraged the Baron as just then Lady Jane Molesworth entered the room.

"Ah! Lady Jane, lovely to see you again; it's been far too long." A warm embrace ensued.

"Come, let's sit by the window, gentlemen, and catch up on all the news from Gaulstown."

Chapter 4

George junior second born was named after his father as was the Rochfort tradition. He had just completed two years of a three-year course at agricultural college and to everyone's surprise seemed to be enjoying the experience; however, that fact alone would not alleviate the feelings of jealousy he harboured towards his older brother for the realization that Robert would inherit everything and he would not would not go away – it meant he would always be Robert's subordinate and forever indebted to him. No matter how hard George tried to suppress his negative feelings they were always there bubbling just under the surface. The transition from boy to man only amplified his feelings of resentment and with the passage of time his urge for revenge only grew stronger. George often recalled occasions when a young Robert displayed his true nature. One occasion stood out: it happened when Robert was thirteen years old, one year after killing the family cat and three years before he raped Sarah.

The three brothers were catching pinkeens in a rock pool they had created on a small tributary of the river Derry using embroidered linen they had pilfered from Catherine Murry's linen cupboard, then stretching it over a circular piece of wire plundered from Patrick Cleary's workshop. The result was a net of sorts in which they hoped to catch millions of the small fish and it worked a treat: the evidence was there in the preserve jar, all twenty-two of them. Everything was well that day until Robert became bored, shouting, "Does anyone want to see a fish swimming in a circle?"

"What do you mean?" asked George.

"I mean this–" then proceeded to rip one of the pectoral fins off the pinkeen then placed the tiny fish back in the pool, at the same time laughing excitedly at the pinkeen's obvious distress. Arthur was paying no attention; he was at the other end of the pool. George could not understand how Robert could take so much pleasure from such a cruel act saying, "You are cruel, Robert; I shall tell Mother what you have done."

Robert's response was instant – pouncing like a crazed animal he grabbed George by the hair and forced his head under the water. Arthur, on hearing the commotion, looked up to see the wild look on Robert's face. He immediately dropped everything and ran in a state of panic. Robert didn't notice Arthur run – he was too preoccupied trying to drown his brother. Then in a flash Robert let go his vice-like grip and with vacant eyes watched George as he scrambled to the riverbank coughing, spitting and running at the same time.

George never did tell a living soul for fear of Robert's temper and Arthur went straight to his room fearing Robert had drowned his brother.

For one so young Robert had displayed his trademark ability to change personalities in a split second. As time went by George learned to live with the memory but he would never forget the level of violence involved. But life must go on and at this moment in time George was more preoccupied with the enormous challenge of managing the entire Gaulstown estate comprising one thousand four hundred acres, some in tillage but pasture and parkland dominated. The Baron left George in no doubt, if he was to be trusted with the management of the estate he would have to excel at college. George fully understood his father's expectations and so far had proved more than capable, gaining excellent grades in all subjects, proving to his father he was up to the challenge.

The estate had one of the largest herds of Angus beef in Ireland, numbering six hundred, a herd of non-native fallow deer numbering eighty-seven give or take a few, for no matter who or how many attempted to count the herd they invariably came up with differing numbers. Finally, a flock of sheep two hundred and twenty strong; the herds all grazed freely on the estate which meant a large workload for any manager. George knew he had the best herdsman in Ireland in Joseph Brophy; and in Michael Clancy, he was confident Gaulstown had the best farm manager, but George still worried about the enormity of the task ahead. Gaulstown has the best labour force, the most fertile land, the best beef and lamb plus access to some of the best fishing and hunting in the whole of Ireland – 'what could go wrong?' he thought.

Arthur was the youngest of the siblings and at no time did he ever covet the title or lands, he was quite prepared to let his two older brothers joust for position; Arthur was determined to live his life as stress-free as possible. On turning twenty-one Arthur would receive a monthly salary plus a drawdown on his inheritance every five years; substantial amounts of money were involved, as far as he was concerned his future looked rosy indeed. Arthur's only passion was reading and at every opportunity he would seek the comfort of the vast Gaulstown library. Maybe it was the perceived warmth – he felt a warmth that seemed to emanate from the oak and ash shelving that consumed this enormous room, from floor to ceiling, wall to wall, the entire space was filled with the combined intellectual genius humanity had to offer, forged on paper and bound in leather from the Greek philosophers to William Shakespeare and all in between, it was all here, right here at his fingertips.

He would spend hours perusing the large volumes of classical works and liked nothing more than lounging on his favourite baroque couch strategically placed in front of the large bay window that overlooked the estate, and from time to time he would lift his head from the reading material to appreciate the spectacular views of the rolling countryside that attempted to mimic infinity.

Such a serene view. It was hard to imagine that only a few years earlier Arthur's grandfather Lt Col Prime Iron Rochfort had been involved in one of those dark events that were buried deep in the bowels of Gaulstown. Arthur had found correspondence in a secret compartment hidden behind a section of shelving he had discovered by accident while searching for a volume of works by Sir William Darcy, who for many years held the office of Vice-Treasurer of Ireland. Arthur intended to peruse a volume written by Sir William, the Decay of Ireland, a movement for political reformation in Ireland, but instead discovered writings that described the downfall of his ancestor Lt Col Prime Iron Rochfort. Stated in print, the Colonel challenged his fellow officer, a Major Turner, to a duel that was staged on the grounds of Gaulstown Hall. But sometime later it was discovered that the charge in Major Turner's pistol was tampered with and after a lengthy trial Lt Col Rochfort was found guilty of his murder and executed in May 1651 just before the birth of his first son Robert, a sign of things to come perhaps. Arthur was very proud and disturbed by his discovery – shining a light, however faint, on a period in Gaulstown's history that everyone wanted to keep buried might not be in his best interests. True to his nature Arthur replaced the offending documents in their place of rest.

Chapter 5

London

Robert had completed two years of his three-year course at King's College London in what he termed intense study; feeling a sense of accomplishment Robert had no misgivings about the next chapter of his life and was planning to enjoy it. King's College was a prestigious seat of learning in 18th century England – members of the nobility were drawn there like sperm to the egg, survival of the fittest, a mantra repeated over and over in Robert's head plus the fact that at any one time you were guaranteed to rub shoulders with some of the most powerful this great nation had to offer including Royalty. He gained excellent grades in all his studies except Latin – quite boring and of no significant relevance he thought. At twenty-two years of age Robert felt it was time to sample the abundance of pleasures this great metropolis had to offer – after all, he was in London, the epicentre of life on earth, for those with wealth and status that is, but for the less well-off it was hell on earth. That fact was lost on the aristocracy for in their opinion the peasantry was placed on this green and pleasant land for no other reason than to serve the Aristocracy, their masters; a filthy necessity was the common conversational thread in aristocratic circles.

Gaulstown

Mrs Doolin was busy preparing the evening meal of home reared prime beef for the exclusive pleasure of the Baron and her Ladyship; the rest of the household would have to make do with her famous Irish stew. The ingredients of this masterpiece comprised four to five pounds of lamb stewing meat, mutton to be precise, cut into substantial chunks with onions, parsnips, carrots, potatoes, stock from the master's prime beef roast, sugar, salt, pepper, bay leaves and fresh basil sourced from the estate gardens.

The smell of mutton stew wafting from her kitchen never failed to entice Barney the Irish wolfhound and it took a lot to shift the big lazy lump from his favourite spot under the wooden stairs in the courtyard. How he could smell the mutton from such a distance baffled Mrs Doolin as it never happened at any other mealtime.

Mrs Doolin took great pride in upholding the Rochfort tradition of domestic staff never eating from the same menu as their masters – mind you, on mutton stew days downstairs were the winners. Mrs Doolin knew better than to break the rules; her Ladyship would often visit the kitchen unannounced to make certain she was keeping with tradition, like this morning for instance. Ned was indulging himself in one of his unofficial tea breaks with the full agreement of Mrs Doolin – she often got bored listening to the silly chatter of the kitchen maids and when she wanted to hear some real news, like what was going on outside of her kitchen on the estate, she would invite her favourite to keep her company while she cooked. Ned was just the man to keep the housekeeper up to date with events.

"Ah! Me favourite mutton stew," said Ned, as he entered the kitchen holding his large nose high in the air to inhale as much of the aroma as possible.

"I could smell it all the way from the low pasture, Mrs Doolin."

"I know when you're after something, Ned Flanagan."

"Honest the god, Mrs Doolin, it's not a word of a lie."

"Mind you," added Mrs Doolin, "it's hard to tell you two apart at times."

"Whah me and Barney sure were the spit of each other," laughed Ned, "twins."

The kitchen maids loved the banter Ned brought to the kitchen but Mrs Doolin liked Ned for lots of reasons; in her opinion it was his forthright attitude – that man is as honest as the day is long she would often say.

"Christ," yelled Ann Quinn, one of the parlourmaids and daughter of Patrick Quinn, as she rushed into the kitchen in a state of panic. "Her Ladyship is on her way." That news meant a certain roasting if her Ladyship caught Ned in the kitchen at this time of day, a roasting he could do without as he raced past the pantry door and out onto the courtyard.

"Good morning, Mrs Doolin, may I see the cuts being prepared for dinner this evening?"

"Yes, my lady," as she led her to the pantry where her Ladyship inspected the cuts and made just one comment: "continue".

"Yes, my Lady," replied Mrs Doolin and as soon as her Ladyship had left the kitchen Ned poked his scrawny head around the courtyard door.

"Is she gone?" But before he could chide Mrs Doolin she threw whatever she had in her hand in the direction of Ned's big head only to see it drop at his feet. Ned picked up the offending item that happened to be a carrot, blessed himself and thanked god it wasn't Mrs Doolin's favourite knife. Relieved, Ned took a bite from the carrot and seeing his ever-ready grin Mrs Doolin couldn't help herself.

"Jesus, Ned, you look more like Barney every day."

This brought laughter and much appreciated light relief to all.

"Come in and finish your tea, ya big eejit."

Ned and Mrs Doolin had a unique bond, especially after what happened to his niece maybe in a different time or a different life they might have married. In their off-duty moments they could be seen chatting in the kitchen till the wee hours discussing both current and past events, some good and some not so good. On one such occasion

Ned recalled the time some thirteen years earlier when he caught Master Robert spitting into her Ladyship's favourite pudding, one Mrs Doolin had left cooling on the pantry shelf. When Ned confronted Robert and told him he was going to inform her Ladyship, Robert replied with venom.

"Do so at your peril, Ned Flanagan, but before you go remember one thing, I shall be your master one day and you shall be my slave. Now go tell your story to the old witch, I dare you."

Ned could hardly believe this seven-year-old could be so wicked and felt compelled to report the incident. He decided to go through the proper channels and informed the head butler James Clarke. He reassured Ned that he would inform Lady Elizabeth and promised the appropriate punishment would be meted out. At the same time he warned Ned not to speak of the incident to a living soul.

But of course Ned did confide in someone: Mrs Doolin. She immediately threw the pudding into the bin and made a fresh one, saying no one need ever know. James Clarke never did inform her Ladyship, preferring instead to say nothing in the hope that Ned would forget the incident and the entire household could proceed in relative harmony. Only time would tell.

Chapter 6

London

Robert, despite his arrogant persona, had made some friends at King's College, two to be precise. Richard Lambert at twenty-three years of age was heir to the Earldom of Cavan, he was a tall handsome looking man with a facial expression that hardly ever changed. This appealed to Robert as he felt something comforting in a powerfully constructed face. Richard was on a parallel journey to Robert – maybe that's what facilitated their rather quirky friendship, for Richard was very happy to study hard and prepare for the day he would inherit the title "Earl of Cavan". He was not driven by the same demons that Robert undoubtedly was, but by a very strong sense of duty; that was the overwhelming force that spurred Richard on. But now two years into his studies he also agreed with Robert it was time to live a little and sample the forbidden fruits London had to offer. James Hamilton, on the other hand, was a bit of a cad, almost twenty-one, the son of Major General Christopher Hamilton, a veteran of many successful foreign military campaigns for which he now reaped the benefits.

The Major was held in high regard in Whitehall and for his long service to the Crown was bequeathed a magnificent estate in County

Kildare, just a three-hour carriage ride from Gaulstown. James knew he could never emulate the achievements of his father, nor did he wish to, and yet here he was going through the motions of becoming an officer in his Majesty's infantry. Deceit was a word that popped into his head now and again, but secure in the knowledge that he alone could access his inner thoughts thought, 'fuck them' – he was not prepared to give up his precious life for a German invader; instead he continued to do what he always did best, run with the hare and hunt with the hounds. James was prepared to settle for a gentleman's privileged position in society; he intended to live off his father's reputation and wealth. James Hamilton was six feet four inches tall, another handsome-looking man, but a couple of days after Richard introduced James to Robert he voiced his concerns.

"Are you happy with the fact that James has common blood running through his veins?"

"You are such a snob, Robert. James is after all a gentleman; you will grow to like him, I am sure, but if you still harbour such feelings when we complete our tenure then you don't have to see him again, ever."

"I accept your advice, Richard. I shall give it some time."

One week later

Richard was already at Robert's lodgings waiting for James to join them, primarily to discuss where their first serious hunt for the forbidden fruit should commence.

"Lieutenant James Hamilton," announced Charles.

"Good afternoon, gentlemen, I hope I have not missed news of any importance?"

"Not at all, James, welcome to the lion's den," said Richard.

"That sounds promising," answered James as he took his place on the only available seat by the open window. "I presume this shall be my seat for the duration of our acquaintance."

Richard smiled at James as if to agree with his assumption, but no such confirmation was forthcoming from Robert as he continued to stare into the empty fireplace as if hypnotized. James reached for the cigar box, deciding to help himself to one.

"What are you doing?" asked Robert, turning to look at James.

"Trying one of your fine cigars, Robert."

"You presume to be a gentleman yet you forget your manners; maybe that's how you conduct your affairs in Kildare but in my chambers you ask the host's permission before you take a favour."

"Let me apologize, Robert," then he pretended to replace the cigar back in its box for a moment. "I thought the cigars were meant to be smoked but if you have a more sinister use please do tell." James decided to elaborate, knowing Robert looked down on his common ancestry.

"Or maybe it's the fact that I am a mere commoner that you take every opportunity to remind me of that fact."

"No," answered Robert, "I was simply referring to your manners, James."

But James was not satisfied and continued.

"The Rochfort family may be one of the wealthiest families in Ireland, Robert, but until such time you inherit the lands and title you remain a gentleman just like me."

You could cut the tension in the room with a knife. Robert now suspected Richard of informing James as to the content of their conversation a few days earlier, if looks could kill. Always quick on his feet, Richard broke eye contact with Robert and directed his laser like gaze at James and said:

"That's quite true, James with one exception."

"What might that be?" enquired James.

Richard's reply, although said in jest, had a certain truth as he continued.

"Robert will one day be a Baron, I one day will be an Earl, but you, James, you will always be a cunt."

Laughter filled the room and any remaining tension quickly vanished up the chimney with the sweet-smelling cigar smoke and

Robert's snobbery.

With a wry smile Richard declared, "Now that we have become bosom friends we have two important issues to decide: first we must establish a name for our little cabal, second we must decide where we should commence our journey to debauchery. Gentlemen, ideas please."

"I have no idea," offered Robert still sulking and still harbouring suspicions that Richard had betrayed his confidence by revealing some of their private conversation. James, feeling the tension, decided to move the conversation along.

"Just stick a pin in the map, Richard, I am sure you will prick a cunt or two."

"A brilliant idea, James, but I have a better one," replied Richard.

"I propose Covent Garden as the location for our first foray into London's worst kept secret. I have heard so much about it I can hardly suppress my libido – what do you say, Robert?"

"I say the map has well and truly been pricked."

'Robert is still sulking,' thought James; 'I'm beginning to tire of his arrogant moods' and instead directed his attention to Richard.

"Covent Garden it is then."

"One last item on the agenda," said Richard. "Our collective name."

Robert now sensing Richard had also lost patience with him, decided it was time to join in.

"How about the aristocrats?"

Both James and Richard glanced at each other trying not to betray their inner laughter, James pretended to give Robert's suggestion some thought when in fact he was regaining his composure.

"A great idea," said Richard while averting his eyes to the floor as he answered, "but what we need is something original, spiritual even. Any other suggestions, gentlemen?"

"I've got it," shouted James.

"Well don't keep us in suspense," said Robert trying to make amends for his childish behaviour, attempting to prove he really was over his sulk as he started to pull on the bell cord shouting "champagne". Richard seemed in tune with Robert's thoughts and was already pouring three brandies while shouting "Proceed, James". James stood upright raised his glass and in a solemn voice declared: "From this day hence, we shall be known as the trinity." Robert and Richard enthusiastically stood, raised their glasses in unison and cried out: "TO THE TRINITY."

Covent Garden was a unique place, by day a bustling market with stalls selling everything from fruit to bric-a-brac of every description, but come the hours of darkness the garden was transformed into something very different, a place where both aristocracy and the lower classes were blended in a human stew. The Aristocracy used the cover of Drury Lane to conceal their true intentions and the lower classes didn't care who knew. Drury Lane was an extension of Covent Garden, a vibrant area consisting mainly of theatres and restaurants but with a slightly better reputation. Covent Garden, on the other hand, comprised mainly brothels that sold alcohol. Illegal gambling gave the impression of being everywhere and dog fighting was also prevalent up there with prostitution and opiates.

With such a seductive menu available, it was no mystery the vermin of London, both peasant and noble, regularly frequented this place – after all, rats like to rummage in the sewer and a sewer it certainly was both literally and metaphorically, the entire area was teaming with deviants of every denomination, all drawn there for no other reason than the exploitation of each other. The following Saturday was chosen to be the Trinity's opening night and when it eventually arrived they were blessed with a warm summer's evening. They got there early, four pm, just as the transformation from flea market to flesh market was getting under way.

"Let's find a good ale house," suggested James.

"The Shakespeare Tavern on the north side of the Piazza is a good place to start," offered Richard.

"Been here before, have we?" enquired James.

"Never, my good man, but I know someone that has," answered Richard.

"The Shakespeare Tavern it is then," agreed James and as the Trinity made their way through the masses they were accosted by all manner of pond life.

"Rabble," cried Richard as he tried to clear a path, but Robert was more forthright as he fended them off with a stiff jab of the snake's head while shouting, "Make way, you filth". The Shakespeare Tavern was almost full but through the thick smoke James could see a table that appeared to be free.

"This way, gentlemen."

Richard struggled to gain the attention of the landlord, but eventually succeeding he shouted:

"Three tankards of your best wine, landlord, if you please."

"Certainly, my lord, only the best for gentlemen such as yourselves."

Three more drinks in quick succession followed and as the evening grew darker the din of noise both inside the Tavern and outside on the Piazza grew even louder and bawdier. Robert was by now feeling the effects of the wine and could wait no longer.

"Gentlemen, I feel somewhat inebriated; is it not time to seek out and sample this forbidden fruit I have heard so much about?"

"What's the rush? Let's finish our wine then we can take a stroll through this famous garden, maybe pick a flower or two," laughed Richard.

Exiting the Tavern, the Trinity once again had to fend off approaches from all fronts, until James homed in on a young woman no more than eighteen years old. She was holding a bunch of red roses in one hand while waving a single red rose in the other.

"Buy a rose for your sweetheart, luvvie," she cried.

James could not resist and made his move.

"Good evening, young lady, may I smell your flower?"

"Certainly, my lord," as she gently placed the rose under his nose then looking directly into his eyes she teased. "For a mere shilling, my lord, you can kiss my rose."

"I may well partake of your exciting offer, my dear. What's

your name?"

"Anabelle, my lord."

"My sweet Anabelle, we the Trinity that appears before you require not one rose but three."

Richard, watching with interest, decided it was time to get involved in the conversation.

"Young lady, can you recommend a house of ill repute? It must have a well-stocked wine cellar, mind."

"Yes of course, gentlemen, please follow me, tiss just around the corner in Kings Street."

"How appropriate," laughed Robert as he enquired, "does it have a name this Tavern?"

"Black Betty's tiss called," answered Annabelle.

"Please lead the way, sweet Annabelle," cried James.

Annabelle skipped along in front intentionally imitating innocence as she dropped rose petals with a provocative slow sweep of her arm while at the same time pouting her bright red lips; the scene only intensified the Trinity's lust. Black Betty's was indeed a rough looking inn from the outside and even worse on the inside, the stale smell of beer mixed with thick smoke and what Robert described as cheap cologne, to which James replied:

"What do you expect, Robert?" Then recalling his earlier jousting bit his tongue. The Trinity managed to find space in an alcove under the stairs that led to the rooms above. The tavern was dark except for two foul smelling oil lamps that threatened to burn the establishment down; scorch marks on the low ceiling was evidence enough of that and the black slate floor only added a feeling of coldness. Black Betty's rooms were available to rent, not for the wary traveller mind you, but for the sole use of the flower girls and their clients. James gained the attention of what he thought was a young boy picking up the empty jugs but instead turned out to be a three-foot four inch fifty-year-old man.

"Yes, what can I get you, gentlemen?"

James, trying not to stare, replied, "Three tankards of your best wine, my good man," his voice barely audible over the din that was Black Betty's. The sight of lace bodice plus the intentional flash of flesh could not fail to instil great desire.

"Have I died and gone to heaven?" enquired James.

"No just gone to heaven," replied Richard and after a couple of hours consuming rather dubious wine Robert was feeling a little worse for wear as he reached across the table trying to touch Annabel's thigh, slurring his words:

"Let's have a look at your rose, girl."

Richard's intervention was timely as he gently took hold of Robert's arm to which Robert took great offence.

"What are you doing, Richard?"

"I meant no disrespect, Robert." At this stage James was tempted to intervene but thought better of it, deciding instead to blame the alcohol for Robert's discourteous actions. Richard need not have bothered as Annabelle was quite used to dealing with all manner of sinners.

"Not so fast, me lord," as she brushed his hand away, "first we must arrange a fee for me services like."

"Quite right, Annabelle," said Richard. "Shall we agree to open negotiations?"

Both parties agreed a fee almost immediately and with the financial details agreed, Annabelle took her leave to secure the services of two more girls. Robert continued to behave like the pompous spoilt brat all at Gaulstown knew to be the case, and Richard had to intervene one more time after Robert called for another round of drinks, shouting, "Goblin, move your disgusting form."

James attempted to calm the situation as he pleaded with Robert, "Please Robert, apologize or we shall be asked to leave."

Robert staggered as he raised himself off his seat, moving towards James until his face was only inches from his then raised his voice saying:

"Apologize? Have you gone completely mad, James? Let's get one thing clear: my name is Robert Rochfort, I will say what I like when

I like to whom I like." Then almost falling back in his seat while at the same time fumbling through his purse and taking two shillings out, he dismissively threw the coins into the spittoon at the end of the counter and turned to James.

"Is that apology enough, James? You see, everyone has their price, even that grotesque little man."

The dwarf was now shuffling his deformed body towards the spittoon, he seemed to interpret what was intended to be an insult as a compliment saying, "Thank you, my lord," as he sifted through the mess. The dwarf eventually retrieving the two shillings, equivalent to a week's wages and proceeded to wipe the phlegm from the coins on his already filthy sleeve.

"Don't forget to wash your hands before you serve me again, you filthy little man," added Robert.

The demon has taken up residence, thought Richard – an astute observation as Robert was not finished just yet. Slurring again, he directed his bile at James.

"If the landlord did not defend his employee, why should you, James?"

Stunned, James decided to make no further comment for fear of ruining what promised to be a "climax" worth waiting for. Richard on the other hand felt like strangling the little ponce but with great restraint he also held his temper and his tongue in check. When Annabelle returned she had indeed brought two more perfectly formed roses.

"What's your preference, ladies? Wine, ale?" enquired Richard as he beckoned to one of the girls "come here".

Robert was still in a cantankerous mood and interrupted once more saying, "Pay no attention to him, my sweet, come sit on my knee."

The young flower girl pretended not to hear Robert's request and sat on Richard's knee instead.

Robert with a dismissive wave of his hand just said, "Sit where you like then."

James now tried to pour water on the smouldering embers as he continued.

"What's your name, my little flower?"

"Mary."

Robert interrupted once more. "Mary, my sweet Tudor rose, we the Trinity shall follow tradition and name you "Mary-Rose". Do you like that name we have chosen for you?"

"Yes, my lord, tiss indeed a fine name."

"Would you know the significance of which I speak, Mary-Tudor Rose?"

"I don't know what you mean, my lord."

"I thought as much," chuckled Robert as he continued. "Without conducting an impromptu history lesson, my dear, let's just say you shall go down like your famous namesake."

Richard and James, while still livid with Robert's arrogance, had to laugh at the historical innocence displayed.

"You made a joke, Robert," laughed James, "a welcome change of mood I might add."

Robert raised his tankard in mock acknowledgement, spilling a little wine in the process. Fearing she might lose her lucrative arrangement, Annabelle decided to do whatever was required to concentrate minds on the task ahead and proceeded to raise her petticoat high enough to reveal a glimpse of stocking and just a flash of her most prized asset. It certainly concentrated minds.

"You have beautiful legs, Annabelle, are they twins?"

"Alas not, my lord for I've had a few in-between."

"Quite witty, would the Trinity agree?" laughed James.

Robert now behaving as if nothing inappropriate had ever happened joined Richard and James as they raised their tankards.

"To the Trinity."

"My name is Alice if any of you gentlemen are interested."

"What a lovely name, sweet Alice, are you feeling left out, my dear? Well don't, for you are mine tonight. Tell me, Alice, have you by any chance got a younger sister?"

Richard, realizing the direction of the conversation, stood and pointed to the ceiling declaring, "Heaven is this way, gentlemen."

That night the Trinity were baptized in the Church that was Black Betty's.

Chapter 7

Back at Gaulstown

Mrs Doolin was busy preparing a menu that her ladyship had suggested for the visit of Viscount Molesworth and Jonathan Swift: beef and lamb reared on home pastures; brown trout fresh from Lough Ennell, hopefully sourced by the fishing party depending on their luck. The Baron and her Ladyship stood at the entrance to Gaulstown as the carriage carrying the two dignitaries came to a halt. Ned dressed in his Sunday best offered his hand as support first to Viscount Molesworth who refused; in contrast Jonathan Swift smiled and said, "Hello Edward and how is the best gillie in Westmeath?" That small gesture made Ned feel ten foot tall.

"Gentlemen, welcome to Gaulstown," enthused the Baron. "This way, you must be famished after your journey, what time did you leave Dublin?"

"Very early, George. Jonathan and I prefer to travel in the hours of darkness with the specific intention of arriving early, we both love the mornings at this time of year," the Viscount replied.

"It makes rising that much more pleasurable. Refreshments?" Turning to Ned, he added: "See to it that his lordship's driver gets a hearty breakfast and take good care of the horses."

When Ned had finished the tasks allocated to him he immediately made his way to the sanctuary of Mrs Doolin's kitchen with the intention of scrounging a cup of tea and armed with that big grin he yelled.

"Good morning, Mrs Doolin, you're looking well so ya are, suppose an ould cup a tea is owada question."

"Don't Mrs Doolin me, Ned Flanagan, and you just out of your bed, still now that you're here ya might as well have one, go on sit down, ya useless fecker and ya better have a bit a news for me mind. Catherine, pour the ould divil a cup of tea, sure he must be parched after all the work he's done this mornin."

The girls in the kitchen could hardly suppress their giggles even though they witnessed sparring like this on a regular basis.

"Ah! That's a grand cup of tea, Mrs Doolin."

"Well I'm waitin, where's the news? Did the Viscount have anything to say?"

"Ta tell ya the truth, Mrs Doolin I don't think he knew I was even there, not a word of thanks from the poncey ould bastard."

"Now, Ned, I'll have none a that."

"Sorry, Mrs Doolin."

"Did Mr Swift have anything to say?"

"Mr Swift is a grand man, a proper gentleman, Mrs Doolin, he even remembered me name so he did, would ya credit that."

"Well you're right for once, Ned Flanagan, you can't bate a bit of manners that's for sure." A bell was now ringing, one of many spring bells situated just under the cornice. "Theresa, drawing room needs more refreshments, please see to it; off with ya, Ned, can't ya see we have work to do not like you ya idle git." With a sly wink she continued, "The next time you darken me kitchen door, Ned Flanagan, ya better bring me a bit of juicy gossip."

"Thanks, Mrs Doolin, that was a grand cup a tea so it was." Then he proceeded to swipe one of the steaming fresh scones resting to cool on the pantry shelf.

"Ya cheeky little fecker, honest the god one of these days I swear–" as they all giggled.

London

"Today could be the best day of my life," exclaimed Robert.

"That's a big statement, Robert, please back it up with some facts," encouraged Richard.

"Prince Frederick attended one of our lectures this morning. I find it incredulous you did not observe all the commotion."

"I was in the library for most of the day asleep," answered Richard. "I am still recovering from our foray to the garden of Eden, but I fail to understand how a visit by a member of the Royal family could be considered one of the best days of your life. May I guess what the subject of the lecture entailed?"

"If you must," answered Robert.

"The history of the German Monarchy."

"Be serious, Richard, this is important, we were looking at events relating to the period from the 12th to the 14th centuries and when I realised the significance of the dates I felt compelled, I had no choice but to interrupt proceedings."

"Why would that particular time period excite you so?"

"My ancestor played a significant part in the coronation of King Henry the 3rd in the year 1216."

"That's more like it, Robert, now you really have got my attention," as he raised himself from his chair saying, "I am all ears."

Robert excitedly explained. "When the opportunity presented itself, I had no choice but to embrace it with both hands."

"How did you instigate the introduction?" asked Richard. "And please tell why the dates are so important as I am still at a loss."

"All in good time, Richard, first things first. I stood and directed my attention directly to the Prince and said, 'may I be so bold as to address your Royal Highness directly?' and after a short pause Prince Frederick turned to establish who had the temerity to interrupt, then with a Royal wave he said, 'It better be important, proceed'.

"'Your Royal Highness, my name is Robert Rochfort and yes this is extremely important to both me and the entire Rochfort family as the years 1216 to 1220 falls within the period we happen to be concentrating on today, your Highness. My ancestor Peter de Roches was pivotal in bringing King John's son and heir Henry the 3rd to the throne in 1216, that was a year after the signing of the Magna Carta also known as the Charter of the liberties.'

"'I am acquainted,' interrupted the Prince.

"I offered my apologies to the future King and continued. 'My ancestor Peter de Roches was instrumental in bringing the warring parties together and promising to abide by the principles of the Charter, the peace that followed paved the way for the coronation of King Henry the third after the death of his father King John from dysentery that same year.

"'It was my ancestor Peter de Roches in his capacity as Bishop of Winchester that placed the Crown on the young King's head, a fact the Rochfort family are proud of to this very day.' I then directed a curtsy to the Prince, apologized once more for my rude interruption and waited for some sort of response."

"Quickly, man, what did he say?" enquired Richard, looking rather excited now.

"He waved his hand and said, 'What did you say your name was?'

"I replied, 'Robert Rochfort, your Highness'."

"'I enjoyed your interlude, Robert Rochfort, it made a boring history lesson bearable. Come join me, tell me all about your family I have a feeling we shall become good friends.'"

Richard Lambert, the future Earl of Cavan, was now standing with his mouth open as if frozen in time, eventually blurting out: "Destiny, Robert, destiny, you could not have engineered such a consequence in one million years. You never mentioned you had an ancestor with such a significant Royal connection."

"Now you know why I had to take the opportunity afforded to me."

"Yes of course, Robert, I agree with your assumption this is without doubt the best day of your life, to date I might add. I have a distinct feeling things will get much better now that you have made such an impression on the future King of England. We must inform

James at once."

"Yes of course, Richard, I shall instruct Charles to send a messenger immediately."

Chapter 8

Lough Ennell

B aron Viscount Molesworth and Jonathan Swift rode in the
lead carriage driven by Ned Flanagan. Patrick Cleary travelled
behind with the picnic hamper and fishing tackle. The short carriage
ride from Gaulstown to the hunting lodge on Belvedere took
approximately twenty minutes. The lodge was constructed from
walnut logs sourced on the Belvedere estate, set back on a hill to
encompass the best possible view of Lough Ennell – the result can
only be described as stunning. Standing on the decking one could see
the vast natural beauty of the lough six miles long three miles wide;
on a clear day the opposite shore was visible from Belvedere and the
Lough's ancient islands were complemented by the vast parkland that
surrounded this jewel, truly a place of tranquillity. It was a long walk
from the hunting lodge to the boat house on the shore, some three
hundred yards or thereabouts – guests almost always preferred to
walk rather than take the carriage ride along the rough bumpy path
and as they walked the conversation invariably turned to the topic of
nature and the natural beauty of the Belvedere estate.

"What a beautiful day," commented the Viscount. "I sense
the Ennell trout seeking a place of refuge at the very sight of our

approach."

"You have always underestimated the Lough Ennell brown," replied the Baron.

"Yes, Robert, I do seem to remember the last time I fished Ennell saying something similar and catching fresh air for my arrogance."

"Don't despair, your Lordship, your luck is bound to change," said Jonathan Swift. "What a wonderful clear view of the opposite shoreline; don't the people look tiny?"

This brought loud laughter from the Baron and Viscount Molesworth.

"They are three miles away, Jonathan," laughed the Baron.

Patrick and Ned were walking just behind carrying the fishing tackle and supplies including the all-important picnic hamper; they were also laughing at the reference to the tiny people.

"Yes, you can all laugh, but there is no denying they do look tiny!" when the giggles subsided.

"What is the name of that area I refer to just there?" pointing.

"It's called Lilliput," answered the Baron.

"What a magical name," replied Swift.

Ned and Patrick emerged from the boathouse in Old Faithful, a large rowing boat constructed from larch again sourced from trees that once grew on the Belvedere estate. Old Faithful would keep them dry for the next six hours or so depending on how hungry the trout were and how realistic the fly.

"Edward my good man, take us to the Ennell brown using your uncanny knowledge of this mysterious lough," requested Swift. Ned chuckling to himself thought 'if they only knew, most of the time it was pure luck'.

"What bait are we using today?" enquired the Viscount.

"The choice is yours, me lord, fly or grasshopper," said Ned.

Chapter 9

London

James Hamilton arrived at Robert's accommodation intrigued by his note with the promise of some very important news.

"Good evening, gentlemen. I got your message, Robert, sounds mysterious – pray tell what have I missed?"

"You inform him, Richard, while I wallow in my good fortune," instructed Robert.

"My pleasure," answered Richard, "but where to start? Robert has engineered an introduction to a very high-ranking member of the Aristocracy."

"I fear we may need your magic pin one more time, Richard," said James bemused.

"Put the poor man out of his misery," instructed Robert. Richard stood to deliver his synopsis.

"His Royal Highness the Prince of Wales…" then waited for James to react.

"One removed from the summit; I agree that certainly is high! You are full of surprises, Robert."

"I think you should hear it from the horse's mouth," said Richard and after Robert had relayed his story James' first thought was tread carefully, now that the fox had entered the hen house anything was possible. James now regretted recently reminding Robert of the fact that he did not hold a title, especially now that the Rochfort family had Royal connections dating back to the 13th century – the possible consequences of that fact coupled with such a significant introduction was indeed a serious advancement to Robert's ambitions. James could now smell a title and decided to proceed with extreme caution.

"Congratulations, Robert, but I fear this may spell the end of the Trinity," added James.

"Far from it, James," replied Richard, "for the Trinity are invited to the Masquerade ball at the Haymarket Opera House in two weeks' time, and that's not all. Robert has promised to introduce us to his Royal Highness Prince Frederick."

"I am at a loss for words," said James, his mind racing now as he grasped for a witty response. "A visit to the haberdashers then" was all he could manage as the Trinity dissolved into laughter.

Gaulstown/London

The Baron and Lady Elizabeth had decided it was time for Robert to marry. Their choice was Elizabeth Tension, the only daughter of a rich Dublin merchant with a reputation of transporting rather dubious cargo. The Baron informed Robert on one of his visits to London in his official capacity as Baron of the exchequer and MP for the County of Westmeath but Robert did not take too kindly to this.

"It's Mother's idea, I am certain of this."

"Robert, it was a joint decision. We both agreed it was in your best interests," explained the Baron.

Robert, raising his voice to match his rage, declared:

"Father, I am twenty-two years old; don't you agree I should have some say in relation to whom I will spend the rest of my life with?"

"It is the tradition, Robert, your Mother thinks–"

Robert furiously interrupted once more. "I knew it was the witch's hand that was stirring the cauldron," he screamed.

"Enough, Robert, enough. You will marry Elizabeth Tension and that's final."

Robert continued to argue with his father until the realization slowly dawned it was futile to continue with his objection. If he was to inherit the estate he would have to agree with his parents' wishes; Rochfort tradition would always prevail at least for now. Robert, although slowly conceding defeat, was at the same time plotting a path to his future success and in that surreal moment a calmness came over him. Even the Baron could sense that something fundamental had just changed in Robert's demeanour, something foreboding. Robert then began to speak in a calm, controlled voice.

"I shall submit to the witch's demands and marry this Tension woman, but please let it be known I do so under duress." At that precise moment the Baron feared for the future.

Lough Ennell

"Wow! This feels like a big one," cried Jonathan Swift as he shifted his weight from left to right trying to compensate for the bobbing motion of Old Faithful while at the same time pulling hard on the fishing line, desperate to land what he hoped would be a whopping Ennell brown.

"What bait are you using, Jonathan?" enquired the Viscount.

'What a fucking time to enquire about bait – can't you see Mr Swift is busy trying to land a fish you wanted to catch?' thought Ned. In both Swift's excitement and determination to land the fish he never heard the Viscount's question, pure concentration etched on his face. Ned decided to answer for him.

"Tiss a grasshopper, me Lord," as he ducked under the fishing line.

"The bugger has made his way under the boat. Move, Robert, quickly, my Lord." Just then the wily trout changed direction. 'I must not lose this fish,' thought Swift while releasing enough line to let the fish take the bait and run.

"There he goes, Mr Swift, now play with him, give him some

slack, that's it, let him run and tire himself out."

The Viscount interrupted once more.

"Did I hear you correctly, Edward: grasshopper?"

"Yes, me Lord–" while thinking 'sit down, ya fat bastard'.

"I thought we were using fly," replied the Viscount.

"Please sit down, your Lordship, we don't want you falling overboard. I'm sure I mentioned both grasshopper and fly, me Lord – did ya not see Mr Swift attach the blow line, me Lord?"

"No, I was too busy trying to tie this dammed fly."

"Well, me Lord, I have a selection of fly plus some grasshoppers I caught this very morning; again the choice is yours, me Lord."

"What are you using, George?" enquired Viscount Molesworth.

"Fly, Robert, maybe we should all use the grasshopper – it seems to be working for Jonathan."

Swift still feeling some resistance on the line but not enough to suggest the fish could continue the fight for much longer, now felt confident enough to instruct the gillie.

"Ready the net, Ned, time to land this beauty."

"Easy, Mr Swift," said Patrick.

"Thank you, Patrick." Just then a flash of silvery brown broke Ennell's surface, a spectacular sight.

"Nice looking fish, Jonathan, must be three or four pounds, a record for you I think, well done," commented the Baron.

"Let's wait till this bugger is landed, my Lord."

"Got ya," said Ned as he gently placed the net under the stunned fish. Applause echoed across the Lough to a chorus of well-done, me Lord.

"Please, gentlemen, refresh your bait for I fear one brown trout will not feed the top table this evening," encouraged the Baron.

"May I have the juiciest grasshopper you have, my dear man," requested the Viscount.

"I will take one as well," said the Baron.

"You, Mr Swift?" asked Ned.

"Fly for me, Edward, I shall continue to swim against the tide – it has served me well so far."

"We are drifting towards Croinis Island, me Lord," said Ned. "We have about an hour before we break for lunch. If it pleases your Lordship we can set a fire there for the ould cup a tea."

"Certainly, Edward, if Croinis was good enough for Saint Malachy surely it is good enough for us."

Bobbing along on minor waves, Old Faithful continued on its trajectory to Malachy's. Silence had taken hold of the entire fishing party each in a world of their own until suddenly the calm was shattered by a squeal. "Here we go again!" The Viscount was now muttering under his breath, 'not another one'. Jonathan was standing again, trying to negotiate the rocking motion like a seasoned angler as he chuckled, "two for me two for me".

"It's not landed yet, Jonathan, it's not landed yet," said the Viscount.

"You have done it once already, Mr Swift, concentrate, it's your day today" was Ned's honest advice. Encouragement was now being offered from all directions but again it all went over Jonathan's head as he pleaded with the fish to run and tire himself out.

"What fly did you use, Jonathan?" enquired the Viscount for the second time.

Ned noticed Jonathan Swift had not heard a word the Viscount had said and decided to answer for him once more.

"Grasshopper, me Lord."

"Oh! Yes, I remember now."

Patrick Cleary stood ready with the net, anticipating that flash of silvery brown and he did not have to wait long – there about six inches under the surface a flash of underbelly exposing the trout's weakness as the exhausted fish expelled what reserves of energy he possessed in one last attempt to escape Swift gently raised his rod high to help facilitate the landing.

"Ya beauty," enthused Patrick as another fine fish was landed to the obligatory chorus of applause.

"Perfect timing," said Ned as he engaged the oars. "Malachy's hideout it is then."

London

"What a night, Richard, I must say I did enjoy the Masquerade ball; do you know what struck me the most?" added James.

"The sheer grandeur of it all," replied Richard.

"No nothing so lofty but it felt like we were in a foreign country – most of the entourage were conversing in their native tongue. Quite disconcerting, don't you think?"

"Not in the least, James, they are German, after all," chuckled Richard.

"Yes, but to witness the future King of England scarcely able to converse in the King's English, it just felt strange, there must be an ulterior motive," insisted James.

"Why would you think that, James? I don't understand what you mean."

"I am not entirely sure myself, but I am certain of one thing: the passage of time will provide the answers."

"Out with it, man, for I fear your reasoning is somewhat more basic. Admit it, you don't like Robert."

"I never said I did not like him; in a strange way I find him intriguing like a puzzle, but at this moment in time I find it hard to extend trust where Robert is concerned," replied James. "There I've said it, there's something about him, I just can't put my finger on it. Observing Robert cosy up to that German Ponce makes me wonder. Don't you have reservations, Richard?"

"Let me remind you, James. You will soon take the oath of allegiance and that, my friend, is a solemn promise to be loyal to the British Monarch and his or her heirs and successors. Are you prepared to make such a commitment to the father of this German ponce that happens to be your King?"

"I was not expecting that, Richard, but of course I am a professional soldier, I will perform my duties as an officer in his Majesty's infantry to the best of my ability, although I would much prefer to extend my loyalty to the House of Stuart rather than the House of Hanover, it's quite simple."

"I must admit I was not expecting that either, you do have a valid point," said Richard. "But to answer your question, do I have reservations about Robert? And to be honest I do have reservations; he can be a devious individual; he is pompous, arrogant, selfish and who knows maybe even dangerous."

"Wow! You kept that to yourself," chuckled James.

"Let's just say Robert's mind works very differently from ours. James, my advice is to take him as you find him on any given day, it's all we can do for now and a point worth remembering. James, Robert pays for most if not all the entertainment we both enjoy. I suggest we let him use us as we shall use him, just like sweet Annabelle, my friend, for we are all prostitutes. May I make one further suggestion, James?"

"Of course, Richard."

"I suggest we never speak of this again – is that understood?"

"Yes, fine by me." But in his mind he knew they would return to this very conversation one day.

Lough Ennell

Sitting in a small clearing on Malachy's Island the fishing party were relaxing in the shade provided by the many birch trees. Ned was busy stoking the fire, trying to encourage the flame to grow and boil the water, muttering.

"Boil, ya bastard. I could murder a cup a tea. How about you, Patrick?"

"Would a dog sniff a bitch, Ned?" Both men were now trying to suppress their laughter.

"What's so funny, you two?" enquired Jonathan Swift.

"Ah nottin really, Mr Swift, it's just Ned here actin the eejit as usual."

"Tea is ready, gentlemen," shouted Ned and as all five men settled down on a fallen birch tree, one of many ripped from its roots by the cruel northeast wind and overtime stripped of its branches by anglers that trod this path before, maybe Saint Malachy's ghost was sitting on it right now. Ned and Patrick were busy laying the picnic hamper, a Mrs Doolin special consisting of a large pork pie at least eight inches in diameter, homemade cheese, tomatoes, onions, lettuce all sourced from Belvedere's walled gardens and to crown it all two bottles of Marquis de Segur that his Lordship had sourced from a London wine auction on one of his official visits. Last but by no means least the star of the show, Mrs Doolin's homemade mustard.

"Tis a visit by the devil himself," said Ned as he passed the fiery paste to Jonathan Swift.

"It should come with a warning, gentleman," added the Baron.

To complement the splendid food was a rather unusual flat bread – Mrs Doolin had baked the bread in Gaulstown's new outdoor oven, a folly some called it when it was first built, a waste of time. The oven had been constructed a few months earlier after his Lordship received a drawing from the internationally renowned German explorer Adam Brand. He was a guest of his Lordship's whilst on a lecturing tour of Ireland, and he made the rough drawing on one of his trips to the Russian interior.

The oven resembled an upside-down beehive; it had a rough clay mortar type plaster covering the exterior, simple in design yet very effective – the bread was delicious and soon became the talk of the village, silencing the critics once and for all.

"Eat up, gentlemen, let's share this bread that was conceived in mighty Russia and now consumed on the ancient Island of Cronis here on Lough Ennell where Saint Malachy also broke bread with the widow of the high King of Ireland, Brian Boru, maybe on this very spot where we sit now. They say Malachy and his followers built a ring fort right here on Cronis after the battle of Clontarf in 1014; the King died in that battle and Malachy became high King of Ireland and went on to marry Brian Boru's widow; the story goes he died on a crannog just there–" pointing to a rocky inlet not more than one hundred feet away.

"We learn something new every day, what an amazing legend," commented Jonathan Swift.

"Not a legend, Jonathan, but a historical fact, my dear man."

"In that case we are truly privileged, imagine Saint Malachy may have sat where I sit; my god, I'm sure I felt a reassuring hand on my shoulder just now!" as they all laughed.

"Whilst we are on the subject of Kings, there are rumours circulating that your son Robert has made the acquaintance of the heir to the throne, Prince Frederick – is there any truth in that rumour, George?" asked the Viscount. "Fact or fiction?"

Two rather large sets of ears stood to attention as both Ned and Patrick could not afford to miss a word – they knew Mrs Doolin would lead the interrogation later that evening.

London

The Trinity were meeting back at Robert's one week after the Masquerade ball but this time it felt different – both Richard and James could sense it, Robert was in buoyant mood... Prince Frederick said this, Prince Frederick said that, and Richard knew it was only a matter of time before James would say something that would shatter any chance of civil conversation so he decided to take pre-emptive action with a slight movement of his eyebrow, unnoticed by Robert but intended to warn James not to respond. James being James decided to throw caution to the proverbial wind, asking Robert:

"How did you communicate with Prince Frederick?"

"What do you mean, James?"

"From my observations, Prince Frederick could hardly speak the King's English, ironic, don't you think?"

"I could not care less what language they converse in; my only concern was to take advantage of the opportunity to befriend the future King of England. Let me advise you, James, not to concern yourself with my affairs."

Richard decided to intervene and back his impetuous friend, sensing Robert was about to land a fatal blow to the Trinity's existence.

"I happen to agree with James – it is a valid observation, idiotic in conception I must admit, but in my humble opinion it does not deserve such a harsh rebuke."

Robert was slightly taken aback but not entirely surprised. He held his tongue for longer than he would normally, giving his brain time to catch up and weigh his options.

Did he want to face the last few months in London without any friends at all? Having to depend entirely on the fickle whim of his new friend Frederick? After some careful thought Robert decided to err on the side of caution as he continued.

"I was somewhat expeditious in chastising you, James. What I meant was that it is incumbent on Richard and me to encourage a respectful attitude towards the Monarchy, as we represent the Aristocracy. I mean no disrespect to your lineage, James, I was just stating a fact."

Robert continued to stare directly at both men – he was up for a fight if it materialized. After a short pause Robert proclaimed:

"Shall we agree to disagree, gentlemen?"

James, recalling the advice Richard had dispensed some days earlier – 'take him as you find him on any particular day' – decided to act on it, tipping his forehead in a mock salute plus a slightly raised palm from Richard seemed to Robert to be an indication of submission. It was anything but.

Gaulstown

Mrs Doolin was busy supervising the preparations for that evening's dinner party making sure everything was the way she liked it: spotless linen, sparkling glassware and a silver service laid out in proper order.

"Ann Mary, the mirrors need polishing, not a speck of dust; are yez paying attention?"

"Yes, Mrs Doolin."

"Where's Catherine Murry?" Then turning to see her standing behind her. "There ya are, Catherine, this will be your job one day – prove to me you are capable."

"Yes, Mrs Doolin." Catherine then proceeded to demonstrate to the parlour maids how to present a proper table, something she had done on many occasions in the past.

"That's more like it, Catherine."

Just then the head butler walked into the dining room.

"Everything on schedule, Mrs Doolin?"

"Yes, Mr Clarke," as she scornfully looked over the rim of her glasses to see the head butler run his white gloved finger over the full length of the side cupboard. Noticing her obvious glare he immediately scurried from the dining room muttering "good job, Mrs Doolin, excellent work, continue". Under her breath she was heard to comment:

"I'll give ya continue, it would answer ya better to polish the brasses on the front door there an absolute disgrace; now remember, girls, make sure everything is perfect, her Ladyship will be on the lookout for mistakes; any excuse to make our lives miserable. We have an hour to prepare – chop chop."

Chapter 10

Lough Ennell

"Yes, Viscount, to answer your question, Robert has made the acquaintance of his Royal Highness. Correspondence from a month ago implies a strong friendship was indeed in embryonic form."

"How was the introduction manufactured?" asked the Viscount.

"They met at Kings College, I believe. I don't know the precise details but one thing led to another, the result he and two of his friends were invited to a ball, I will have to wait for Robert's return to understand how it all transpired."

Patrick and Ned were once again on high alert while at the same time wrapping what remained of the picnic in a fine linen cloth. Mrs Doolin would have their guts for garters if a single detail were to be left out.

"Your son seems to know exactly what he wants and now has the conduit to pursue his agenda," added the Viscount.

"Life has a few twists and turns in store for all of us, of that I am certain," answered the baron.

"That's very true, Baron," interrupted Swift. "Maybe even another four-pounder!" That put an end to the Viscount's inquisition and brought more laughter.

"Ready, gentlemen, the trout are waiting, we have three hours to catch the monster that will outweigh Jonathan's fish."

"Not a chance," replied Swift. "I could put some of that Russian bread on my line and still win."

"It's not over till it's over," said the Viscount.

"Remember, gentlemen, we must not be delayed for dinner this evening; if the matter is not settled by 5pm then maybe you two could settle it with a duel at dawn." Prophetic words were often spoken in jest.

London

"Good evening, gentlemen and how are we this fine evening? Just a few more months and it's back to the Emerald Isle," said Richard.

"How do you gentlemen intend to pass the time while you both wait to inherit your lands and titles?" enquired James.

"I intend to manage the estate and hopefully gain the requisite experience for when that time comes, I am quite content to wait, I can assure you."

"What about you, Robert?"

"I have a rather evil plan, James, I intend to poison my father, seize control of Gaulstown and become the youngest member of Parliament."

"Be serious, Robert," chuckled Richard.

"Seriously, I shall supervise my younger brothers as they adjust to their new responsibilities and like you, Richard, I shall prepare for the day my father meets his maker."

"You, James, have you had any indication where you might be posted?" enquired Richard.

"No idea, I shall be informed of my posting the day I receive my commission. That reminds me, gentlemen, I hereby invite you both, it's in two months' time."

"I would be honoured to witness your finest hour, James; will your family be travelling over from Ireland?" enquired Richard.

"Yes, Father can hardly believe I have completed the course – he was expecting me to capitulate I think."

Robert was now looking down at a poorly printed leaflet that he was holding in his hand, something he had picked up in the street encouraging political agitation, referencing the possible return of the Catholic King James and he seemed disinterested in the conversation.

"What about you, Robert"? enquired James without raising his head. Robert spoke with an air of indifference.

"Let me think about that, James; it is still a couple of months away but if my calendar allows then I would be glad to attend."

Richard looked at James with that trademark raised eyebrow, do not rise to the bait. James knew better and proceeded with great restraint.

"What's the agenda for the Trinity this weekend, gentlemen? Is it not time for our next adventure? Any ideas, Robert?"

"I'm afraid I will not be able to join the Trinity this weekend, I shall be otherwise engaged."

"What could be more important?" asked Richard.

"Both of you were very interested in my communication skills regarding Prince Frederick – let me inform you as to the thread of our conversation."

"Peter de Roches," interjected James.

"No, James, it was about our little foray to Covent Garden and I might add the Prince was very interested, in fact he insisted I take him there this weekend."

"That's brave – what if someone was to recognize him, would he not be in mortal danger?"

"Not everyone is a Royalist, Robert," added Richard.

"I did convey that very point to his Royal Highness."

"Did he not seem apprehensive?" asked Richard.

"No, he intends wearing a disguise to resemble the pond life – they would never expect a member of the Royal Family to frequent such a sewer. He also mentioned his bodyguards staying at a discreet distance."

James could not let the opportunity slip.

"Prince Frederick's command of the English language has improved somewhat and before you boil over, Robert, I say that in jest."

Richard was now on his way to the annex laughing to himself.

"I am gradually getting used to your sense of humour, James, but as you can observe I do not find it quite as funny as Richard."

When Richard returned James exclaimed:

"Observe, Richard, no blood on the floor!" That made the Trinity laugh a little more.

"May I suggest you take James as extra security," advised Richard. "After all, he is a trained infantry officer – look at him, big, strong and beautiful; just what Prince Frederick needs, maybe even craves."

"That I believe is some form of mirth, Richard, you two certainly complement each other."

"Forgive me, Robert, I could not help myself."

"It looks like it's just you and me tomorrow night, Richard," sighed James.

Lough Ennell

Old Faithful creaked under the combined weight of the fishing party and Ned still had to climb onboard. With a final heave he swung his leg over the side, splashing the Viscount in the process.

"Damn you, man, you should be more careful."

"We are on a lough, after all," said the Baron in recognition of Ned's hard work.

"I apologize, Edward, there was no need for that."

Ned on the other hand was thinking 'I should scull the ould bastard with the oar, make it look like an accident', then with a soft chuckle confined that idea to the depths of Lough Ennell and that wasn't very deep.

"May I have a grasshopper, Edward?"

"May I have one also, my good man?" asked the Viscount.

"You, my Lord, any preference?" asked Ned.

"Whatever Jonathan is using; it seems to be working for him," answered the Baron.

After drifting for what seemed like only minutes but was just over one hour, Jonathan Swift was standing again pulling hard on the line, shouting.

"I hate to inform you, Viscount, but this one feels more like nine pounds in weight – would you like to land him for me?"

With that the Baron burst into laughter and it was infectious, even the Viscount joined in. Ned was now ready and gently eased the net under the exhausted fish and exclaimed 'fish landed'. Jonathan Swift took hold of the net, raised it high so that everyone could appreciate the specimen and through tears of laughter declared, "A pinkeen". The echo of laughter could be heard as far away as Lilliput.

"Gentlemen, that's enough for today, I can't take any more."

Patrick knew what the Baron meant and taking hold of the oars he began to steer Old Faithful in the direction of Belvedere. On the carriage ride back to Gaulstown the conversation was all about the ones that got away.

"Lady Elizabeth will be pleased," suggested the Viscount.

"Yes, two nice fish," complimented the Baron.

"What do you estimate the combined weight, George?" the Baron added.

"My guess is four, maybe five pounds."

"What's the heaviest trout ever caught on Lough Ennell?" enquired the Viscount.

"That is in dispute, Robert, a gentleman from Kilkenny named Reid I believe claims to have caught a 7lb 8oz off Clongowney on the far shore; unfortunately, the only witness died a few weeks later, casting doubt. Another gentleman from Mullingar, a doctor, his name escapes me for the moment, he caught a verifiable 6lb 10oz near Lilliput. To answer your question, 6lb10oz stands as the official record. I remember now, Michael Seery was the doctor's name."

CHAPTER 10

Back at Gaulstown

Mary Clarke nearly knocked the door off its hinges in her rush to inform Mrs Doolin that the fishing party were halfway up the avenue.

"They're here, they're here, Mrs Doolin."

"Ok, girl, calm down, I heard you the first time." As the carriage came to a halt Ned jumped down ready to lend a hand only to be greeted with a grunt from the Viscount, a modest nod from the Baron, a firm handshake from Jonathan Swift – Ned immediately felt the cold shilling in his roughhewn hands.

"Thank you, Mr Swift."

"No! thank you, Edward, the best gillie in Westmeath."

"Edward, take the fish to Mrs Doolin and ask her to perform her usual magic," requested the Baron.

"Yes, me Lord," as he hurriedly made his way to the kitchen.

Patrick Cleary, just pulling up behind with the equipment and seeing Ned make a break for the sanctuary of Mrs Doolin's kitchen, shouted:

"Hey Ned, no sly cups of tea de ya hear me, we have work to do."

"Ok, Patrick just taking the fish to the kitchen, won't be long."

Chapter 11

London

Robert reassessed his decision not to include his two friends on his secret Royal excursion to Covent Garden and decided the wise move would be to enlist the remaining members of the Trinity to help chaperone the future King – 'the extra security might just come in handy,' he thought.

"If I take you both tomorrow afternoon you must promise me, especially you, James, not to attempt any form of irreverence – do you both agree?"

"Understood," as they raised their glasses.

"A question: where shall we meet?" asked James.

"We are meeting outside Lincoln's Field Theatre at 3pm and be precise, gentlemen – is that understood?"

"I have another question: won't people be wondering why the Prince is in Covent Garden at three in the afternoon?"

"Have either of you ever heard the name Johann Christoph Pepusch?" enquired Robert.

"No."

"He is a famous German-born composer and he happens to be conducting rehearsals at Lincoln Fields in preparation for the opening night of the Beggar's Opera."

"Convenient," said James, "German and Beggars in the same sentence."

Richard laughing now continued or attempted to continue with composure.

"You promised, James," laughed Richard, "you gave your word."

"So I did, don't worry, gentlemen, I shall be on my best behaviour tomorrow afternoon. One last question, where do you intend taking him?"

"Covent Garden, of course, Black Betty's to be precise."

"Good idea, as we know the lay of the land so to speak," added Richard.

"The plan is to arrive at the Opera House at 3pm sharp, watch rehearsals for ten minutes or so, then retreat to one of the dressing rooms where the Prince will discard his Royal robes in favour of something less conspicuous – that should be enough to convince the rabble."

"Sounds like a good plan; may I offer a little advice?"

"For god's sake, man, what is it now?" sighed Robert.

"Please advise his Royal Highness that when he converses with our favourite rose he should remember to say yes."

"What's your point this time, James?"

"I was just thinking Prince Frederick might be tempted to inadvertently resort to his mother tongue yaaaa."

"Enough, James" was Richard's stern reply.

Gaulstown

"That was an excellent meal, one to remember," said the Viscount as he secretly undid a button on his breeches.

"I agree, Mrs Doolin has proved once more to be the most accomplished cook in this fair county," added Jonathan Swift. "May I visit downstairs to convey my compliments to Mrs Doolin and her staff?"

"If you wish," said her Ladyship. "I shall have your brandy and cigar taken to the drawing room."

Downstairs had just finished their meal of chicken stew and Mrs Doolin's fine apple pie, all now chatting in small groups, some catching up on news from the village hoping to hear a wee bit of scandal, others about the day's events on the estate.

Mrs Doolin was well into her interrogation of Ned and Patrick regarding the day's fishing adventure when she heard the knock on the kitchen door, looking up to see Jonathan Swift standing in the doorway. Legs were quickly removed from the cross members that helped support the weight of the large kitchen table, uniforms were straightened, backs positioned upright and cigarettes were hurriedly stubbed in ashtrays, chatter was instantly halted.

"Sorry to interrupt your meal, I just wanted to thank you all, especially you, Mrs Doolin, for that excellent meal. The presentation was a joy to behold."

Mrs Doolin's cheeks were now taking on a pink hue as she stood.

"Thank you, Mr Swift, for your kind words."

"I caught the fish myself," added Jonathan Swift proudly.

"Yes, Ned told us all about it, well done, Mr Swift."

"A shilling for you, Patrick; I have already rewarded Ned; and two shillings for you and your girls, Mrs Doolin." The entire kitchen stood to thank Jonathan Swift as he took his leave. Making sure he was out of ear shot, Patrick stared in the direction of Ned Flanagan as he slowly raised himself from his seat.

"Come here, ya little bollox, when were you going to tell me about the shillin?"

With that ever-present grin Ned shouted: "I was going to tell you after dinner, Patrick, honest ta god."

"After dinner me arse," said Patrick as the two men chased each other around the large kitchen table to shrieks of laughter. Then the dreaded bell.

"That's enough, you two, stop your messin; the dining room won't clear itself," commanded Mrs Doolin.

Back in the parlour the conversation invariably turned to Robert.

"When do you expect Robert's return?" enquired the Viscount.

"Four more months," answered Elizabeth with a sigh.

Trying to cover Elizabeth's obvious indiscretion, the Baron immediately intervened.

"Yes, four months; just enough time to arrange his marriage."

"Oh! You have chosen a bride for Robert."

"You sound surprised, Viscount," said Elizabeth.

"No, not really, Elizabeth, one has to discharge one's duty I understand that, if I am to be honest I had harboured hopes that maybe one day our two families might join in matrimony but alas it's too late for that now."

"Maybe not?" offered Elizabeth. "I presume you were thinking of a match between Robert and your beautiful daughter Mary?"

"Yes, that was our hope, Elizabeth."

"I shall be in the library," interrupted Jonathan Swift.

"That won't be necessary, Jonathan," said the Baron.

"Yes it is," smiled Swift already on his way.

Elizabeth continued.

"We did discuss the possibility of a union between Mary and Robert, but considering the age gap we had no choice but to dismiss that option as we both felt Robert needed direction in his life sooner rather than later. May I suggest you and Lady Jane consider a union between Mary and our youngest son Arthur as they are closer in age."

"With no disrespect to Arthur or your very kind proposal, Elizabeth, but I feel I must be honest, I owe you that much. The fact that Arthur will not be inheriting your lands and title–" now looking directly at the Baron, "I am sure you will agree it is my duty, no my obligation to find a suitable partner that fulfils the necessary criteria."

"Yes of course, Robert, we understand your dilemma entirely and we wish you well in your quest. Mary deserves a fitting partner; she is such an accomplished young lady."

The Viscount was now eager to change the subject for fear of displaying his disappointment further as he proclaimed:

"What a wonderful two days we have had and I want to thank you both for your generous hospitality, I look forward to the next time we visit Belvedere. I also live in hope that someday my luck will change and maybe catch a fish or two. You must visit Brackenstown as soon as possible, Elizabeth, Jane so enjoys your company. Let's not leave it so long next time, agreed?"

"Yes of course, Robert."

Jonathan Swift walking back into the room whispered, "Safe to enter?"

"Yes, quite safe. I was just saying what a wonderful time we have had, especially you the supreme angler."

"Yes, Jonathan, a great day's fishing," said the Baron. "We know how hard it is to trick the Ennell brown – well done, my good friend."

Downstairs.

The bell was ringing now just as Patrick Cleary had laid the last card in the next hand of poker.

"This won't take long and don't touch those cards, Ned, I'm warning you."

"I wouldn't do such a thing, Mr Clarke." But he was no sooner out the door when Ned had his cards turned over revealing the head butler's hand. Ace of hearts, three of diamonds, five of spades, nine of diamonds and the seven of clubs. Both men looked at each other and at the same time declared "pure shite".

London

Saturday was indeed a fine sunny day in London. Covent Garden was in the process of its daily transformation from flea market to flesh market; some stall owners were busy dismantling what can only be described as piles of rubbish, others aesthetically more pleasing to the eye were doing a brisk trade. Throngs of people poured into Covent Garden, some sauntering, others moving with purpose, some doing God's work but the majority doing the Devil's. The Trinity's carriage arrived outside Lincoln's Field Opera House at 2.30pm, plenty of time to prepare for the arrival of Prince Frederick.

"Shall we partake of a sly ale, gentlemen?" enquired James.

"No, I won't join you," replied Robert. "I shall start the necessary preparations."

His Royal Highness arrived on time, entourage in tow. They entered Lincoln's Field Theatre by a side entrance to very little public interest. James and Richard were feeling rather nervous; German or no German he was heir to the throne. After introductory formalities were complete, the Trinity began the process of transforming a Prince into a pauper.

In the background Johann Christoph Pepusch together with the English writer John Gay were overseeing rehearsals for their upcoming opening night of the Beggar's Opera, written by Gay who was very well known for his many satirical works, but this was Gay's first attempt at lampooning the Italian Operatic style with his very own English Opera, set to popular broadsheet ballads mixed with Opera arias, Church hymns and bawdy folk tunes popular all over London. Prince Frederick was standing with his eyes closed in a trance-like state, moving his hand in a wave like motion whilst listening to a piece by Handel. Richard and James were concentrating so much on the job in hand they hardly noticed the exquisite melodic composition filling the entire space, they were too busy applying the finishing touches to the newly created sewer rat. At last the Prince looked more like a swamp dweller than a future King. James, armed with his unshakeable reservations about this unlikely friendship that was blossoming between Robert and the future Monarch, was now concentrating hard straining to listen to the conversation between the Prince and Robert.

"I am ready now for our meeting with this young woman Anabelle, are you absolutely certain we can trust her, Robert?"

"Yes, your Highness," as he glanced first at James then at Richard as if to transmit the instruction 'don't you dare'.

But to Robert's surprise both men seemed to be keeping their word, that is until the next unsettling exchange between the future

Monarch and his newly appointed pimp. Robert was now trying to coax the Prince away from anyone that might have the opportunity to overhear the content of their conversation.

"This way, your Highness" as Robert ushered Frederick in the direction of the only mirror that happened to be on the opposite side of the room. James was not about to let this opportunity pass.

"Let me help," pleaded James, as he looked for any excuse to stay close.

Frederick continued: "Robert, the implications of betrayal are too alarming to contemplate – we must be certain we can trust this woman."

Robert was now trying to muffle his voice whispering, "Can anyone be trusted one hundred percent, your Highness?"

"Speak up, man, I can't hear a word you are saying."

Robert raising his voice ever so slightly answered.

"You can never have certainty, your Highness, but let me assure you, if she did decide to abuse my trust and sought to rise above her station then I will deal with her personally."

"How do you intend to deal with her?" asked Frederick.

"The Thames can be a very cold and dangerous river."

"Excellent," said Frederick. "One more thing, if the boy looks older than sixteen our contract shall be void, is that understood?"

James turned and stared at Richard in dismay then whispered, "Now I understand why Robert was so reluctant to invite us here today. I did raise my concerns with you, Richard. I told you Robert had to have an ulterior motive – he was only ever interested in one thing, 'power', after what we have just witnessed he intends to comply with any request from the future King to attain that power, no matter how repugnant."

Richard nodded in agreement and said, "Let's make our excuses, we do not want to be witness to this nauseating arrangement."

Chapter 12

Gaulstown, some months later

Preparations had barely started for the return of the prodigal son. "What time are they expecting Master Robert?" asked Mrs Doolin.

"Sometime today, anytime now, Mrs Doolin," answered Mr Clarke.

"That's no help, Mr Clarke, no help at all, how are we supposed to prepare with so little information? Do you know if her Ladyship is in the family room?

"I don't think her Ladyship has left her bedroom today, Mrs Doolin."

"I'm not surprised to hear that after the conversation I witnessed yesterday between her Ladyship and his Lordship."

"May I enquire as to the content? If I may be so bold."

"As you well know, Mr Clarke, I'm not one to gossip, but in this instance I shall make an exception, her ladyship was saying now that Robert had completed his time at finishing school as she likes to call King's College maybe he had mellowed."

"Let's hope for all our sakes that she's right but I'll not hold my breath. Did the Baron reply?"

"Yes, and with a comment that surprised me, he said leopards don't change their spots."

"Robert's carriage is on the avenue," shouted one of the parlour maids.

"God almighty, Robert is here and we're not nearly ready. Theresa, gather all available staff and take them to the entrance hall, now hurry, girl, run, we have about eight minutes to avert a very public war between her Ladyship and Robert."

"Elizabeth, there is a commotion downstairs," shouted the Baron, "and that can only mean one thing."

"I will be down presently."

Robert's carriage was now at Sullivan's corner, named after a former estate manager Henry Sullivan who some years earlier had fallen from his horse and died on that very spot. It was the last slow turn on the avenue before the main hall.

"Five minutes!" cried Mrs Doolin as she shooed everyone outside onto the steps as quickly as she could, then looking up to the sky she commented, "it's gone quite dark, looks like rain. I hope it's not an omen."

As Robert's carriage came to a halt Patrick Cleary was on hand to attend the carriage door.

"Welcome home, master Robert, I hope you had a pleasant journey."

No acknowledgement was forthcoming as Robert gingerly placed his left foot on the tiny stirrup step for fear of falling and ending up in a crumpled heap, a vision that would not lend itself to the plan he was about to unleash on his unsuspecting audience; and as he surveyed the scene Robert could see that almost the entire household were assembled on the steps of Gaulstown. 'Perfect' he thought.

"Welcome home, Master Robert" was the cry led by the head butler as the entire household clapped.

The Baron slowly approached his son and as they awkwardly embraced he said: "Welcome home, Robert, we were not expecting you until later this evening. James was just about to organize the bunting."

"That's of no consequence, Father, it's good to be home at last."

Lady Elizabeth was standing on the steps fifteen to twenty feet away. She offered her hand and waited for her son to come forward and take it. Even on occasions like this, Lady Elizabeth liked to give the impression she was the power behind Gaulstown. With an exaggerated flowing bow, Robert greeted his mother.

"Good afternoon, Lady Elizabeth, I hope you are in good health; did you miss me?" Loud enough for the entire household to hear.

Her Ladyship stood still, just like the Ennell brown staring at the bait thinking shall I take it or shall I leave it; Elizabeth, feeling she needed more time to figure out the strategic elements of this new game her eldest son had just invented, decided to leave it. Robert perused the assembled staff and thought, 'just the way I envisaged it'; this was indeed the perfect stage to launch his devious plot. He began by addressing his younger brother George.

"Good afternoon, George, I hear you have excelled at agricultural college and Father has elevated you to the position of estate manager – you must be feeling quite indispensable."

Then turning to his youngest sibling Arthur.

"Good afternoon, Arthur, our very own Archimedes–" and with a slight glance in his father's direction made his point. "Father in all his wisdom decided to elevate you to the powerful position of financial controller, in my humble opinion a most important position. May I take this opportunity to congratulate and remind you both of one very important detail: every decision you make or every decision you may wish to implement will have to be sanctioned by me. Is that understood?" Then he waited for the inevitable.

Robert's intentional public display of disrespect sparked a reaction from the Baron rarely seen at Gaulstown, precisely the reaction Robert was hoping for as the Baron hollered.

"Robert, you are not yet master of Gaulstown; have you forgotten your place? How dare you!" as he struck his son hard on the face. Her Ladyship was now screaming at the assembled staff instructing them to return to their duties immediately. Robert continued to implement his ghastly plan by pretending to apologize profusely amid the mayhem but in his mind was thinking, 'this is proceeding well'.

"I meant no disrespect, Father, what I meant was in the future when you–"

"Stop right there," commanded the Baron. "Never mind your lame excuses, Robert, remember I know you too well and what just happened was meant to happen. Now get out of my sight before I say or do something I shall regret."

Lady Elizabeth was now looking directly at Robert with serious contempt in her eyes, but Robert just grinned at his mother safe in the knowledge the Baron could not see his face from where he stood.

In the family room later that evening the Baron, Lady Elizabeth, George and Arthur gathered to discuss Robert's outrageous behaviour. George, sensing his opportunity, however slim, decided to try and capitalize on what he assumed to be a fatal mistake on Robert's behalf. Meanwhile downstairs the entire staff were in shock and extremely upset.

"My god, what was that all about?" asked Mrs Doolin. "I've never seen the like, but if you ask me Robert knew what he was doin."

"I agree," added Mr Clarke, "very strange, very strange indeed."

One man had his own unique take on the events the entire household had just witnessed: Ned Flanagan and he was not about to hold back as he fumed.

"Why would he do that especially in front of the entire household, he's up to sometin, we all know too well what that devil is capable of, looks like the horse has bolted and I fear we are in for a wild ride."

"That's enough, back to your duties, go, well what are yez waiting for? Go on all of yez, I need me kitchen back."

"Father, you simply cannot allow Robert to evade punishment as he has done so often in the past; you must re-establish your authority at once," insisted George.

"I fully understand your frustration, George and I also agree with your conclusion. That is precisely why I intend to indulge in a period of reflection, I need time to determine the appropriate punishment," the Baron replied.

"Disown him, Father. Robert will never change, surely you have eyes to see that," added George.

"Reflection!" laughed Elizabeth. "I agree with George, perish your period of reflection, you should disown him now."

"What about you, Arthur, what do you think we should do?" enquired the Baron.

"I agree with Mother and George, you should banish Robert for I fear he has embarked on a very dangerous path."

Robert having retreated to his quarters immediately after initiating his plot was now laughing as he drained the last drop of brandy from the decanter, feeling quite pleased with the way his opening gambit had played out. 'A couple of weeks in Dublin would give all at Gaulstown the time to recover', he laughed.

After three weeks of decadence in various Dublin Inns and whore houses the intentionally dishevelled Robert returned to Gaulstown eager to continue his charade. He was confident his untidy appearance would lend the impression that he had undergone great anguish over his dishonourable behaviour.

'Timing is everything,' he thought as he requested a meeting with her Ladyship and the Baron. The message was delivered by James Clarke.

"You can leave now, James, I shall ring if we require refreshments." Elizabeth waited for the butler to vacate the family room before she delivered Robert's message and when she was satisfied she began to read the contents of the note to the Baron.

"My dear father, please forgive me; I did not intend to be treacherous my only intention was and has always been to alleviate some of the administrative pressures I so naively presumed to be the case. I now realize my error and sincerely beg your forgiveness; I beg you, Father, grant me one last audience. Your loyal son Robert."

"Our son is even more devious than I thought possible; surely you do not believe his empty words," cried Elizabeth. "You of all people know what we are dealing with. Banish him, now is your chance to cut this cancer from our midst. You will live to regret it, I tell you, if you grant him another chance and you suggest we take time to reflect. Well let's do that, let's reflect. Is your memory so bad that you have forgotten his previous indiscretions or should I say evil acts – maybe I should refresh 'your' memory, my dear?"

"That won't be necessary, Elizabeth," shouted the Baron, but Elizabeth continued.

"I seem to remember you saying a leopard does not change its spots, if you truly believe that sentiment you have no choice but to proceed directly to punishment – if you are man enough, that is."

The Baron now shook with temper as he felt his authority was being undermined by all as he hollered:

"I am Baron George Rochfort, master of Gaulstown and Belvedere, don't any of you ever forget that. I and I alone have the authority to decide Robert's destiny."

"I know what's coming: one last chance," shouted Elizabeth. "How many is that?" And she continued. "Robert has had too many squandered chances, is it not time for a safe pair of hands like George? This is our opportunity to rid the Rochfort family of what we both know to be a disease before it destroys us all."

"That's enough, Elizabeth, Robert is the rightful heir and I intend to accommodate his request for an audience. If my decision is to lead to Robert's banishment from this family then I need to be certain. Summon Mr Clarke."

Later George and Arthur were sitting in the library discussing the proposed audience the Baron had just arranged with Robert; the certainty of the outcome only compounded the hatred George now felt for his older brother.

"The snake will wriggle out of this trap with ease; after all, it's a trap of the snake's own design. If this is not evidence enough of Robert's treachery, then surely Father is blind. Say something, Arthur."

"I don't feel the need as you have already laid bare my inner thoughts."

After weeks of self-confinement Robert felt confident the dust had settled to such a degree that it was safe to resurface and start the process of mending relationships, not with sincerity but with deception. Having expressed fallacious remorse at every opportunity, Robert was now pinning his hopes on the proven fact that time would cure all ills. George and Arthur reluctantly accepted Robert's inept apologies – they realized there was no point continuing hostilities now that the Baron had decided not to punish Robert but instead to extend him one last chance. That being the case the only course of action open to both George and Arthur was to continue to pretend all was forgiven and proceed as normal. To undermine the Baron's decision would prove futile and only play into Robert's hands, but there was another very important factor: Robert was still destined to inherit everything; George and Arthur knew they would have very little influence in any future decisions regarding the path the Rochfort family should take once Robert was head of the family.

Chapter 13

Observing his siblings' lack of fight gave Robert the impression that he could manipulate them even further but for now he decided the best option was to continue as if normality had returned to Gaulstown. Weeks passed and during that time the family tried their best to avoid each other, easy in such a large house. After six weeks of hide and seek Robert decided it was time to banish the feeling of boredom that weighed him down and inject some urgency into his plan. He realized Arthur would be in his sanctuary, the library, for he seldom left it; he decided now was as good a time as any to arrange a clear-the-air meeting with his siblings. He sent James to inform George and Arthur that he would like to meet with them in the library; he engineered the meeting, intending to muddy the waters with smoke and mirrors.

'When I have finished weaving my veil of deception no one will be able to distinguish truth from fiction,' he thought. As he entered the library both George and Arthur rose from their seats, conveying a feeling of submission, at least in Robert's mind.

"Please, gentlemen, please sit. I would like to extend my appreciation for agreeing to meet with me, if I have not completely ruined our friendship with my clumsy homecoming speech for which I once again offer my sincere apologies and seek to make amends."

Arthur interrupted abruptly.

"It's done, Robert, it's over; you have demonstrated both your regret and your determination to make amends on more than one occasion. We, that is the rest of your family, have agreed to leave the matter where it now belongs, in the past."

George on the other hand decided to play devil's advocate and rolled the dice.

"I feel I must be totally honest if we are to salvage our friendship, Robert. The only reason I have agreed to this meeting is the fact that Father has assured us that you are on probation; once again Father has promised the remaining members of this family that one more transgression will lead to your banishment from this family and may I add you will only have yourself to blame."

Robert replied, "We have cleared the air, so to speak or should I say you have, George. Can we shake hands and commit to a fresh start?"

The three brothers proceeded to shake hands in less than convincing style.

"Thank you, gentlemen, for both your honesty and your willingness to afford me one more chance. I will not let you down."

"One last chance," corrected Arthur. As Robert left the room his only thought was, 'now that you have had your say, gentlemen I shall have mine'. George was first to comment.

"It's only a matter of time before Robert shows his true nature. We are both aware of his unnatural appetite for ungodly conduct; the most we can hope for at this juncture is that Father retains good health well into the foreseeable future. Can Robert continue his charade of being the reliable trustworthy sibling we all know not to be the case... time will tell."

Arthur feeling rather despondent reluctantly agreed with George and decided it was in their best interests to pretend normality had returned to Gaulstown. The next day the three brothers found themselves in the family room at the same time. Arthur decided to break the ice and start a conversation, any conversation.

"You mentioned in your correspondence that you and Prince Frederick attended opera together?" he enquired.

Robert was glad to start a normal conversation for a change.

"Yes, Arthur, as you may know I have made two new acquaintances."

"Yes, Father did mention that fact," said Arthur.

"Richard Lambert, the future Earl of Cavan and James Hamilton, an officer in his Majesty's infantry, we had the pleasure of joining Prince Frederick's entourage for the opening night of the Beggar's Opera."

"How did you meet? The Prince I am referring to," added Arthur.

Robert decided by way of recompense to relay the entire events as to how he gained the friendship of the future King and after hearing Robert's account George proclaimed:

"It is faith, Robert, for I distinctly remember the day you left Gaulstown for London, you promised Father that you would seek to enhance the Rochfort family name and you have kept your promise it seems. Although we await the evidence with great intrigue."

"I shall have to tread with care knowing your memory is so vivid, George. May I enquire: do you remember as clearly events from our early years and all the good times we shared?"

George replied, "Yes, Robert, the good and the bad."

Both brothers stared deep into each other's eyes until Arthur interrupted once more, fearing the situation just might spiral out of control, precisely what George was hoping to engineer. Robert, sensing what George was up to, issued a final apology for the indiscretions of his youth, hoping it enough to keep George in his place and his leadership challenge at bay, at least for now. Robert disengaged eye contact with his younger brother and took up a position under a large classical portrait of their ancestor Peter des Roche with the intention of delivering a statesman-like speech. But if Robert hoped to project a classical pose intended to enhance his stature, he failed miserably. The large open fireplace dwarfed his rather small frame. Realizing just in time, Robert slowly moved to one side and took up a more fitting position beside a Maltese walnut writing desk, the perfect height for Robert to rest his left hand. He then manoeuvred his right hand inside his purple three-quarter split velvet coat resting it just under his left breast and delivered his conciliatory homily.

"Gentlemen, I hereby promise to make the Rochfort family wealthier and more powerful. It is my true intention to ensure all members of this great family benefit from my introduction to the Royal household, but more importantly the future King. I have already enlightened his Highness on the history of the Rochfort family and make no mistake our name will not be forgotten in the corridors of power, I promise. When you have friends in high places you gain status, when you have status you gain what every Aristocrat dreams of, 'Power' and when you acquire power–" now looking at his brothers directly he proclaimed: "Need I say more?"

George, now trying desperately to suppress both his anger and his jealousy for his instinct screamed 'lies'. He knew Robert had no intention of sharing riches or status and certainly not power. Arthur seeing the look on George's face moved the conversation forward at pace.

"That is indeed great news, Robert, may we have that promise in writing? I say that in jest, of course, for we both know you would never tell a lie." Not giving Robert time to respond Arthur continued. "We have also been informed of your impending marriage – your thoughts on that subject should be interesting."

Robert now trying hard to hold both his tongue and his temper in check continued.

"Yes, gentlemen, I am to marry Elizabeth Tennison. They say she is very pretty, the daughter of a rich merchant, a widower I believe. Mother has arranged the marriage to keep me occupied or maybe as a punishment, she intends to teach me a lesson."

Then taking in a deep breath he stated with force: "It is of no consequence, in time that issue shall be dealt with."

"What precisely do you mean?" probed George.

"You will understand in time," answered Robert.

"Do you mean to find an avenue not to marry Miss Tennison?"

enquired George as he probed a little deeper.

"No, I shall abide by Mother's wishes and marry this Tennison woman, but it does not follow that I must spend the rest of my life with her."

"Do you intend to forge a reason to divorce her?" enquired Arthur.

"Something like that." Robert walked to the large bay window, stood for a moment taking in the striking view, then turned and again muttered "something like that". Little did they know but this was as good as it would get between the siblings.

George decided to take this opportunity and let his brother know that some of his secrets were in fact public knowledge as he continued. "Maybe you should spend some time in Dublin before Mother decides to apply the hand braces. I'm sure you will find respite there like you have in the past–" but before Robert could answer...

"May we join you, gentlemen?" as Lady Elizabeth and the Baron entered.

"Yes of course, Mother, please take my seat," encouraged George.

"Father, you take my seat," encouraged Arthur.

"Now that we have you all in one place your father and I intend to take this opportunity to resolve some outstanding issues. First you, Robert, you know how I feel regarding your inheritance, your father in all his wisdom has decided on a course of action that keeps you in line to inherit everything. I hope your father lives a long and healthy life and by that time you may have matured sufficiently to take your place at the head of this family."

The Baron interrupted:

"Now that you understand the seriousness of your situation and the need for you to mature, we have arranged your marriage with the intention of helping you construct a firm foundation. You will marry in one year; it is time for you to meet your future bride. Miss Elizabeth Tennison will travel to Gaulstown this coming Saturday for the formal introduction, she will be accompanied by her widowed father. If you have any objections please offer them now."

Robert fearing one more outburst would surely seal his place and send his father over the edge continued to implement his plan.

"Yes of course, Mother, I am so looking forward to meeting Miss Tennison."

The Baron and Elizabeth glanced at each other in dismay, both thinking this cannot be the same Robert who had displayed such arrogance on the steps of Gaulstown a mere six weeks earlier. Turning her attention to George junior, Elizabeth continued.

"You, George, will live at the Hall until we can source a suitable site for you on Belvedere."

Then the Baron turned to address his youngest son.

"Arthur, we intend to renovate Belfield House on the estate for your sole use; when completed it will rival the best Westmeath has to offer. It's close to the main hall and quiet there, that should help you concentrate on the financial wellbeing of the estate. Is everyone in agreement?"

"Yes" was the unified answer.

The Introduction

The library was chosen for the introduction, the ambience and subtle reference to both knowledge and status would in Lady Elizabeth's opinion add a degree of authority.

"May I introduce Robert Rochfort," announced James Clarke.

Elizabeth Tennison stood beside her father; she wore a tight white satin bodice with panned sleeves lined in pink with a matching petticoat. Her hair was worn in a mass of tight curls, pearl drop earrings and a matching necklace paid compliment to her pale complexion. She stood so still one could be forgiven for thinking you were gazing at a porcelain Aphrodite, quite stunning. Her father Clarence was dressed in typical gentleman's apparel, an imposing figure as he stood six feet seven inches tall; even at the ripe old age of thirty-eight Clarence emanated the aura of a man not to be trifled with.

He wore the most fashionable wig, a collarless deep purple coat with deeper cuffs and a matching waistcoat, a ruffled white linen shirt neatly tucked into his breeches – they were a lighter shade of purple and stopped just below the knee where they were held in place with a one-inch collar of pale blue elastic. Silk stockings and buckled shoes complemented a most dashing figure.

Robert strode into the library with purpose stopping two yards from his future bride. Bending his left knee and bringing his right foot behind his left whilst adding an exaggerated flowing movement with his right arm he then stood upright and declared:

"It is indeed a great pleasure to meet you at last, Miss Tennison," taking her hand and kissing it, then turning to Clarence Tennison.

"May I say what a great honour it is to make your acquaintance, Mr Tennison," and shook his hand with vigour.

Her Ladyship and the Baron were seated on Arthur's favourite baroque couch watching proceedings with the obligatory stiff backs in full compliance with strict protocol essential on occasions such as this. Elizabeth not quite believing what her eyes and ears were witnessing turned to the Baron and whispered, "We must tread carefully, my dear. Robert is up to something, again."

The bell was ringing downstairs. Mrs Doolin was her usual calm self – she loved occasions like this, the more chance of something going wrong the more she enjoyed the challenge.

"Ann Quinn, there you are, go get the champagne from the cold shelf in the pantry and take it directly to the parlour. The introductions are complete. Mr Clarke will serve. The rest of yez have twenty minutes to prepare for service. How is the prime beef, Catherine?"

"Just perfect, Mrs Doolin."

"Who's on duty upstairs?"

"Mr Clarke and Ned, Mrs Doolin."

"Good, the right man in the right place. Ned won't miss a thing."

"I just laid eyes on Miss Tennison, she's gorgeous so she is," said Ann Quinn.

"Only beautiful," replied Theresa Staunton. "You can see who's getting the top of the milk and it's not Miss Tennison," as they both giggled.

"What are yez laughing at?" enquired Mrs Doolin.

"Nottin, Mrs Doolin."

"Can't be nottin, tell us."

"Well, Mrs Doolin, Ann was just saying that the beauty has just been introduced to the beast."

"Well for once I agree with yez," as they all laughed.

One week later the Baron fulfilled his promise to Elizabeth, George and Arthur. He had promised them that he would stipulate in the strongest terms in a written contract that all family members were required to sign. This binding document stipulating the conditions under which the Baron was prepared to retain Robert as heir apparent, he summoned members of the family to the library for this very important meeting.

"Your mother and I have agreed to make this a formal statement witnessed by the most influential members of the Rochfort family," and he started to read the contract aloud.

"Robert, it is my duty to warn you especially after recent events. If you intentionally or unintentionally commit one more indiscretion that brings the Rochfort family name into disrepute then I, Baron George Rochfort, will have no choice but to elevate George to the position you currently hold, that of heir apparent to the Rochfort lands and title. If such circumstances should arise, George and not you will lead this family into the future," and finished by saying: "do you understand?"

"Yes, Father, I fully understand and thank you for the chance afforded to me. I realize I have made mistakes in the past and I also realize there is no room for mistakes in future. I am at present formulating a plan that I fully intend to implement."

"May we enquire as to what your plan entails, Robert?" asked the Baron.

"I am still working on it, but I can assure you, Father, you will be the first to know."

"For your sake, Robert, I hope it reflects the strict uncompromising rules of the Rochfort dynasty."

"Uncompromising it will be, Father."

"Bring the plan to me immediately you have finalized the detail, your mother and I will have to sanction it one way or the other. Now that we have established the ground rules going forward and it has been witnessed and signed, let's move on to more cheerful matters.

"When will we meet your new friends, Robert? I hope we don't have to wait until the wedding. You should invite them both to Gaulstown, maybe take in a spot of fishing on Lough Ennell. As you are all aware the renovations to the lodge on Belvedere were a great success so please feel free to use it at your leisure."

"A very good idea, Father, I shall contact Richard and James to arrange a visit as soon as possible."

"Excellent, we are all looking forward to making their acquaintance."

Downstairs

"That smells lovely, Mrs Doolin, can I have a taste?"

"No, you can't, Ned Flanagan."

"What's the special occasion?"

"Have you not heard, Robert's friends are visiting for the weekend and my instructions are to make it a special one."

"Oh! I did hear something but I thought that was next week; anyway tell us what's in the ould oven?"

"The aroma, Ned, is a combination of smells as you like to call them, suckling pig, pheasant and brown trout?"

"Well for some, Mrs Doolin. Suppose we'll have to make do with chicken stew again."

"What's wrong with me chicken stew, Ned Flanagan?"

"Nottin, Mrs Doolin, I only meant..."

"I know what ya meant, ya big lump; what are ya doin in my kitchen this time of day anyway?"

"I thought I might scrounge an auld cup a tea."

"We're too busy at the minute, Ned, off with ya – can ya not see we have work to do? Oh! I nearly forgot, take that linen wrap with ya."

"What's in it?" enquired Ned.

Mrs Doolin, now almost whispering, replied, "It's a roast pheasant, Ned, take it to the village with ya. It's your night off, isn't it? And remember, not a word."

"God bless ya, Mrs Doolin, I always said there was a heart in there somewhere."

"Off with ya before I take it back."

Once again the kitchen girls got great enjoyment as they witnessed Ned and Mrs Doolin share a love lost.

Upstairs

"Father, may I introduce Richard Lambert, heir to the Earldom of Cavan."

"Richard, welcome to Gaulstown."

"This is James Hamilton, a commissioned officer in his Majesty's infantry."

"It's a pleasure to make your acquaintance, gentlemen. Elizabeth and the boys are anxious to meet you both, this way please."

September now and autumn had well and truly arrived. The Belvedere estate was awash with colour, varying shades of brown infused with orange, red and pink, a natural canvas awaiting the hand of the cosmic artist, a carpet of autumnal colour stretching as far as the lake shore, a sight to lift even the heaviest heart. Elizabeth was busy writing invitations for this year's Belvedere hunt but still had time to wonder at the sheer beauty of nature – being a member of the organizing committee meant she had to take on the extra workload as this year's event promised to be the largest gathering of nobility Westmeath had seen in many a day.

"George, I have almost finished the guest list; is there anyone else you wish to include this year?"

"How many are on the list?" asked the Baron.

"Forty-seven including family members."

"I am sure you have included everyone, my dear. Oh! I nearly forgot, please invite Jonathan Swift – he promised he would attend this year's event."

"That surprises me, George. I was under the impression he did not approve of such cruelty as he put it."

"He has mellowed with age, Elizabeth; I presume you have included the Molesworths."

"Yes of course, George! Did you need to ask? You can be so tiresome at times. The Countess informs me Mary is eager to attend her first hunt."

"That is indeed good news. I look forward to introducing Mary to Arthur – you never know, Elizabeth, maybe we could convince the Viscount and Lady Jane that Arthur is after all a suitable match for Mary. It is my opinion she would make an excellent wife; she is so accomplished yet still only sixteen years of age."

"Yes, she has a wonderful presence," added Elizabeth. "I agree, George, we must apply all our cunning to progress that wonderful idea. Did you know she has already taken to the Dublin stage; amid rave reviews I believe?"

"Really, I am not at all surprised. I did inform you as to her virtuosity on the piano – do you remember I mentioned it the last time I visited Swords? Mary played a piece from Amor d'un'ombra e gelosia dun'aura – it was magnificent.".

"It was a mouthful, you mean, and yes I do remember, you were quite taken with her rendition."

"Your recollection is accurate, Elizabeth; translated it means the love of a shade and the jealousy of an aura by the Italian composer Domenico Scarlatti. I happened to see the Opera at the Haymarket Theatre. If we are to convince the Viscount and Lady Jane that the union is a viable proposition then we should pamper them more than usual. Please ensure that the Viscount and his family have the guest suite on the east wing this year."

"There may be a problem with your request, George, as my brother always takes the east wing when he visits."

"Well not on this occasion, Elizabeth."

"I agree, George. I shall find a reason to accommodate the Earl on the west wing."

"It's not like we are imposing inferior rooms on him, my dear; your brother is simply too lazy to walk the extra distance from the west wing."

Robert, feeling both restless and bored after months pretending to be normal, decided enough time had been wasted, he was now ready to implement the next phase. 'As soon as the Belvedere hunt has come and gone I shall take the first available opportunity that presents itself and strike. If I must suffer this boredom for much longer I will go insane,' he thought.

Chapter 14

The hunt

September the 8th was a bright sunny day as the cream of Westmeath Aristocracy arrived at Belvedere. The hunting lodge today looked more like a home from home as the servants attended to their master's every whim, but before the hunt could proceed all new members had to undergo the ritual of 'the blooding' where the hunt master would smear the blood of a fox on their cheeks and forehead.

The last of the five new members to undergo this important ritual was Mary Molesworth and as she stood before the master of the hunt Baron George Rochfort it was plain to see she was enjoying every minute of this noble ritual, unpleasant as it may seem. When the Baron smeared the blood on Mary's cheeks signalling the end of the initiation ceremony there was much whooping and applause. The next tradition to be observed was no less important; it was meant to symbolize the equality of all, present domestic staff not included of course. The master personally served a fine scotch malt from solid silver trays to the hunt members while on horseback and when everyone had their tipple the master called the hunt to order and got proceedings underway.

"Remember, ladies and gentlemen there are many coverts and

brush on Belvedere where the fox may lie. I encourage you all to seek the scent in such locations and please, ladies and gentlemen, take very little risk, be safe." Then the sound of the horn to indicate the start of this year's hunt accompanied by the obligatory shouts of "Tally ho, Tally ho, cast the hounds".

Downstairs

The smell wafting from Mrs Doolin's kitchen was delightful. A large prime beef roast plus a selection of wild fowl enough to feed five members of the Rochfort family plus Elizabeth's brother, the Earl, his wife and the three members of Viscount Molesworth's family. Mrs Doolin had strict orders to serve dinner at 7pm.

"Half hour till service, how are we doin?" hollered Mrs Doolin.

"Grand, perfect timing, Mrs Doolin," answered Catherine.

"There's the bell; they'll be wantin more champagne. Catherine, take two bottles from the larder and make sure they're chilled, go on, hurry, girl, Mr Clarke will be waiting."

Upstairs

Lady Elizabeth had arranged the seating plan which meant Mary Molesworth was seated next to Arthur. They both seemed to be enjoying each other's company; there was lots of laughter as they chatted enthusiastically – maybe there was a chance after all.

"I have been informed you play the piano with the skill of a seasoned professional?" enquired Arthur.

"You have been misinformed, Arthur, my skill at the piano is adequate at best," answered Mary.

"But you have played on the Dublin stage, I believe."

"Yes, that part is true but a seasoned professional I certainly am not, although I have been asked to play again."

The conversation at the table was robust, dominated by the day's events. The hunt had been a great success; everyone wanted to relive every exciting minute of it. Robert, on the other hand, found it all quite boring.

"Pity it only lasted fifteen minutes or so," commented Robert, "after all the months of planning by the organizing committee. It just seems to me a waste of time and energy."

"That's because you are a poor horseman, Robert," offered his uncle the Earl.

"I may well be one of the less skilful horsemen, Uncle Richard, but from the time the pack picked up the scent to the actual kill was only fifteen minutes, maybe less; my point was merely to shed some light on the fact that so much hard work was repaid with so little enjoyment."

"It's called a hunt for good reason, Robert, sometimes the hounds get lucky. I have participated in many hunts; some have lasted as you say, Robert, fifteen minutes, other kills have taken up to three hours – your argument is flawed, nephew."

"But is not the preparation to be seen as part of the enjoyment or indeed our gathering here this evening," interrupted Mary as she looked directly at Robert.

"Mary, my dear, you have decided to include us in your conversation," cajoled Robert.

"No," answered Mary, "I have decided to join yours."

Robert looked directly at the Viscount saying, "Feisty little mare you have there, Viscount; does she bite?"

Mary raised her voice.

"I am over here, Robert, you can deliver your misogyny directly."

Turning to look at Mary, Robert coyly replied: "I meant no disrespect, Mary, quite the opposite in fact. I have always encouraged the younger females to assert themselves."

"I may be sixteen, Robert, but your analogy between youth and maturity, especially when dealing with the female mind, is not determined by the intellectual prowess of any one man but by the level of maturity of that particular individual; as for me I am a woman," sniped Mary.

Robert waited patiently for the giggles to subside

"Forgive me, Mary. I simply meant your youthful appearance conceals your implacable fortitude; I apologize if I have offended you."

"Apology accepted," as she turned to Arthur and picked up the conversation where they had left off.

One month later

Now that the Belvedere hunt was over all Robert had to do was wait for his opportunity to take the Rochfort name to the next level, but to achieve his goal he knew he would have to get his hands dirty. However, his plans were dealt a blow and would have to take a back seat at least for now after he received a letter by special delivery – the Royal seal obvious for all to see. Inside was one sheet of Royal stationery with the words in bold letters. *Return to London immediately our flower girl has become a liability* signed Frederick. That can only mean one thing, he thought and within two hours he was on his way to Waterford. Robert decided to use this adventure as a rehearsal, for he suspected his dark side would be required to assert its brutality soon. On his arrival in London a Royal escort was waiting to whisk Robert to Kensington Palace. 'This is not looking good,' he thought, 'what has Annabelle been up to?' He did not have to wait long for his answer. Prince Frederick was standing at the east end of the Kings Gallery directly under a large imposing portrait of King Charles the 1st on horseback.

The largest and most prestigious room, the Kings Gallery boasted some of the most important paintings in the Royal collection. The high walls were painted a deep terracotta above the chair rail lending a feeling of warmth to what was in fact a cold room; the carved oak door casings seemed to grow from the solid oak floor, a magnificent yet imposing room. Robert could feel the tension as he stood at the entrance and if proof were needed then a glance to the far end of the room confirmed his feelings. Frederick was standing waiting for his pimp and he looked angry.

As Robert started the long walk, he could not help but notice the magnificent ceiling. The seven hand painted scenes from the life of Ulysses were just stunning and as he approached he lowered his gaze from the ceiling and looked directly at the Prince. Immediately he could discern from the expression on Frederick's face that this was going to be a meeting with only one outcome.

"Your Royal Highness, you requested my presence."

"Yes, Robert and I take no pleasure in recalling you so soon, but as you will come to understand I had no choice. Remember you said we could trust this harlot, Robert."

"Your Highness, I need to know precisely what has transpired; only then can I make a judgment."

"Annabelle has resorted to extortion," replied Frederick.

"Annabelle does not possess the intelligence or courage to organize something like this, she must be working with an accomplice," answered Robert.

Frederick continued.

"I too must accept some responsibility for I did visit Black Betty's on one occasion without you, Robert, but I was in disguise."

"Your Highness, you broke the rules that you yourself put in place to prevent such a situation arising, but I shall not waste time on that – what's done is done. Did Annabelle recognize you?"

"How could she? I was wearing a disguise."

"She must have recognized you, your Highness; maybe she followed you to your carriage."

"No, Robert? Our transport was more than half a mile from Black Betty's. I did not disrobe my disguise until I was in my carriage behind closed drapes."

"A very strange decision for a young woman to take, for I left her in no doubt as to the possible consequences," assured Robert.

"How could she know my true identity?" enquired the Prince.

"I suspect Annabelle is quite ignorant as to your identity, your Highness, but I suspect her accomplice or accomplices know exactly who you are. For the present let's assume this is simply an unsophisticated attempt at extortion, blackmail, call it what you will. Your Highness, how did she make contact?"

"A note was handed to one of our party."

"By Annabelle's hand?"

"Yes."

"Where is the note now? Do you still have it?"

"Yes of course."

After reading the note Robert stood and stroked his chin, then looked up and said: "In my opinion Annabelle has no idea who she is dealing with, your Highness, I fear another hand is engineering this attempt to acquire financial gain. Let me talk to Annabelle and find out precisely who she thinks she is blackmailing."

"May I offer a little advice, Robert, or should I say motivation intended to make certain you solve this conundrum?"

"Yes, your Highness, your advice is always welcome."

"Maybe not this time, Robert. If I am implicated in any way you will lose your head."

"I shall keep that in mind at all times, your Highness."

Robert left Kensington Palace with a very real feeling of trepidation; the only course of action he could envisage was not one to be taken lightly. That's when Robert decided he would need the assistance of his most trusted cabal, the Trinity.

Six days later the Trinity gathered at Robert's temporary accommodation in Kensington Palace to discuss a way forward.

"Gentlemen, we have a problem, Annabelle has been in touch. She is demanding payment for withholding Prince Frederick's name from printed pamphlets she intends to make available to the public if her ransom demand is not met."

"That girl is playing with fire. What do you intend to do, Robert?" asked Richard.

"There is only one course of action that will contain this attempt at blackmail and you, my good friends, will play your part."

"Sounds both ominous and dangerous, Robert. When do we execute this plan of yours?" enquired James.

"Thank you, James, and for your loyalty Prince Frederick has arranged a series of commissions that will grant you status beyond your expectations."

"If that is to be the consequence of loyalty, so be it. Time to plan our strategy, gentlemen," encouraged James.

Black Betty's

One week later the Trinity were once again embroiled in the murky world of Covent Garden's underbelly, but this time the stakes were much higher. It did not take long for Annabelle to make her entry.

"Good evening, gentlemen, may I join you?"

"Ah! Sweet Annabelle, come sit by me," encouraged Richard. James sat on his own far enough away to have an unobstructed view of the entire Tavern. Through the poor light and the acrid smoke, James noticed a man acting suspiciously near the door and decided to keep his eye on him.

"Annabelle, why have you decided to take this course of action? Did we not adequately reimburse you for your service? Are you embarking on this path of your own volition?"

"Yes, my Lord, but I am in need of money for an abortion. I could see no other way." James was now studying the man by the door for Annabelle frequently locked her gaze in his general direction. Robert continued.

"Annabelle, do you realize whom you are dealing with?"

"You, my lord."

"Do you know who I am?"

"No, my lord, not really but you have lots of money."

"Who is the source of this information?"

"Well I'm not blind, my lord, I know you and your friends are rich. I'm doing this of my own accord for the reason I just gave you, my lord." Again raising her eyes in the direction of the stranger at the bar.

"Annabelle, I have sympathy with your situation; that is why we have decided to pay the amount you requested with a caveat."

"I don't know what you mean, my lord."

"With a condition. You must give me your word of honour never to pursue this course of action again. Will you extend me your word?"

"Yes, my lord, you have my word. Do you have the money?"

"No, Annabelle, it would be foolish to carry that amount in person; we will have to arrange a suitable place for that transaction, don't you agree?"

"I'm not sure, me Lord."

"Do you need to consult with someone before we arrange a suitable place for the handover?"

Annabelle may have had limited intelligence but she was not a fool. Realizing Robert was baiting a trap, she continued with caution intending to seek advice from her co-conspirator.

"If you don't have the money with you, then I see no other way except to arrange a place for the handover," replied Annabelle.

"Excellent, I have taken the liberty of writing a date, time and place for the handover. This is non-negotiable, Annabelle. If you want the money then meet me as specified."

"I shall have to think about that, your lordship."

"I will be at that place at that time and I shall bring the specified amount of money. It is up to you now."

Annabel secreted the piece of paper, saying, "I will be here two nights from now, I will let you know then." She vacated her seat and left the premises.

James, after receiving a nod from Richard, was already moving through the crowd keeping the stranger in his sights and when Annabelle left Black Betty's the stranger followed at pace. Keeping a safe distance, James decided to shadow both the stranger and Annabelle while Richard trailed all of them desperate to uncover the extent of this plot. 'How many are involved?' thought James, 'time to find out.'

Back at the palace Prince Frederick and Robert waited anxiously for James and Richard to return, preferably with news that could lead to the identity of those involved in the blackmail plot. The more people that knew about it the more intricate the solution would have to be. Two hours later...

"Good news, your Royal Highness, from our observations Annabelle is working with one other, a man in his late twenties; James observed the pair enter a tavern on Charing Cross Road," informed Richard.

"Excellent, Richard, I always had faith in James," commented Robert. "Have you got any idea as to the man's identity?" Richard was tempted to remind Robert of his outright hostility towards James when he introduced them but decided against it

"Yes, Robert, that was the easy part. After they both left we plied some of the patrons with free wine; we now have an address for the cohabitating couple. We got lucky, your Highness; I am certain no other persons are involved."

"Then you must proceed with gusto, Robert. I want this to go away, now deal with it."

"Yes, your Highness. We intend to plan our strategy this very night."

One week later the Trinity, after observing the blackmailer's movements over a period of days, decided it was time to implement their plan. After some careful strategic military planning by James, arrangements were now in place for the ransom handover. Robert was in a hurry to complete his task – as far as he was concerned no one was going to interfere with his future. No one.

When the evening of the handover arrived it was raining heavily. 'Perfect,' thought James as he secreted himself behind one of the massive wooden supports put in place to facilitate repairs to Waterloo bridge, work that was due to start soon. At the same time Richard was waiting for Annabelle and her accomplice to leave the hovel they were living in and when they appeared he followed at a discreet distance. The site chosen was meant to allay any feelings of anxiety the blackmailers might have had; it was a short walk from their hovel on Charing Cross Road to the Victoria embankment and on to the location chosen for the payment of the ransom money, a location the Trinity had explored with great care over the previous days. The terrain conditions under Waterloo bridge were perfect with lots of bramble brush and undergrowth should the Trinity need it for cover; the heavy rain kept potential witnesses to a minimum, another reason to be grateful. Deserted on this cold wet October night and Robert was drenched to the skin as he stood by a rusty old gate just under the Bridge at a point where the cold water of the Thames pushed with tremendous force on the base of this massive structure creating a crescendo of sound, unnerving to say the least. The force of thousands of gallons of water rushing past at great speed had garnered everyone's attention. The next few minutes would determine what direction the Trinity's future would take; tonight would test each man's resolve to the limit.

Robert gave the gate a slight shove and it almost disintegrated it was so badly maintained. If it was meant to keep the public away from the dangerous tides then it failed miserably. After clearing the debris, Robert carefully picked his footsteps over the obstruction revealing a narrow rough path through the undergrowth and down the muddy bank to the cold filthy water of the Thames. Annabel's male accomplice left her side early and as she approached the bridge, he took up a vantage point in some bushes no more than twenty yards from where Robert was hiding.

James and Richard were waiting for Robert's signal before springing the trap. As Annabelle slowly approached, Robert vacated his hiding place and walked out onto a partially lit section of road that pedestrians used all the time, during the day that is. Robert gained her attention by waving his arms in the air.

"Over here, Annabelle."

But when she surveyed the scene before her she stopped dead in her tracks – she had to be certain in her own mind that Robert was alone. Her accomplice was watching through the foliage a short distance away but the heavy rain was making it extremely hard for him to see things clearly.

"I do not feel safe here," shouted Annabelle. "Please can I have the money?"

Taking a package from his satchel, Robert offered it to Annabelle, calling for her to come closer while at the same time touching his forehead with the serpent's tongue; a signal to the other members of the Trinity. When Annabelle got close enough to reach out for the package she felt it instantly, the cold steel as it forcefully entered just under her ribcage and finished buried deep in her heart. Her startled eyes betrayed her. Death was almost instantaneous. At the same time James was putting his military training to good use as the young man's neck snapped like a twig.

The Trinity had to work hard and fast, removing any evidence that could be used to identify the remains, stripping the clothes from their bodies. The Trinity proceeded to bludgeon the blackmailers' faces beyond recognition. It was hard work dragging the remains to the riverbank but once there they could let the natural strength of the river do the rest.

"Gentlemen, that was exhilarating; time for a celebration." Robert had tested his dark side and found it competent.

Gaulstown

Robert returned to Gaulstown feeling more powerful than ever, the next phase of his plan would once again test his dark side but he looked forward with renewed vigour; he was ready for the task ahead, especially after Waterloo.

Two Months later

"Father, would you care to join me in the family room, I have acquired a fine Scotch whisky that I sourced in London. I would like to share it with you," invited Robert.

"With your mother visiting family in Drogheda and your brothers in the city I don't see any reason not to."

Three hours later and one bottle of whisky consumed, Robert

instructed James Clarke to bring another bottle from the cellar and not just any bottle.

"You must try this whiskey, Father, it's Irish."

"Irish whiskey!" exclaimed the Baron. "There's no such thing."

"I knew that would gain your attention," Robert, looking at the label, declared. "Distilled in County Antrim, Old Bushmills I believe."

"Irish whiskey that's a first and about time too, the Scots have had it their way for far too long. How could I refuse an offer to taste some of our very own? Let's see how it compares with the Scottish variety," slurred the Baron, then almost dropping his glass on the floor, "Oops thank heavens I am home and near my bed for I fear I may have taken too much alcohol."

"We are not finished yet, Father, it's the turn of the Irish now; only then can we decide on the character of the combatants."

"Well let's not waste any more time, pour. Who is on duty downstairs, Robert? I have a feeling I may need help getting to my quarters tonight."

"Both James and Patrick are on duty, Father, but don't worry, we shall see you to your quarters and safely to your bed."

Two more hours and the result of the whiskey tasting was in.

"Father, I cannot separate these two whiskeys. The Scotch displays a hint of peat on the palate, very distinctive, whilst the Irish is lighter in colour with a slight hint of fruit. What's your opinion, Father?"

The Baron was asleep.

Robert summoned the servants and instructed both James and Patrick to take the Baron to his chambers and see to it he was placed safely in his bed.

"Make sure the Baron is on his side and prop a pillow at his back, we don't want him getting sick in the night."

"Yes," replied James. "Shall I sit with him?"

"No, that won't be necessary, I shall look in on him later."

Chapter 15

Dublin

C larence Tennison had purchased one of the first houses to be
built on North Great Georges Street, Dublin, in the reign of
King George the first. A splendid example of Georgian Architecture,
three storeys over basement, very popular with the Aristocracy and
high-ranking members of both leading faiths. Clarence was a self-
made man albeit with a lot of help from a dowry received when he
had married Aoife Burk, the daughter of a successful tanning factory
owner from Tallagh.

Clarence used the dowry as a down payment on a merchant
sailing ship and for the past twelve years had been plying his trade
transporting cargo from Bristol to the African continent. From there
the crew would load up with fresh cargo bound for the Caribbean
where they unloaded that cargo and replaced it with spices, coffee,
sugar and a verity of exotic plants before sailing back to Bristol. It
was a well-documented triangular trade route. Clarence never set
foot on African soil nor did he ever experience the beauty of the
Caribbean. Instead he spent most of his time in what he referred to
as his office but was in fact a large dingy space formally used as a
warehouse to store animal skins imported from around the globe.

Apart from Aoife Burk's dowry, which was substantial, she had also inherited her father's fortune when he died suddenly from a suspected heart attack just four weeks after her wedding. That opened a whole new avenue of possibilities and Clarence was not going to let the opportunity pass him by. Apart from the financial windfall, Aoife also inherited a large warehouse and her father's tanning factory in Tallagh. Clarence Tennison's luck or misfortune depending on how you looked at it kept changing. His wife Aoife died of cancer two years after her father, leaving Clarence a very wealthy man and he wasted no time consigning Aoife Burk's memory to a very tiny space somewhere in his subconscious mind.

Although partitioned many times since its original intended use, the warehouse still carried a faint musty smell; the only way to rid it of its legacy was to burn the dammed place down. The warehouse was situated in a rundown part of Dublin's docklands on the north bank of the river Liffey at Ringsend. He often thought about relocating to a more fashionable area – after all, money was not the issue – but he always dismissed the idea for he had a deep affinity with the old place, one that he never quite understood.

3am. Clarence was sat at his desk under a very dim light from the inadequate number of candles placed around this large space; the large open fire was of little help as earlier Clarence had packed it with slack to help sustain the spark through the night. Straining his eyes, trying to make sense of a letter that had just been hand delivered, he raised his voice in frustration. "Damm! I must install this new gas lighting everyone is talking about." Then sliding his armchair closer to the nearest available source of light he began to peruse the correspondence. It was from the Royal African trading company. It read:

Dear Mr Tennison. You may not be aware of the pending article in the Dublin newspaper 'Pue's Occurrences', a popular source of news for the average City dweller. It is due to hit the streets of Dublin this very morning and it is my duty as chief executive to warn you of the significance within the content and to offer you some advice on how to reflect the accusations printed therein.

"Damn, that's all I need, the fallout from such innuendo could have far reaching consequences," as he jumped up from his leather armchair to fetch another large candle from the small writing table by the door then taking his seat again and sighed, ah! that's better; a quick poke of the large coal fire disturbed the scab atop the red-hot coals, the result was a higher level of comfort but more importantly light. The coal now burned with that familiar white orange glow, flooding the immediate area in front of the large black slate fireplace, creating a sphere of bright orange light that stretched no more than eight feet from the source; the rest of the large room was in complete darkness except for the odd flickering candle. Picking up the letter once more... "That's better, maybe now I can make some sense of this drivel." On reading the complete contents of the letter drivel it most certainly was not. "If I am implicated in this article the simplest way forward is to deny everything and stick to the tried and tested formula as advised in the correspondence from the Royal Africa Company; after all, it has a certain authority, the seal of the 'Royal Charter'." Clarence decided to use the next few hours before dawn to prepare for any eventuality. "My line of defence shall be:

"I ship textiles, copper and on occasion gunpowder to Africa and return with sugar, tobacco, rice, rum and indigo from the West Indies. What I transfer from Africa to the West Indies is clearly stated on the ship's manifest.

"I shall stick to the official statement; it would be almost impossible for any newspaper to acquire the evidence with which they could disrupt this glorious and advantageous trade." Only now did Clarence realize that he was talking aloud. Dawn broke just as Clarence returned to his home on North Great Georges Street exhausted. He sat by the fire that his daughter had kept alive from last evening.

"I taught you well, my dear, you make great slack; let's crack the scab and see if your handy work has been a success." A couple of pokes later and the fire burst into flames.

"Father, you are working too hard, you never slept last night, I heard you come home, Papa, and you look worried. Can I get you a glass of wine? It may help you sleep."

"Thank you, Elizabeth, I would like that, come join me by the fire." And after catching up on the previous day's events Clarence decided to take this private moment to try and unlock his daughter's true feelings with regard to her betrothed.

"Tell me how you feel, Elizabeth, about your future husband I mean?"

"To be honest, Father, I hardly know Robert, but from what I witnessed on the occasion of our introduction he seems odd."

"What do you mean?"

"I mean he is short in stature yet he exudes the aura of a much more powerful man or should I say pompous man. I am not quite sure yet, Father, but if I was to summarize my feelings at this moment I would say that I am, 'somewhat optimistic'; and you, Father, what is your opinion?"

"Like you, Elizabeth, I remain cautiously optimistic, one has to live in hope. I have worked very hard to organize this union with the best of intentions. I hope we never have reason to regret it."

Gaulstown

Robert pressed down on the pillow with all his strength and soon began to realize just how hard this was going to be – not in any emotional way, but the sheer physical strength required did surprise him. His initial reaction to the inevitable fight for life was to place his right knee across the legs of his victim whilst at the same time applying all his strength downwards on the pillow. Every ounce he could muster was now required as he tried to avoid the flaying arms of someone fighting for their very existence. A moment later he thought 'It's getting easier now, just a jerk or two, almost done, but to make certain Robert held the pillow firmly in place for what seemed like an eternity. Then in an almost caring voice he whispered, "there there, sleep". Robert, feeling quite jaded now, slowly eased the pressure on the pillow and in that surreal moment he began to wonder why he felt nothing, no empathy, no remorse, no regret, no sorrow, nothing. Any rational answer would have to wait for a more convenient moment for Robert's cold callous heart was looking forward to analysing the expression on his father's face and as he slowly removed the pillow the first thing to strike him was the Baron's open eyes staring accusingly at the monster he was warned to banish. Robert moved close almost touching his father's cheek and again whispered, "Even in death, Father, your eyes accuse me, but I must admit you do have good reason on this occasion, I grant you that."

Robert positioned the pillow just behind his father's left shoulder then placed two fingers on his eyelids as he unceremoniously closed the Baron's eyes then proceeded to gently stroke his father's face as if to chastise him, saying, "You should never have threatened me with banishment, Father; did you not understand it was my birthright? And to that end I claim it now. For I neither have the time or the patience to wait a moment longer. My time has come, Father, say hello to the new MP for the County of Westmeath – oh! I nearly forgot to mention – and master of all I survey."

Robert then proceeded to pour the remains of the Bushmills into the Baron's open mouth saying aloud: "At least you perished on a good Irish whiskey, Father." Standing to observe the entire scene Robert felt satisfied there was enough circumstantial evidence to convince the village doctor that the Baron's death was a tragic accident and sign the cause of death accordingly. Robert retreated to his quarters unheard and unseen to await the inevitable mayhem.

The village of Rochfortbridge was in shock; down at the inn the locals couldn't understand how the Baron, considered to be a relatively fit man, had died so young. Then the rumours began and almost to a man Robert was the prime suspect. Larry Cleary, one of the village elders, gave his verdict after consuming a few tankards of ale, resulting in a more animated display.

"Robert Rochfort murdered the Baron, of that I'm sure; they say he died in his sleep but I don't believe that for a minute."

Another of the village elders told Laurence to hold his tongue until the doctor had a chance to determine the cause of death.

"Well I have just told yez the cause of his death, it's Robert Rochfort – he couldn't wait for the Baron to die of a natural cause, simple as that, hungry for power I tell ya."

The landlord told both men to calm themselves and wait for the official diagnosis, adding, "Ned Flanagan will be in soon – maybe he can shed some light on the events up at the big house. For now, gentlemen, instead of blaming anyone we should all pray for the repose of the Baron's soul, god rest him."

But Larry Cleary was not finished yet.

"I'll tell yez another thing, yez are all wasting your time and prayers on that Sassenach for the whole Rochfort family are cursed."

"Ah shut up, old man, you don't know what you're talking about. Why couldn't it be an accident? They happen all the time. Dr Sweeney is up at the hall right this minute; he'll get to the bottom of this and they're French."

"French, me arse," shouted Laurence, "and as for that charlatan Sweeney he will do what Robert Rochfort instructs him to do and I bet a few pieces of the King's gold will change hands as well. Don't yez all know Sweeney is nearly as bad as me self with the drink."

"Jesses, Larry, hold your tongue, will ya."

"Why?" shouted Larry. "Everyone in this inn knows all about Sweeney, anyone with any sense would go onto the pass for a decent doctor, go on, ask any of them."

"For feck's sake, Larry, any more of that ould talk and I'll have to take your drink off ya or make ya drink it outside. What's it going to be?"

Up at the big house Mrs Doolin's kitchen was awash with tears and in between sobs the assistant housekeeper Catherine Murry was telling everyone that only yesterday his Lordship had agreed to grant her an extra day off because of her influenza.

"A grand man was the master. What will become of us all?"

"Now now, girls get a grip of yourselves, everything will be fine;

it's not us that needs to worry." Just then Ned entered the kitchen. "I thought you were gone to the village, Ned, is it not your night off?"

"Sure, how could I, Mrs Doolin, with all that's happened?"

"Now that you're here tell us what's going on upstairs?"

"Don't really know, but I think the doctor is finished. I saw him have words with Robert."

"Does anyone know if Mistress Elizabeth and the boys have been informed?"

"Yes," answered Ned, "Mr Clarke sent messengers straight away."

"Does anyone know how his Lordship died, was it his heart?"

"Mr Clarke overheard the doctor say he died in his sleep, choked on the drink or sometin. Mind you that's very likely cos his Lordship drank a good sup last night. Sure me-self and Patrick had to take him to his bed."

"Did Robert play any part in putting the Baron to bed?"

"No, Robert had a good few whiskeys himself and went straight to his quarters, but not before he told us to place a pillow behind his Lordship's back. I think he was trying to avoid this very thing."

"Did yez put the pillow behind his back?" enquired Mrs Doolin.

"Yes, we followed Robert's instructions and when we left the Baron was sleeping soundly."

"That's a relief, at least he was grand when ye left, sure he must have somehow turned over on his back in the night and got sick, that's the only thing that makes any sense."

"That's what the doctor thinks," said Ned.

"It's an unfortunate thing to happen, god rest his soul," cried Catherine through her tears.

George and Arthur, on hearing the devastating news, travelled the relatively short journey from Dublin to Drogheda to collect their mother and take her to Gaulstown. They spent most of the journey time trying to comprehend how their father could have died so suddenly.

"He was fine when we left not more than forty-eight hours ago, what could have caused it?" asked Arthur.

"I don't know but I have my suspicions," added George.

"I know what you are thinking, George, but when Mother joins us may I suggest you hold such accusations until we talk with the attending physician."

"You have your suspicions, just like I, Arthur and don't pretend otherwise."

"I did not say that, George," replied Arthur.

"But it does look rather sinister, you must agree," added George.

"I shall reserve judgment; at this moment I will not entertain the possibility of what you are suggesting – it is too horrendous to contemplate."

"Have you forgotten how frightened you were that day at the pond, when he tried to drown me? Do you remember?"

"How could I ever forget, George? Yet to think Robert could have a hand in such a vile callous act – his own father – that, George, disturbs me greatly."

"But Robert has a lot to gain by Father's death, do you not agree?" added George.

"Enough, George, enough," sighed Arthur.

Robert was waiting on the steps of Gaulstown as the carriage carrying Elizabeth, George and Arthur arrived back. Robert knew what they were thinking and decided the best form of defence was attack.

"Why this horrendous event took place when I happened to be the only member of this family present, I will never know. After the year we have just endured, I feel the gods are conspiring against us one more time."

"Are you certain it is the gods we should direct our anger at?"

"Let me assure you, Mother, the first I knew of Father's death was this morning when I heard the screams of the chambermaid on discovering Father had passed. I just want you all to know that Father and I had a very cordial conversation last evening enhanced by some splendid Irish whiskey. I might add I will go as far as to say we both enjoyed great conversation. When we retired I instructed

Edward and Patrick to escort Father to his chambers and see to it he was made comfortable in his bed and after speaking with them both this morning they assured me they had followed my instructions to the letter. Dr Sweeney estimates the time of death between four and five this morning."

"Robert, we have just alighted from our carriage, why do you take such a defensive posture?" enquired Elizabeth. "No one has accused you of any wrongdoing, yet your words sound like the words of a guilty man. God knows you have committed enough evil acts in the past to suggest you are capable of such a deed. After all, you have the most to gain from an event of this magnitude, yet I cannot believe you would sink to such depravity as to take your own father's life. No, I will not entertain such evil again. I shall speak with the doctor as soon as possible; there has to be a rational explanation. For now I grieve for my beloved husband. I need time to come to terms with and understand the implications of such a tragic event."

"Yes of course, Mother, can I get you something to drink?"

"No, Robert, no alcohol, I feel I shall need all my propensity to deal with this awful tragedy."

George and Arthur just stared at Robert but declined to say a word except to encourage their mother to take to her bed.

"How can I sleep? This is the darkest day of my life?"

"Come, Mother, let us escort you to your quarters," interrupted Arthur.

Chapter 16

Christmas came and went. The events of four months earlier were lessened to a degree with the passage of time, but not entirely forgotten. The wedding was now beginning to take everyone's attention away from the untimely death of the Baron; the spotlight was now firmly fixed on the newly appointed member of parliament.

Robert was now the most powerful man in Westmeath and arguably in Ireland, but that was not going to satisfy Robert's hunger for substantial power. The title 'Baron of the exchequer' died along with his father but that did not trouble Robert. He promised himself he would soon reap the rewards from seeds planted together with Prince Frederick in Covent Garden not that long ago, but for now the most important item on the agenda was Robert's maiden speech to the House of Parliament in two months' time. He spent the next six weeks putting the final touches to the most important speech he would ever deliver, a speech he was certain would cement his position in the eyes of the only family that mattered: the Royal family. The cunning plan Robert had instigated on the steps of Gaulstown Hall a mere twelve months earlier had so far yielded the most favourable results. The next phase was to enlist the help of his Royal connections. Robert left Ireland for London on the 15th of April in the year of our lord 1731, leaving his mother to oversee the affairs of Gaulstown.

London

Robert's maiden speech to the House of Parliament was an outstanding success. Prince Frederick was most impressed as the speech was a homily to the Royal family. Frederick sent his private carriage to Parliament to take Robert to the palace and when he arrived he was escorted straight to the Prince's private quarters where he was warmly greeted by Frederick.

"I must congratulate you, Robert, on your maiden speech, probably lost on most of the common rabble that peruse the House of Parliament, or should I refer to it by its proper name house of 'commoners'. No place for a man of your stature, I might add, but nonetheless one must endure what one must endure to keep the illusion of democracy alive."

"Thank you for your kind words, your Highness, it is indeed a great honour to receive a private audience," as he performed an elaborate curtsey.

"I was sad to hear of your father's death, Robert, he was quite young; but you know what they say every cloud has a silver lining. You are now Member of parliament for–" 'pause'– "I've forgotten, remind me again, Robert."

"The County of Westmeath, your Highness."

"Yes, that sounds familiar but knowing you as well as I presume to, I am not entirely convinced you are satisfied with the title MP for the County of–" 'another pause'– "forgive me, what was the name again?"

"Westmeath, your Highness."

"Yes, Westmeath, but you must not despair, my good friend, for I have plans for you, Robert, but first I must ask you to indulge my penchant for young men one more time."

"Young men, your Highness?" cajoled Robert.

"I have no need to elaborate further, Robert, for we both know the intent."

"Yes of course, your Highness, I apologise for my inept attempt to generate mirth."

"I promised to repay you, Robert and I fully intend to keep my promise. I have arranged for us both to attend a private lunch with the King here at the Palace tomorrow evening and I can give you assurances that my father will accommodate any request I may make of him, within reason of course. When we have completed our forays into the bowels of this great Metropolis you will see my gratitude in tangible terms and soon."

Robert stealthily combined his official duties with his unofficial to the satisfaction of both the British establishment and the Royal inner circle. Robert returned to Gaulstown a more powerful man than even his immediate family suspected, and he was determined to test his power the only way he knew how. His lust for young girls had not dissipated over the years and when that uncontrollable urge took over no female was safe, young or otherwise. Who was going to be his next unfortunate victim?

The young chambermaid entered Robert's quarters intending to carry out her duties as quickly as possible but to her horror Robert was waiting.

"I can come back another time, me lord. Mrs Doolin said you were out riding; I'm not supposed to be in here when you are."

"Come here, what's your name, girl?"

"Lilly Sullivan, your lordship, please, me lord, Mrs Doolin will–"

"Did you know we once had an estate manager; his name was Sullivan also, any relation?"

"Yes, me lord, he was my grandfather."

"How old are you?"

"Sixteen, me lord, please sir I'll be in trouble if–"

"Come closer," demanded Robert.

Lilly was in shock as she obeyed her master's request. Slowly, nervously, she started to walk to the night stand that Robert was pointing to. After glancing up to see the look in Robert's eyes the young girl was terrified and felt very vulnerable. She instinctively knew she had to try and find a way out of this dangerous situation and attempted to make a hasty retreat.

"I forgot to bring the bucket and mop, please excuse me, your lordship, I won't be long." And she started to walk to the door.

"Stop right where you are, girl." Lilly froze.

"Now turn around and put your hands on the nightstand with your back to me and do not make a sound."

"But your lordship–"

Robert placed his hand over her mouth saying: "Stay quiet, girl and in a few moments you can return to your duties," then he began lifting her petticoat.

"I do not intend to hurt you, but if you resist I will have no choice but to evict you and your entire family. Do I make myself clear?"

When Lilly felt his hand caress her inner thigh, she bolted for the door but did not cry out. Robert grabbed her by the arm and almost tore it from its socket, then slapped her hard in the face shouting, "You will do as I say, is that clear?" Taking his silk handkerchief from under his frilled shirt cuff, Robert roughly wiped the blood that was now trickling from her nose saying, "Shall we start again?"

Lilly stood with her hands tightly gripping the edges of the nightstand. She was so terrified she could not speak, let alone move. Lilly, now sobbing, cried out, "Please sir, you're hurting me." She knew in her heart it was of no use to resist, the master could do what he wanted with impunity; she had no choice but to succumb, it would soon be over she hoped. Robert viciously raped the young chambermaid knowing that he could get away with practically anything.

When he finished he callously said: "Back to your duties, girl and before you do make yourself presentable, now go." The young chambermaid was not the first and she would not be the last to brush herself down after an encounter with the devil. She kept Robert in her sights as she slowly walked backwards in the direction of the door and relative safety, but she need not have worried as Robert had already turned his back. His mind was now firmly on his upcoming wedding to Elizabeth Tennison, just four months away now. Robert approached the inevitable with gusto, his primary motivation was to get the marriage over with as soon as possible.

The marriage had been arranged in what felt like another lifetime, one when the Baron was master and Lady Elizabeth Rochfort had some degree of power, but that was no longer the case as Elizabeth appeared a shadow of the woman she had been a mere twelve months ago.

That fact was not lost on her family back in Drogheda, but the new Earl was dealing with a family crisis of his own; he was kept busy attempting to rebuild the shambles that was the Earldom of Drogheda. After the death of Elizabeth's father Henry, the third Earl of Drogheda who had squandered almost the entire family fortune on women and gambling, accordingly the estate fell into debt. The last hope for the Moore dynasty lay with Elizabeth's brother and her mother, the Dowager Countess of Drogheda. The Dowager encouraged her youngest son Edward, the fourth Earl, to sell enough of the Moore family estates in County Louth to meet Henry's outstanding liabilities of more than £180,000 and now that the estate was clear of all debt, the Dowager at last felt able to offer moral support to her beleaguered daughter at Gaulstown. Her intention was to live at Gaulstown Hall for as long as was necessary.

On hearing this news Robert was not at all pleased, but decided to accept the situation and settle for a period of calm; after all the mayhem of the last few years it might be wise to let things pursue a more natural course; it might help to mend some rather badly constructed bridges. His logic was, if the Dowager was predisposed with the affairs of the Moore family and did not interfere with the affairs of the Rochfort family, then everything could proceed in a cordial atmosphere.

Even after all this time Robert could sense the family animosity that still hung heavy in the air. The Moore family were incensed with Robert's treatment of Elizabeth, George and Arthur. By way of insincere recompense Robert decided to ask George to be his best man, soliciting the advice of his younger brother Arthur; the advice he received was not what he had hoped for but was expecting. Arthur tried to explain that George had not forgiven Robert for his disrespectful outburst on his return to Gaulstown from London.

"Not only did you disrespect Father, you also diminished our status before the entire household."

"But I thought we had put all that behind us, Arthur."

"George is finding that very hard to do," answered Arthur.

"Thank you for your honesty," replied Robert. The next day he instructed James to summon George to the library.

Library

"Good afternoon, George, care for a glass of wine?"

"A little early for me, Robert, but I shall make an exception. Have I done something wrong, Robert? It's quite unusual for you to seek out my company."

"No not at all, George, I have nothing but praise for the way you and your staff are managing the estate, excellent reports, excellent. No that's not the reason I summoned you, George. I want to ask if you would do me the honour of being my best man, but before you answer let me just say: I know we have not always seen eye to eye but believe me, George, I would like to wipe the slate clean and start afresh. What do you say? Shall we shake hands?"

George paused for a moment thinking 'how can I trust this man after everything I have witnessed and the fact that I still hold him responsible for the death of our father' but rather than make his own position at Gaulstown untenable, George agreed to be his best man – 'what other choice do I have?' he thought.

"Yes, Robert, I agree but on one condition. May I enlist your good friend Captain James Hamilton to help plan the entertainment? I do not have sufficient experience of the Dublin social scene."

"Splendid, George, although I shall be a little apprehensive if James Hamilton has any involvement, for I know how much he would like to pursue a humorous agenda and more, coincidently Captain

Hamilton happens to be in Ireland enjoying some long overdue leave and will visit Gaulstown in the coming weeks – a perfect opportunity for you both to plot my stag itinerary, with you making the final judgement, George; I shall relinquish any such negativity regarding his involvement. Let us summon Arthur to his favourite hideout and celebrate our new beginning."

Chapter 17

The Stag Party

T he stag party's carriage arrived outside the Grey Goose tavern
in Temple Bar, an area situated on the south bank of the river
Liffey directly in the centre of Dublin. Once located outside the old
city walls – it was called Saint Andrews then – but the area had fallen
into disuse because of attacks by the native Irish. It could be compared
with Covent Garden, thought Robert, smaller but no less potent.
Richard and James were on their second ale as they both sprang to
their feet to welcome the Rochfort siblings.

James enquired, "How is the doomed man?" Then turning to
George and Arthur asked if they were ready for the night of their life.

"Yes indeed, good evening."

"Well, gentlemen, now that the pleasantries are done, let's get
down to the serious work," suggested James as he shouted, "Five ales,
landlord if you please."

"I hope you have nothing too outrageous planned for tonight?"
enquired Robert.

"How could I hope to emulate the highs of Covent Garden,
Robert? Nothing could come close. Still we shall give it a try. Has your
big brother told you he is a member of the Royal inner circle now?"

"Yes, he did mention it," said George, "but I'm sure we are not party to the entire facts."

"I fear you will need the skills of the inquisitor Generalis Tomas de Torque to extract the full facts, or should I say "secrets", that your brother shares with his Royal Highness Prince Frederick," chuckled Richard.

"Who is Thomas de Torque?" enquired George.

"He spearheaded the Spanish Inquisition," said Arthur.

"I must visit the library more often," said George.

"My brother must be hiding some serious secrets to invoke such a historical brute," commented Arthur.

"Just teasing, gentlemen, for we all have secrets to protect. Is that not so, Robert?" No response was forthcoming.

"Cheer up, Robert for it's your night," encouraged James as he placed a friendly hand on Robert's shoulder only to be rebuked with a forceful brush of Robert's hand. James then decided to direct his attention to the rest of the party.

"Drink up, gentlemen, for we have a strict schedule to follow. In less than two hours I intend to place the Trinity plus two in the capable hands of the floozy that sucked the noble cockles off the second Earl of Milltown. The lady in question hails from your neck of the woods, Robert, 'Westmeath'." James then raised his glass and proposed a toast to the groom. Two hours passed in what felt like minutes for the merriment was frantic. "Ok, gentlemen, it's time for our appointment with destiny, I believe our cab is waiting."

"Peg Plunket's den of iniquity, my good man, do you know the establishment?"

"Certainly, gents, every Dubliner knows Peg's Palace."

"If that be true can we make haste for it is almost the witching hour."

The smell of horse manure was everywhere, and no amount of cologne could mask its potency nor deflect its nuisance.

"This city is indeed sinking in the dreadful stuff; goddam that smell," mumbled Robert through his cologne-soaked monogrammed cotton handkerchief.

"You are not the only one to raise that issue, Robert for only this very morning the esteemed editor of the Dublin Gazetteer was calling on the public to apply coercion to their political representatives, demanding they eradicate this very problem," added Richard.

"I will not hold my breath," said James, "for I fear half of our political representatives cannot wipe their own arses, present company excepted, Robert."

"You, Robert, are one of our representatives yet you complain; raise the issue, man," demanded Richard.

"I fear the alcohol has emboldened your distain for authority, gentlemen." Arthur passed a silver hip flask containing a fine malt as James continued.

"The sooner we arrive at Peg's Palace the sooner we can clear our nostrils of horse shit and fill them with the sweet smell of pussy." Let's drink to that was the chorus.

Peg's Palace

Heaving was the only way to describe Peg's establishment, three floors packed to capacity with men of varying shapes and sizes, from tradesmen all the way to nobility.

"Gentlemen, please peruse the menu and make your choice while I discuss commerce with the famous Madam," said Richard.

Peg's Palace was decorated in the style of a North African Bedouin tent; the ceilings and walls were loosely covered in fine silks, every conceivable colour and more besides transporting one's senses into a surreal dream-like state. A couple of hits from the ever-present Opium pipe certainly helped to encourage not only visual perception but also eliminated any remnants of historical prudence. Peg certainly gave value for money. Chaise longues, leather sofas and what seemed like hundreds of exotic cushions were scattered everywhere; Peg's girls were using every trick in the book striving to entice the clientele to make haste – time was money.

The sooner they could extract the money and complete the transaction the sooner they could move onto the next client. Turnover was the key to Peg's wealth; her motto was 'get them in, get them out'. Arthur was lying on a bed of cushions staring blankly at the ceramic pipe bowl, caressing the curves as if he were caressing the female form.

"Wake up, Arthur, the real thing is right in front of you," encouraged James. Arthur slowly came around and as his eyes adjusted to the scantily clad flesh laid before him, he had no choice but to succumb to the intense temptation.

"This way, darlin," purred a young sexy brunette as she took him by the hand. George was next to fumble his way in the direction of what he described as an Angel.

"Look at his little face," laughed James as the young man was led away by a pair of very large breasts.

"That just leaves the Trinity, gentlemen, let's make ourselves comfortable. Opioids anyone?"

"Yes please!" as the Trinity continued to observe and drool.

The available girls were parading in various stages of undress.

"A sight to behold," mumbled Robert.

James motioned to one of the girls who particularly caught his eye, a beautiful dark-haired vixen that oozed sex from every pore. She slowly moved closer while all the time swaying her hips provocatively inviting his touch with her eyes. James could no longer resist as he slowly lifted her petticoat exposing a tantalizing glimpse of the young woman's most valued possession.

"May I take a closer look, my dear?"

"Help yourself, darlin, I'm waiting."

James was now almost touching the prize with the tip of his nose as he whispered, "Use your fingers, my dear, I like to see what I am paying for." That was the cue for the remaining members of the Trinity to make their choice and find a room.

3am and Arthur was the second to extricate himself from the boudoir as James was already waiting on a pile of cushions with two bottles of Jean-Louis Champagne and five glasses. He tried to gain Arthur's attention through the seemingly growing clientele shouting, "Arthur, over here."

"Wow," said Arthur, "that was the best night of my life, thank you, James."

"It's only starting, my friend, the night is still young," as he slapped the young man on the back saying, "there's more to come, if we can drag the others away from the honey pot, that is." George and Robert were next to surface.

"Champagne, gentlemen," invited James.

"Can we please do that again?" asked George.

James then turned to Robert and enquired, "Was she young enough for you, Robert?"

"I don't know what you mean, James. Where's Richard? Has he not finished yet?"

"Arthur, go find Richard as we need to make haste," pleaded James.

"You have something else planned?" enquired Robert.

"Yes, back to Temple Bar, gentlemen, for I have sourced a certain house where the Madam specializes not only in the art of the Kama Sutra but also in the art of chemistry. Do not fear, gentlemen, our host is very experienced in the art of magic potions, opiates mainly. Ah! there you are, Richard and judging by that big grin on your face I can only conclude you had a very satisfying encounter," as he handed him a glass of champagne.

"Drink up, gentlemen. I have one last trip planned, "trip" being the operative word."

"What are you talking about, James?" enquired Richard.

"No sleep tonight, gentlemen. I shall explain on the way. But look on the bright side, we have one week to recover."

Exiting Peg's establishment, they were greeted by the cold night air.

"Cabbie, Temple Bar and drive like the devil."

As dawn broke over Dublin

and night turned to day
Peregrines against the grey sky
seeking out their prey
seeing love lose out to lust
the meek began to pray
there was nothing left to ponder
nothing left to say

Chapter 18

Autumn leaves now covered the avenue as guests began to arrive for the wedding Robert hoped would never happen but having promised to abide by Rochfort tradition there was only one way out of it and that was to go through with it; a Rochfort paradox of which there were many. There was great excitement in the village of Rochfortbridge and for two days the curtains twitched feverishly; everyone wanted or needed a glimpse of this great spectacle. Carriage after carriage carrying the elite of Irish society passed through their little village and on through the gates of the Gaulstown estate. Elizabeth's brother Edward Moore, the 4th Earl of Drogheda and his new wife Sarah Margetson were first to arrive. Followed by Robert's good friend Richard Lambert, accompanied by his father the 4th Earl of Cavan. Major General Christopher Hamilton was next accompanied by his wife Neibh and their son Captain James Hamilton. Next to arrive was Viscount Robert Molesworth and his wife Jane. One by one the cream of Irish nobility graced the halls of Gaulstown.

The wedding reception would be held in the Great Hall, where three hundred guests could be seated in relative comfort. As the guests began filing into the Great Hall some gasped at the sheer size of this massive room. Guests stood gazing in amazement at the two depictions of the Rochfort family history; on the left were oil paintings in the style of the old masters and opposite a synopsis of the Rochfort family history depicted in large stained-glass windows.

The distribution of crisp sunlight through the copious amounts of small irregular panes of coloured glass, appeared to bring the complete autumnal season into this vast space. Shades of red, blue, yellow and green bounced around this great hall like a fairy dance, leading the eye to the gable wall and the largest stained-glass window outside of Dublin. The depiction of Robert's ancestor placing the crown on the young King's head meant to convey a message of power, wealth and status to all.

The guests' interaction with the actual wedding service would be limited; if they were extremely quiet, they might just be able to hear some of the ceremonial proceedings from the tiny chapel. Robert and his best man entered the chapel through the fairy door, the bride would enter from the small vestibule through the courtyard. As Robert waited for his bride whom he had not laid eyes on since their formal introduction just over one year earlier he was now thinking, 'Why should I proceed with this charade?' then quickly banished that thought for he had already made provision for this very scenario when he spawned his evil plan.

Mrs Doolin had no part in the preparation of the wedding feast simply because of the vast number of guests involved. Her instructions today were to supervise the distribution of food and she was in her element. A specialist team of cooks based in Dublin and vastly experienced in organizing functions of this size were commissioned to supply and prepare the enormous array of food. Meats included wild boar, roast sirloin of beef, venison, roast snipe, pigeon, turkey and chime of mutton. A full range of sweet fruits from apples to berries plus a variety of citrus. A selection of home-grown vegetables with just a couple of exotic examples like artichoke and avocado. The meats were cooked on spits that were set up behind the walled gardens then brought to the top table in the main hall.

The desert was by far the easiest to prepare, large trays of what Mrs Doolin simply called "bread pudding". The ingredients were flour, milk, butter, eggs, sugar, suet, marrow and raisins. James

Clarke was busy making sure the thirty or so male staff under his control were kept occupied; most were loaned from surrounding estates, some as far away as Kilkenny. They included senior butlers, under butlers, footmen, carriage drivers, stable hands, even gardeners were drafted in for this one. James Clarke kept them all on their toes ferrying the large trays of roast meats from the walled garden to the top table.

Mrs Doolin was finding her responsibilities much easier supervising twenty-seven female staff, a mixture of parlour maids, chambermaids, kitchen maids; some were her own girls but like the male staff most were borrowed from surrounding big houses across Westmeath. She knew all the girls by name for they had been drafted in for feasts like this on many occasions in the past. The hardest part of her job she was heard to say later was "keeping them quiet", trying in vain to stop them from using the cover of the wedding to gossip about everyone and everything. It was their big opportunity to catch up and share stories about their masters and mistresses. "Drive me mad yez will" was a favourite of Mrs Doolin's but she loved all her girls and protected them like a mother hen.

James Clarke was not quite as relaxed; he was beginning to feel the pressure. The only one that seemed to be enjoying himself was Ned Flanagan, promoted for the day to under butler, a role he made his own.

"You, take this jug of wine to the big hall. Mr Clarke will supervise you from there. And you, come here. What's your name?"

"Thomas, Mr Flanagan."

"Good man, Thomas, take these refreshments to the minstrel's gallery." Then turning to Patrick with that big grin, laughed, "Did ya hear that, Patrick? Yer man called me Mr Flanagan." Ned was having the time of his life; 'I could get used to this,' he thought.

After the wedding ceremony was complete Robert and his new bride entered the main hall in single file through the fairy door, Robert pausing to extend his right arm an invitation to Elizabeth, she accepted by placing her left hand on Robert's elbow then bowing her head so she could pass under the low arch of the fairy door. The procession moved slowly to the top table, where members of both families were seated; much merriment and laughter resounded in the Great Hall.

At the top table Robert was paying very little attention to his new bride, a fact that did not go unnoticed by Elizabeth's father, Clarence. Elizabeth, noticing her father's unease, turned to her new husband intending to allay her father's fears.

"Robert, is it not the custom for the groom to take his wife onto the floor for the first dance?"

"I don't dance" were the only words he offered.

"Come, husband, I will teach you, it's quite simple."

"Are you hard of hearing, Elizabeth? I said I do not dance."

"Am I to be the only bride not to dance at her own wedding?"

Still silence as Robert looked straight ahead.

Elizabeth's father leaned over to his daughter and enquired, "Is everything well, my dear?"

"Yes, Papa, everything is fine."

"I did not hear your conversation, my dear, but your demeanour does not portray a sense of happiness. Are you sure all is well?" Elizabeth tried to hide the sorrow caused by her husband's indifference. Alas the tears that had now formed in her soft green eyes gave the game away.

"Why do you cry then if all is well?"

Lying, she answered, "Father, I was very young when Mother died but I know she is watching over me this day; I am sad she is not with us to celebrate my wedding day."

"There, there, my sweet daughter, don't cry; will you dance with your father and in silence we can invoke your mother's memory?"

"Yes, Father, that would help release the sorrow I feel at this moment."

"Come, sweet Bess, a waltz, your favourite." Sweet Bess was a pet name Clarence used when Elizabeth was a child, reserved for such occasions as a fall or a minor mishap of some sort. Today it was used to show Elizabeth that her father would always be there. Clarence suspected Robert to be the source of his daughter's distress even though she was trying to mask that very fact. Clarence promised himself that fateful day, if Robert Rochfort brought sorrow and misery to his beloved daughter, he would have no option but to take his life.

Clarence accompanied his daughter to the dance floor.

Elizabeth, knowing her father suspected Robert as the source of her unhappiness whispered, "I am wondering if I have made the biggest mistake of my life, Father."

Clarence, trying to ease both her pain and his own, replied, "Don't say that, Elizabeth, we must give Robert a chance, thus give your marriage a chance. Remember you can always come back home to Dublin whenever you wish, for as long as I have breath in my body you will be loved."

"Yes, Father, I know and thank you for all your support. I will always love you too, Papa."

When the waltz was over Clarence escorted his daughter back to her place at the top table where they observed Robert still sitting in the same position they had left him. Elizabeth then remarked that she had not seen Robert's mother saying, "Her Ladyship has not been seen since the ceremony; a foreboding sign, don't you think, Father?"

"Now that you have brought that fact to my attention I am inclined to agree," said Clarence.

"Would ya look at them, Patrick, tearin the food like a bunch of animals," remarked Ned.

"Ay, a bunch of rich animals," replied Patrick.

Just then the bell sounded to let the guests know it was time for staff to clear the centre of the hall for dancing. James Clarke issued the order: "Clear the floor", a command to the entire domestic workforce to remove the wooden benches and make way for the dancing to commence.

As soon as the floor was cleared the minstrels encouraged the guests to take to the floor, a minuet was guaranteed to get the guests to their feet. Emboldened with alcohol the ladies entered the space amidst a flurry of extravagant dresses, a mesmerizing collage of colour moving in synchronized patterns across the floor interrupted on occasion by puffs of powder emanating from some of the rather dubious looking wigs. Most of them slightly askew to one side or the other as some of the guests were a little worse for wear.

The merriment continued unabated for hours and after they nearly drank the place dry some of the guests were too drunk to continue. Luckily Ned and Patrick were on hand to summon their respective drivers to take their masters home. Some got so comatose they slept on wooden benches in the Great Hall. The next morning saw Elizabeth Rochfort with eyes as red as crimson, still sitting in her chamber, still in her wedding dress and still a virgin. Robert had left for London in the middle of the night without telling a soul, the guests had left Gaulstown including Elizabeth's father before anyone knew that Robert had deserted his wife on her wedding night. Elizabeth was so ashamed she created a cover story for his absence. Robert would not return to Gaulstown for two months.

Two weeks after the wedding Clarence Tennison, on receipt of a letter from his daughter telling her father that the marriage had not been consummated, returned to Gaulstown intending to take Elizabeth back to Dublin with him, but Lady Elizabeth promised to find her wayward son and suitably reprimand him.

Clarence turned to his daughter and said, "If you are in agreement with Lady Elizabeth and you want to give him time to explain his actions all I can do is be there for you when you need me." But on leaving he warned that the current situation would not be allowed to continue. Lady Elizabeth was at her wits' end. Where could he be?

When Robert eventually returned to Gaulstown he was confronted by Elizabeth's mother the Dowager Countess who had commandeered the suite on the east wing and was now lending support to her daughter in her time of need.

"That is no way for a gentleman to behave, Robert, have you lost all respect for the Rochfort name? Your ancestors are turning in their graves."

But instead of saying what he wanted to say, Robert bit his tongue and implemented the next chapter in his twisted plot.

"You are perfectly right to reprimand me, Countess, for my actions are the actions of a bounder. I do not know what came over me," then continued to make some very lame excuses. He promised the Countess that he would make things right with his virgin bride saying, "I shall go presently and beg my wife's forgiveness."

Robert did go directly to Elizabeth's chambers; there he profusely begged her forgiveness and blamed his outrageous behaviour on his nervous disposition, relating to the fact that he was still a 'virgin' and did not know how to properly perform his marital duties.

To his great surprise and relief Elizabeth believed his lies. He then proceeded to fumble his way through lovemaking in the manner of a less experienced lover.

The next morning Elizabeth Rochfort sat at her bureau desk writing to her father saying the marriage had been consummated and all was well at Gaulstown. Robert spent the next ten months trying hard to convince everyone that he had changed and become the model husband. The ruse was quite easy for Robert as he had plenty of practice in the art of deception. The fact that he spent most of that ten months carousing bordellos in both Dublin and London under the pretence of official engagements was neither here nor there and he was not finished yet.

Chapter 19

London

Robert had no intention of returning to Gaulstown any time soon. Like a glutton that had consumed food to the point of making himself sick, he had become bored of his visits to Covent Garden and decided a change would do him good. He decided to explore some of the architectural masterpieces of this great city – 'a dose of intellectual stimulation might just fill the void I feel at this junction' he thought. One such excursion brought Robert into the heart of the Metropolis to marvel at Christopher Wren's masterpiece St. Paul's Cathedral. Completed in 1708 it replaced the original St. Paul's that had been destroyed in the great fire. The new building was considered one of the finest in Britain and a fine example of Baroque architecture. The clock tower interested Robert and with the help of his good friend Prince Frederick was accorded supervised access.

The experience although benign acted as a catalyst and true to his nature Robert soon got bored with convention and was back to his old tricks. Instinctively he returned to the darker side of his nature for he felt compelled to satisfy his inner demons. With that in mind Robert decided to seek out other more 'infamous' landmarks. London was expanding at an alarming rate; crime was rampant, resulting in numerous executions. Highwaymen were a crowd favourite; the folklore and legend that accompanied such characters only amplified the excitement.

Robert was intrigued and decided to attend one execution, one that was widely reported in a host of printed pamphlets and newspaper articles. The atmosphere at public hangings was carnival like, that combined with the clamour of the bloodthirsty rabble 'made for a grand day out' thought Robert.

The execution that appealed most to Robert was that of Sir Simon Clarke Bart, a member of the Aristocracy turned highwayman, perfect fodder for the baying crowd. Robert had no intention to rough it with the peasantry, but instead he invited Prince Frederick to accompany him and to his great surprise Frederick accepted. The Prince seemed even more enthusiastic than Robert, thus ensuring a ringside seat with all the security that entailed.

The day of the execution arrived. It seemed the entire population of London had turned out to besiege Newgate Prison, it was a scorching hot day with a definite carnival atmosphere. The place was throbbing with life, glinting market stalls, dog fights, fops, prostitutes and pickpockets all crammed the plaza; street vendors sold everything from scissors to matches. Gamblers cursed as their favourite cock had just fought to the death and lost but it wasn't the end of the world, for fortunes were won and fortunes were squandered, but who cared, there was a hanging to see, let some other poor bugger suffer; but until then it was time for the baying illiterates to fill their bellies and have some fun.

The mixture of aromas now drifting on the sultry summer breeze left no one in any doubt that this was indeed a celebration, a macabre celebration of 'death', 'how magnificent' thought Robert. Men on stilts mingled within the crowd, whether their purpose was entertainment or merely to gain a more favourable view was open to question. The laughter of children fused with the cries of punch as he beat the living daylights out of his beloved wife added an air of anticipation to the proceedings. Prince Frederick seemed to be infected just like the masses and did not hide his enthusiasm shouting, "bring on the traitor, hang him high". Robert was now beginning to feel something approaching the euphoria he felt on the night he took his father's life. The waiting was over and if proof were needed one only had to focus on the outer edge of the crowd to realize that security were laying into the masses as they cleared a path for the carriage carrying the caged accused. With each crack of the leather whip cries of pain rang out, a promise of things to come no doubt. Rotten lettuces and over ripened tomatoes rained down on the prisoner's transport and by the time it reached the foot of the scaffold the cage looked more like an exhibit straight from a zoo.

"Hang the bastard. Cut his bollocks off and shove it up his aristocratic arse" were some of the more reserved expressions of encouragement directed at the masked executioner who stood motionless. Robert turned to Frederick with a question.

"Your Highness, there are two prisoners in that cage if I am not mistaken. I am wondering which one is the fallen aristocrat and what is the reason for the other man's plight?"

Frederick turned to one of his advisers to seek the answer and after a moment he said, "The chubby one is the fallen angel or if you prefer one of ours, the skinny one is about to pay the ultimate price for the murder of his wife."

"A bit harsh for such a small sin," commented Robert as both men laughed heartedly.

Chapter 20

Ringsend

Clarence Tennison arrived at his offices in Ringsend to find graffiti daubed on the entrance door; it simply read "Slave Trader". He assumed it was fallout from the newspaper article one year earlier. 'Strange,' thought Clarence, 'for so much time has elapsed since the publication of the disruptive article'. He instructed one of the workers to make haste and remove the offending words – 'maybe this is nothing or maybe it is an opportunistic attempt to blackmail me; either way I must proceed with great caution'. He had read all the newspaper articles rallying against the slave trade and instinctively knew it was only a matter of time before public opinion was mobilised to such an extent as to severely curtail or at worse ban this exploitation of our fellow humans. He decided to strike while the iron was hot and purchase a second vessel, a much larger three-masted clipper anchored at the Royal dockyards in Deptford, East London. One that could reach speeds of 22 knots with the explicit purpose of outrunning the plague that was "Piracy". Clarence deemed commerce more important than his fellow human being.

London

Robert once more grew wary of London and decided to return to Gaulstown. It was almost one year after his wedding to Elizabeth; time to initiate the next phase of his plan. But before he could say goodbye to his favourite Metropolis he had one important task to complete. It was a request from the Dowager Countess for Robert to bring back some exotic plants, for she thought Gaulstown's large glasshouse would be the ideal environment to encourage their growth.

Robert was of similar mind and decided to visit one of the most famous pleasure gardens in London intending to source suitable varieties. As luck would have it, Frederick Prince of Wales was Vauxhall Gardens' ground landlord and arranged for Robert to meet with the head horticulturist in order to assist him in his quest. When Robert arrived, he was amazed; he was not expecting such opulence.

Vauxhall Pleasure Gardens were not just gardens, they also boasted one of the finest raised open-air pavilions with a private dining room, where one could sit and observe the cabinets of curiosities plus the fairs, puppets, freak shows, ballad singers, menageries and any number of similar amusements.

"What a wonderful place," said Robert as he was introduced to the primary horticulturist and after pleasantries were exchanged both men tucked into a fine meal of roast beef with a selection of fresh vegetables picked that very morning. The food was consumed with gusto and when both men had finished their fine brandies and cigars, Harold Tolworth presented Robert with a selection of exotic plants to take back to Ireland with Prince Frederick's compliments. He pointed to one plant and warned Robert of its poisonous character and to inform whoever might have access, to treat it with respect.

Back at Gaulstown

Robert returned to Gaulstown with little fanfare, for the entire household were enjoying life without the disruption that always accompanied the Member of Parliament. Elizabeth would now have to relinquish any influence she presumed to exert over her remaining two sons, thus taking a back seat. Lady Elizabeth had grown very fond of her daughter-in-law and was dreading Robert's return for she knew only too well how much he had protested the marriage and how disinterested he remained, plus the fact Robert used every conceivable excuse to avoid physical contact with his wife and that as far as Lady Elizabeth was concerned, was a recipe for disaster.

How did Lady Elizabeth harvest such intimate details? Ten months is a long time and it gave both women the opportunity to get to know each other on a more intimate level; many of their discussions were intense and would surely have given them both food for thought. Elizabeth was busy arranging her first wedding anniversary celebration as autumn had well and truly arrived.

"Mrs Doolin, your presence is required in the library, more discussions on the menu I think," chuckled James.

"Not again, I don't know why she bothers. Robert doesn't care one way or the other, I wager you he won't even remember it, the wedding I mean."

"Don't think I'll take you up on that particular wager, Mrs Doolin, for I detest losing money."

"Best pander to the poor girl for I do feel sorry for her," added Mrs Doolin.

Lady Elizabeth and her daughter-in-law were in the library finalizing details when Elizabeth broke down in tears scattering her notes on to the floor saying, "What's the point, Lady Elizabeth, for my husband has barely looked at me since our marriage, if you could call it a marriage – more resembling a sentence," she cried. "I don't mean to disrespect you, Lady Elizabeth" and through tears of sorrow screamed, "Why did I go through with it? My hopes and dreams for a family lie in ruins, if only I had followed my instincts."

"There, there, Elizabeth, let me hold you," and as both women sought comfort in each other's embrace Lady Elizabeth was overcome with a feeling of trepidation. For she knew in her heart that her daughter-in-law's dreams of a family lay elsewhere, not here at Gaulstown and certainly not with her son Robert. Lady Elizabeth tried her best to console Elizabeth, but her words of comfort sounded hollow even to her as she continued.

"Don't cry, Elizabeth, for I am certain all your dreams will come to fruition in time," as she picked up the scattered notes. Lady Elizabeth continued to encourage her daughter-in-law not to give up hope but to try and recover her lost enthusiasm while thinking 'I must try to rectify this situation for all our sakes'.

Robert arrived back from a parliamentary subcommittee meeting in Dublin to find his wife in determined mood to confront him and to extract a statement of intent.

"Good afternoon, my dear. What pursuits have you engaged in whilst I was in Dublin?" enquired Robert.

"Enough of this charade, Robert, if you think you can remove my anxiety with a courtesy visit once in a blue moon and expect me to be grateful – I entered this marriage expecting a husband that would at least try to make it work. We have had marital relations twice in one year – how do you intend to start a family? What are your plans, Robert? I deserve to know."

"My plans, Elizabeth, are no concern of yours. I am the master of Gaulstown. It is your duty to obey to the letter my instruction and to do so with obedience and silence, is that understood?"

"We are not living in the dark ages, Robert; I do have rights as a wife."

"Please feel free to pursue your rights as you see fit, Elizabeth, but proceed with caution. My status is extremely important to me. Do you understand?"

She screamed, "My father is a wealthy man. I do not have to put up with your cruel terms and conditions."

"That, Elizabeth, is a fact and as you so eloquently stated it is also an avenue open to exploration. Now please excuse me I have correspondence to attend to."

Elizabeth now understood her position at Gaulstown and it was not favourable. She decided to write to her father and seek his advice; at the same time she sought discussion with Lady Elizabeth and the Countess hoping for guidance on a way forward. The Countess and Lady Elizabeth listened intently and seemed at a loss for words at yet another despicable display of arrogance.

Ringsend Dublin

Clarence made himself comfortable before opening the correspondence from his daughter. He looked forward to Elizabeth's letters as they normally contained elements of hope, but this was not one of them, this was a subconscious cry for help. Elizabeth did not directly ask her father to intervene but reading between the lines there was no doubting the fact that his precious daughter was reaching out for help. When Clarence finished reading her letter a terrible rage consumed him as he swept the contents of his desk to the floor. 'Robert Rochfort will pay for this' and as he left his office he hollered, "ready my carriage," bellowing "it's time for action not words. Gaulstown, Sean and don't spare the whip".

Gaulstown

Ned Flanagan was busy cleaning the statue of Kratos that stood on the roundabout to the entrance. On hearing a loud noise on the avenue he looked up to see a fast approaching carriage. His first thought was it's out of control, there must be a problem with the harness, but as the carriage got closer he could see the driver was intentionally using the whip. Trouble, he thought, as he ran toward the approaching carriage ready to help, but soon realized it was no runaway as the driver stood on the platform pulling hard on the reins shouting 'woo boy'. As the carriage came to a halt Ned rushed to open the door and was almost knocked over as Clarence Tennison leaped from the carriage shouting, "Where is your master?" as he purposely walked on.

Ned had to raise his voice.

"The master is in London on business, Mr Tennison."

Clarence dug his heel in the gravel turned and said, "What did you say?"

"The master is in London on business, Mr Tennison."

"Is he ever at home. Is her Ladyship available?"

"Yes, sir this way, Mr Clarke will take you to her Ladyship."

"Thank you, my good man," as he made haste. Mr Clarke was in the kitchen chatting with Mrs Doolin when the bell rang, not once but almost continuously.

"Who could that be?" asked Mrs Doolin.

"Well whoever it is it sounds urgent," replied Mr Clarke.

"Best go see what the commotion is," instructed Mrs Doolin, "and report to me as soon as you know what it's all about." But Mrs Doolin did not have to wait long as Ned came rushing through the kitchen door.

"It's Mr Tennison and he doesn't look or sound happy, looking for the master he was but I don't think he's in the mood for talk."

"Ned, hurry, go to Mistress Elizabeth's quarters and inform her that her father has arrived."

Mr Clarke proceeded to open the main entrance door and was surprised to find a somewhat dishevelled Clarence Tennison.

"Oh! It's you, Mr Tennison, how wonderful to see you again."

"I believe the MP is in London on business?" enquired Clarence.

"Yes, sir, but Lady Elizabeth is home."

"Home, you call this a home. Please take me to Lady Elizabeth."

Just then his daughter came rushing down the grand staircase, catching her heel on the lace hem of her exquisite gown, almost falling into her father's arms.

"Father, I hope this is not what I think it is."

"It is precisely what you think it is, Elizabeth. I believe that bounder of a husband of yours is in London again. Is he ever here?"

"Maybe it's just as well he is not home, Father, for I somewhat fear your temper has clouded your judgement."

"Clouded my judgement, I don't think so and it's time the instigator of your sadness be taken to task."

"Please, Father."

"Elizabeth, trust your father. I wish to converse with Lady Elizabeth; please take me to her."

The greeting was terse as Clarence wasted no time venting his anger. Lady Elizabeth sat staring at the large oil painting of Peter de Roche when she placed her hands to her head and said, "I am truly sorry you feel this way, Mr Tennison and I fully understand your frustration, for I fear we have trodden this particular furrow many times. May I appeal to your intellect, Clarence, and ask you to withhold whatever form of reprimand you have in mind for my son Robert and postpone your actions for a period of six months? That way–"

"No, Lady Elizabeth, I did warn you on a previous occasion that I would not allow the mistreatment of my daughter to continue. I have decided to take my daughter back to Dublin for the sake of her sanity. Please inform Robert that he will hear from my legal advisor, my daughter will be seeking a divorce."

"No, Father, that is not my wish, my correspondence was not meant to cause such upheaval. I only meant–"

"Enough, Elizabeth, you know in your heart Robert is not the man you will spend the rest of your life with, you are being foolish if you still harbour hope of salvaging this sham of a marriage."

"Father, I know you are upset and I agree you are probably right, but I would like to give my marriage one last chance and before you say anything, Father, I promise if my husband does not change soon I shall leave Gaulstown and divorce him."

"I know from experience, Elizabeth, there is no art yet available that could encourage you to change your mind when you feel like this. I cannot force you to leave this wretched marriage, but I must state in the strongest possible terms that you should end it now today. Are you certain you want to give it more time?"

"Yes, Father."

"I shall agree on one condition, that in six months' time if there is no improvement you seek a divorce settlement?"

"Yes, Father and thank you for your love and concern."

Clarence continued, "If this last year is to be considered a mistake and cast aside, then Robert Rochfort will pay for that. Let's see how a substantial divorce settlement appeals to the MP and the inevitable loss of status resulting from rumours both true and false that would surely follow."

Chapter 21

London

Robert was obviously unaware of the growing anger fermenting back at Gaulstown and if he did, he certainly did not show it as he placed the monogrammed royal crystal glass to his lips, at the same time a pretty young woman performed fellatio. Prince Frederick on the other hand was in a rather more compromising position accompanied by a young man dressed in the prince's Royal bath robe. Groans of delight from every participant as the yolk of inhibition was cast to the four winds, albeit with the encouragement of opioids. 'Just the way God intended,' thought Robert.

Gaulstown

Robert arrived back in Gaulstown to a very different atmosphere than when he left. He went immediately to his quarters intending to change and prepare for the inevitable confrontation that would surely materialize later that evening when the family sat down to dinner. Ned was on duty the night Mistress Elizabeth scattered her papers to the floor and his first port of call when he finished his duties was the kitchen where the inevitable Inquisition took place, spreading however reluctantly the suspicion that a split was highly likely.

7pm, the bell for dinner rang out.

Robert entered the dining room with a swagger; the rest of the family were already seated. George was first to stand, followed by Arthur, then in turn the three rather angry women slowly climbed to their feet, enthusiasm rather lacking their male counterparts.

"Good evening, everyone, it's great to be back home," then looking directly at George to the exclusion of everyone else enquired, "George, what's been happening while I've been away?" At the same time without looking up he gestured to Elizabeth. "Pass the bread."

"You could have added the word please; I am not a servant." As Elizabeth angrily stood she intentionally kicked her right leg backwards, sliding her chair a couple of feet, then stormed out of the dining room and straight to her chambers.

Looking at the remaining two women, Robert raised and lowered his shoulders saying, "What, what have I done?"

Lady Elizabeth firmly slammed the palm of her right hand on the dining table saying, "Where would you like me to start, Robert? I seem to recall we have been here before, on quite a few occasions I might add."

Robert just sat there intending to block the chatter from the two matriarchal women; that is until he was jolted back to reality with the words...

"He intends to encourage his daughter to sue for divorce and seek a substantial financial settlement," added Elizabeth.

Robert sat there with his eyes closed portraying a picture of calm but inside the volcano was heating up at a rapid pace. The two matriarchs tried to convince Robert to settle down and start a family with Elizabeth as a divorce could be both disruptive and costly. Robert exploded with a force neither women had ever seen before, with a sweeping motion he scattered his untouched food to the four corners of the room. George and Arthur stood and took their leave; this discussion did not concern them.

The different sounds resonating from the cutlery and glass

crashing to the floor were a sign of things to come. The two women instinctively knew that this was the unmasked Robert almost frothing at the mouth as he hollered: "This is the last time I will be chastised in my own home. I am the master of Gaulstown. I and I alone will decide the future direction this family shall take and you, Countess, I have grown bored with your continued interference in matters that do not concern you.

"You have not adhered to our agreement; you gave assurances not to interfere with the day-to-day running of Gaulstown, but at every opportunity you tried to influence its course. Pack your trunk; you are leaving this house directly. You, Mother, are confined to your quarters until I can figure out what to do with you."

Lady Elizabeth now had a bad feeling in the pit of her stomach, a feeling she would have to get used to, a mixture of loss, fear and anger. Either way the Countess and Lady Elizabeth knew not to say another word as they hurriedly left the dining room trying desperately to camouflage their tears.

When George and Arthur had time to digest the day's events they were incensed, but they both knew there was absolutely nothing they could do or say that was going to improve the situation; Robert was the master of Gaulstown and there was nothing anyone could do. Lady Elizabeth went with the Countess to her quarters intending to console her mother.

The Countess started to pack her trunk, saying, "I shall not stay a moment longer in this house, Elizabeth, and I implore you to abandon any hope you may have of salvaging the situation. Please, Elizabeth, come with me to Drogheda; there is no reason to stay here."

"Thank you, Mother, but both George and Arthur will need my support. It is my duty as a mother to stay and help them navigate the inevitable storms that lie ahead. But I cannot see how I shall ever cope with Robert's obvious lack of respect."

"Is that what this is, lack of respect? I would have said Robert's actions were more like the actions of a tyrant."

Just then Mistress Elizabeth entered the Countess's suite and noticing the trunk on the floor enquired, "Why are you packing, Countess?"

"Robert has informed the Countess that her support was no longer required and to leave Gaulstown with immediate effect," shouted Lady Elizabeth.

"Maybe I could try and talk to him."

Both Lady Elizabeth and the Countess looked at each other with incredulity as the Countess answered, "No, Elizabeth, you are naive if you think Robert will change. My advice to you is leave now. Your father will welcome you home, you can start afresh. You shall find a husband that will treat you with the respect you deserve. From what I have witnessed this day, Robert is not to be trusted and certainly not to be relied on."

Lady Elizabeth took her daughter-in-law's hand as she spoke from the heart.

"Remember, Elizabeth, I gave birth to Robert. I watched that boy grow up and now I see the man and I will not pretend any more. My advice to you, sweet child, is to leave him. He is not the husband for you."

Chapter 22

Ringsend

Clarence Tennison was en route to London planning to sign the contract that would secure the purchase of his second clipper with the intention of significantly increasing his already substantial fortune; he still had no idea who was trying to blackmail him. Two days after the graffiti incident came a ransom note demanding one hundred pounds in cash to be handed over on a day and time of the blackmailer's choosing or the blackmailer would make public a document they proclaimed to have in their possession. A document that would prove his complete involvement in the slave trade. Wait for further instructions, the note stated.

Gaulstown

Gaulstown was not a happy place. The banishment of the Countess was still a festering sore and if Robert was to execute the next phase of his master plan then he needed to change his tactics. A softer approach now seemed prudent as Robert entered his wife's quarters.

"Elizabeth, may I have a word?"

"Why have you banished the Countess?" enquired Elizabeth.

"I have made that quite clear from the beginning, Elizabeth, if you care to remember. The Countess could live at Gaulstown if she agreed not to interfere in the running of Gaulstown, but she has done nothing but. I alone will decide Gaulstown's future."

"But–"

"Please let me finish, Elizabeth. I know I have not been the model husband; I realize how dastardly I have behaved towards you, but I will not change my mind regarding the Countess, and as for the witch–"

"Do not refer to your mother as the witch."

"Please, Elizabeth, I am trying to apologize, do not make this more difficult for me than it already is. I brought you a night cap; it will help you sleep; we can discuss the situation in the morning. Good night, my dear."

"I would prefer to discuss our marriage now," shouted Elizabeth. "Why wait for tomorrow?"

"I said tomorrow, Elizabeth, and that is final, now drink your drink and get some sleep," as he pulled the door hard making sure it was closed.

Elizabeth could not believe what had just happened: Robert had never personally served a drink to anyone; he seemed almost human. Her first reaction was to go straight to Lady Elizabeth's quarters and inform her of Robert's apparent conversion, but instead she decided to drink her nightcap and sleep on it.

Ringsend

Clarence Tennison returned from London in great spirits after securing the ownership of the much sought after clipper; he decided to name his pride and joy Sweet Bess. But Clarence had another rather more urgent problem: on his desk was an envelope that had been shoved under the warehouse door sometime during night fall; in it were instructions on where to drop the ransom. It read: 'Tomorrow at noon place the money behind the large rock that marks the spring in the Phoenix Park' adding 'your movements will be observed at all times, if you try to intercept our courier or interfere in any way with the ransom pick up, the incriminating documents will be published'.

Clarence read the ransom demand again thinking, 'maybe I should inform the authorities or maybe I should seek the help of a professional or maybe I should just pay up. If I pay what's to stop him or them from demanding more money?' Clarence decided to drop the ransom money himself and not risk involving anyone that might take the opportunity to betray him later.

Gaulstown

Elizabeth informed her Ladyship of the unfolding miracle of Robert's conversion.

"He came to your quarters each evening with a night cap?" enquired Lady Elizabeth.

"Yes, I am at a loss for words, five nights in a row. What should I deduce from that?"

"What was in the nightcap, brandy, whiskey?"

"No, no alcohol, a herbal sleep remedy he said."

"Has it worked?"

"Unfortunately not, for I feel devoid of energy these past few days," added Elizabeth.

"Don't build up your hopes, Elizabeth. Robert is usually up to mischief of one sort or another; he is not to be trusted. It is up to you now. If you are intent on finding the key to Robert's heart then I fear you shall fumble in the darkness for eternity."

"I shall never forgive myself if I do not try."

"Try by all means, Elizabeth, if it helps you make up your mind one way or the other. You know your father has said he will take you back to Dublin in the event Robert does not uphold his side of the marriage contract. Where is Robert now? I need to discover the contents of the night cap."

"London again, he left last evening for a very important vote."

"Important vote," sighed Lady Elizabeth, "another lame excuse to be anywhere other than here. I will inform one of the maids to take some warm milk to your quarters at midnight; it will help you sleep. Good night, Elizabeth."

Ringsend

Clarence Tennison readied his recently acquired flintlock pistol muttering 'time to deliver a message in person' as he instructed his driver "Phoenix Park and use the Chapelizod entrance I want to minimize the chance of detection". On reaching the drop off point Clarence instructed his loyal employee to secret the carriage in one of the many potential hiding places. He settled on one spot partially covered by foliage approximately three hundred yards from the rock that marked the spring. He then instructed his driver to place the weather resistant container with the ransom money behind the rock as directed. When the driver returned, Clarence took his magnifying eyeglasses from their snug leather case and trained them on the rock saying, "let the fight back begin".

Gaulstown

"Come quick, my lady, please. I can't raise Mistress Elizabeth, please hurry." One could sense the urgency in young chambermaid Aileen Dunne's voice as she implored Lady Elizabeth to make haste and through her tears cried, "I think Mistress Elizabeth is dead".

"Quickly someone go to the village and summon Dr Sweeney, hurry," screamed Lady Elizabeth. The scene at Gaulstown Hall was incredibly sad and deeply shocking.

"What could have happened?" asked Mrs Doolin. "What in the name of God could have brought this on? I know Mistress Elizabeth had not been feeling too well this past couple of weeks but I thought like everyone else that it was just a cold, sure the village is full of it."

"Cold, me arse," said Ned. "There's more to it than meets the eye if you ask me."

"No one asked you, Ned Flanagan keep your poisonous theories to yourself, at least for now."

"All I meant was it could be smallpox. James Horan was saying that he heard about a case of smallpox down in Tullamore only a week ago; well that's what they thought it was."

"Who's James Horan when he's at home?"

"He's a gardener in Doctor Moore's down there."

"Exactly, a gardener not a doctor, don't you dare spread that gossip, Ned Flanagan. Let's wait till Doctor Sweeney makes a proper diagnosis."

"Ay, like the one he made when his lordship the Baron died."

"Enough, Ned."

Lady Elizabeth had no one left that she could confide in, but she had no doubt that Robert poisoned Mistress Elizabeth. Now she had to find a way to prove it before she could make her suspicions known to George and Arthur. In the meantime she did not intend to eat or drink anything that Robert might have touched.

Phoenix Park

Seven hours later. Clarence was ready to give up he was tired hungry and frustrated.

"Have we any sustenance left, Sean?"

"Afraid not, Mr Tennison."

"Let's wait till dusk, it's just another hour or so."

"Yes, sir."

"Wait, look there, that man with the flat cap."

"Yes, I see him, you're right, he is acting strange."

"Precisely, that's twice he has attended to his shoelace."

"You know what you have to do, Sean. I will take the carriage back to Ringsend and we shall meet there when you have completed your task."

"Yes, Mr Tennison," as he exited their hiding place.

Gaulstown

"Dr Sweeney has been up there for three hours and he won't let anyone in," said Catherine Murry.

"That could mean it's smallpox," added Ned.

"That means nottin, Ned, remember what I said."

"Yes, Mrs Doolin."

"Where's Mr Clarke? He might have an idea; he's been upstairs all morning. Go find him, Ned, see if he knows anything."

"On me way." Ned made his way upstairs on some pretence or other and meeting her Ladyship on the landing enquired, "I need to seek advice from Mr Clarke, your Ladyship, have you seen him?"

"Yes, Edward, I have instructed James to travel personally to Mr Tennison's place of work to convey the terrible news."

"Thank you, my Lady, I'm sure Mrs Doolin will know what to do."

"Can I help?"

"Tis a trivial matter, your Ladyship, of no importance."

Both George and Arthur waited patiently in the parlour hoping Dr Sweeney would have a definitive diagnosis sooner rather than later.

"Ah! there you are, Mother, any developments?" enquired George.

"Yes, Dr Sweeney has intimated although not a definitive diagnosis just yet, but he is investigating the possibility it could be smallpox."

"Could be," said Arthur. "Are you sure he is a doctor? He has been up there three hours."

Just then Dr Sweeney entered the parlour. Lady Elizabeth, George and Arthur stood waiting for the official cause of death.

"Dr Sweeney, have you made a clinical diagnosis?"

"Yes, it's my professional opinion the cause of death is smallpox."

"Smallpox," said George, "but Elizabeth did not display the tell-tale spots. You, Mother, you talked with Elizabeth last evening – did you notice any spots?"

"Not spots exactly but Elizabeth's face and upper body displayed obvious discoloration, quite a severe uneven rash, you could classify some as spots."

"Precisely," added Dr Sweeney, "that was my dilemma. I had to ask myself could this be anything other than smallpox and I thought yes, the visual manifestation of a rash including small red blotches could be the result of poisoning from a variety of plants such as water hemlock, deadly nightshade, foxglove, castor bean to name but a few. But after careful deliberation and the fact that none of the above grow on the estate I am left with only one possible cause, smallpox. That is why we must quarantine Gaulstown for a period of fourteen days; no one leaves and anyone that visits will be subjected to the terms of the quarantine. Is that understood?" All nodded in unison. "Furthermore, Mistress Elizabeth's quarters should be stripped of all bedding and clothing, anything she might have touched in the last couple of days should be burned immediately. Is that clear?"

"Yes," answered Lady Elizabeth, "that's quite clear. Should we worry for our own safety?"

"Follow my instructions rigorously and I do not foresee any danger, but it will take at least two weeks before we can be certain we have contained the situation."

"George, inform the household and please make sure panic does not prevail. Tell them as little as possible and do not mention smallpox. I am sure you will invent a believable cause for the extreme actions we are about to take."

"Yes, Mother."

Then turning to Arthur:

"You are the brains of this family. Let's peruse the library, I need your help to research this dreadful disease."

Dr Terrence Sweeney, on the other hand, did not need to refer to any medical journals: he knew the cause of death was not smallpox but he could not be certain who had administered the poison that had killed Mistress Elizabeth. Until he could identify the culprit he was prepared to continue the charade. For all he knew his livelihood and maybe even his life was in jeopardy – he had had his suspicions about Robert after the Baron died so suddenly; he could remember vividly Robert's forceful directions to complete the examination and conclude that the cause of death was asphyxiation and therefore accidental death.

There were veiled threats as to what could happen if he was to stray from that diagnosis. Good reason to open another bottle of whiskey.

Chapter 23

London

Robert Rochfort in his capacity as MP was in Westminster for a very important vote, a vote to protect the trade in home-produced items from competition in the Colonies. The intention was to restrain and control production of colonial trade. Parliamentarians were convinced that firm, but wise regulation was the key to sustaining economic prosperity at home. After the successful vote MPs began to exit their pews when one of the ushers tapped the member for Westmeath on the shoulder and handed him a folded piece of paper which he instinctively placed in his breast pocket.

"May I suggest you read the correspondence, my Lord."

"It can wait, I am in conversation."

"I don't think it can, my lord."

Turning to face the usher intending to scold him for his impertinence, on making eye contact Robert immediately recognized the intensity in the usher's gaze. Realizing the contents of the note were of the utmost importance Robert slowly retrieved the piece of paper from his pocket. On reading the note Robert Rochfort slumped back onto the green leather pew while at the same time raising his hands to his face in what can only be described as abject horror.

"What is it?" enquired his fellow aristocrat and MP for Chester, twenty-four-year-old Sir Charles Bunbury, 4th Baronet, whom he had met on one of his forays into the underbelly of this great metropolis. Both men had on occasion accompanied his Royal Highness the future King while he indulged his passion for younger male company. Both men were sworn to secrecy and for their loyalty were now beginning to reap the fruits of their labour.

"What is it, man? Out with it."

"My wife has died; I must return to Gaulstown at once."

North Great Georges Street

It was dark as James Clarke sat in the carriage outside Clarence Tennison's warehouse in Ringsend. He had been waiting almost seven hours but dared not leave. Clarence had to be informed of his daughter's demise no matter how long it took. Just then a carriage turned onto the quayside at Ringsend. James was surprised to see Clarence holding the reins. He straightened his back, cleared his throat and wiped the sweat from his brow in anticipation of Clarence's reaction on hearing the devastating news he was about to deliver.

Clarence was plunged to the depths of despair, pacing the floor of this semi darkened space except for the lone gaslight that had been recently installed over his small desk in the far corner. Clarence wiped the tears from his eyes with the lace cuff on his right sleeve, his mind was racing now, questions and more questions – how could this have happened?

'I have not been informed of any recent illness, it must be her heart, that's it, a problem with her heart, no, that can't be, she has never given cause to worry about her heart. It's Robert, he is responsible, it has to be his fault, but how could that be? He is in London unless he has employed someone else to carry out his murderous instructions.' "Get a grip of yourself, man," he shouted. Clarence, now crying, pacing the floor not knowing which way to turn, which way. 'Stop, stop, calm down,' he told himself as he wiped more tears from his already saturated eyes. He felt imprisoned in a surreal place as he tried to sit but immediately jumped up again.

"What am I to do now? My beautiful Bessie, I cannot believe, no I don't believe this?"

James just stood there all this time, his hands behind his back not knowing what to do. 'Should I offer some form of comfort or should I just leave?' he thought, but his feet were like lead planted in the floor until Clarence suddenly stopped then looked to James with a distorted face and began to laugh nervously.

"It's not true, is it, who instigated this charade?"

"Please, Mr Tennison, it's no charade, your daughter is no longer with us."

With that Clarence slumped back in his armchair with force, dislodging it from its normal position, the enormity of what just transpired at last beginning to sink in.

Moments later he dismissed James with a half-hearted wave saying, "Go, go now, I need time to evaluate the situation, go and inform Robert Rochfort I shall be paying him a courtesy visit soon very soon."

Relieved, James made a hasty exit. Clarence Tennison's dilemma now was, should he wait for the return of his driver with news of the blackmailer or should he leave immediately for his daughter's interment at Gaulstown? Clarence left a note for Sean explaining his sudden departure and warned him to keep secret his actions until he returned. He then climbed onto the carriage, drew the whip shouting, "let's go, girl" as the crack from the whip echoed across the river Liffey.

Clarence did not believe for a minute the cause of his daughter's death was smallpox – no other cases had been reported and the rushed interment did not please him either – in his mind it all pointed to a cover up. The physician must be involved and so he decided to confront him in the parlour.

"I demand to see my daughter's remains. I do not believe her death to be the result of smallpox, how do you explain the fact that no other victim has come to light? Don't you find that odd, not one other case in the whole county? I demand to see my daughter; I shall have my physician examine her remains. I have the utmost confidence in his ability."

"I not a charlatan, Mr Tennison and I take great offence in you doubting my ability to perform my duties. My diagnosis was reached on the basis of evidence and reasoning."

'I have cast the die,' thought Clarence, 'now let the doubt ferment.'

Clarence returned to Ringsend exhausted and anxious, anxious to know what had transpired in the Phoenix Park. Probably a blessing in disguise that Robert was in London, for a confrontation at that time would not have ended well for both parties. Clarence intentionally displayed a conciliatory temperament towards Robert while at Gaulstown, but in his heart he blamed Robert for her decline into poor health both mentally and physically, leading directly to her death. He was determined to carry out the promise he made to himself on his daughter's wedding day. But he also knew that any act of retribution would have to wait for a more accommodating time.

Gaulstown

Robert arrived back to Gaulstown at 4am, exhausted. The night sky was pitch black as he watched the cab fade from view then he turned to face Gaulstown Hall, all was quiet not a sound. 'I could not have engineered this scenario if I tried,' he thought. Turning his back, Robert walked away from the house in the direction of the glass house and into the darkness. The next morning Robert was informed that his wife had already been interred in the family plot – for obvious reasons her interment could not wait.

"I fully understand," said Robert. "Did the Doctor say how long we should keep the quarantine in place?"

"Six more days," answered Lady Elizabeth, adding, "are you not sad, Robert?"

He ignored her question. In the library George was in one of his darker moods, a sort of melancholy as he tried to come to terms with Mistress Elizabeth's death.

"Do you think it was smallpox, Arthur?"

"I have no reason to doubt Dr Sweeney's diagnosis, George. Why, do you?"

"Yes, I have my misgivings. Do you remember when Robert returned from London with an array of exotic plants gifted to him by Prince Frederick?"

"Yes, I remember, but why would that be of any relevance to our conversation?"

"I am not sure at this time, but I do intend to satisfy my curiosity."

"Out with it, George, I am not a mind reader."

"Poison, Arthur, poison."

Arthur looked up to see George scanning the entire library.

"Poison," said Arthur.

"Yes, poison, what was it Dr Sweeney said? Yes, I remember now, he said that he had struggled with his diagnosis, something about poisonous plants native to both Ireland and England that had the potential to confuse a physician."

"He did mention some native plants if ingested, or in some cases even touched, could bring on symptoms closely resembling those of smallpox." George and Arthur looked at each other with slightly raised eyebrows.

"I think we should pay a visit to the greenhouse and seek the advice of our head gardener," said Arthur.

"Precisely, a gardener he may be, but in my humble opinion a horticulturist Patrick Cleary is not."

"Agreed, but it surely deserves our attention. What do you say?"

"I say it is time to test our head gardener's knowledge. We have an obligation to alleviate any suspicions you may have, I meant we may have. Shall we go?"

Patrick Clearly was busy attending to the many varieties of plants both native and exotic when George and Arthur entered.

"Good morning, Patrick, this takes me back. Do you remember

the fun times we had in here? One in particular still makes me laugh?"

"I'm certain I can recall the incident you refer to, George," interrupted Arthur.

"So can I," said Patrick. Is it the time I slipped and fell into the muck pit while showing you boys how to mix a good base for seedlings?"

"Yes, Patrick, it's still as fresh as if it took place yesterday."

"But that's not why you gentleman are here, is it? What can I do for you?"

George started the inquisition.

"The selection of plants Robert brought back from London; we were wondering how they were settling in."

"Follow me, gentlemen that section is down the far end, there's quite a collection and all doing very well. See for yourself."

"What is that, that one there–" pointing to a very striking plant.

"Oh, that's called Bird of Paradise."

"Yes, I can see the resemblance, and that one?"

"That's called the snake's head fritillary – see the flower resembles the head of a snake."

"Amazing," said Arthur then pointing to another, "that one?"

"Pineapple."

"You certainly know your plants, Patrick, I am impressed," said George. "But there the soil seems to be recently disturbed."

"Yes," replied Patrick. I just noticed that yesterday."

"What's missing?" enquired George.

"Foxglove and for the life of me I don't know where it went." George raised his eyes as he glanced in Arthur's direction while making sure Patrick did not see. Then George continued the conversation to cover the real reason for their visit.

"That one, Patrick, there with the enormous leaves."

"That's a Japanese Banana plant," added Patrick, "pretty, don't you think? Don't worry, gentlemen, I'll take good care of them."

"Thank you, Patrick, I can see you are more than capable," as they made their way to the exit.

Dublin

The headlines were almost identical on all newspapers but one – Pew's Occurrences stood out; it read:

[One of our own shot down in cold blood].

The article went on to describe in detail the murder of one of their own reporters. Terrence O'Malley was shot down in cold blood on his own doorstep after responding to a knock at the door. Currently the police do not have a motive or a suspect.

Clarence Tennison was beginning to come to terms with the death of his daughter, but he had not forgotten or forgiven Robert for the cruel treatment he had bestowed on her and he blamed him for her death. Clarence had on numerous occasions promised to avenge her death and he meant it, but that was for another day when things had calmed down, for now Clarence had a more pressing issue to deal with.

"Sean did you dispose of the weapon as we discussed?"

"Yes, Mr Tennison, it can never be found."

"Good, neither will the note; and for your continued loyalty, Sean, I am making you a partner in my company since I do not have any living relatives. It's just you and me, Sean, you and me."

Chapter 24

Gaulstown two years later

O ut of the blue an invitation was extended to Robert from Baron
George and Lady Elizabeth's oldest friends, Viscount and Lady
Molesworth. Lady Elizabeth dreaded the thought for she knew the
reason such an invitation was afforded to Robert as Viscount and
Lady Jane had previously sought a union between Robert and their
daughter Mary. Lady Elizabeth feared the timing of this invitation
would lead to a marriage and vowed to do everything in her power
to sabotage such a union.

For she knew her own son had the morals of a sewer rat and was
in her mind and in the minds of many a suspect in both the death of
the Baron and the death of Elizabeth Tennison. That fact was never
discussed or mooted as a realistic line of enquiry, at least in public, but
George and Arthur were convinced Robert had caused the deaths of
their father and sister-in-law; however, who was going to be the one
to raise that issue in a public forum? It was useless to try: Robert was
too powerful, therefore such dangerous thoughts were dismissed as
soon as they surfaced.

Lady Elizabeth also suspected her son and felt she had to try
and save Mary from the same fate. Robert was in London again on

official business when the invitation arrived and Elizabeth thought about destroying the dammed thing, but soon realized that would be a mistake – Robert was sure to find out. No, she would have to come up with a more sophisticated plan if she was to be successful in preventing the same fate befalling Mary Molesworth.

Brackenstown Swords Co Dublin

When Mary was informed about the Viscount's plans for her to marry, she voiced her opposition to any formal introduction to Robert and insisted she was a highly motivated young lady and did not need to enter an arranged marriage.

"I have enough talent to make my own way in this world."

"Mary, you are almost twenty years old, this chance may never come again. You will marry Robert Rochfort if he will have you," instructed the Viscount. "He is one of the most powerful men in Ireland, not to mention his fortune; you should be glad this opportunity has presented itself. Is that understood?"

"Yes, Father," as she stormed from the parlour.

Six months later

Robert was summoned to Clarence House – 'probably to arrange another visit to the human cesspit' thought Robert, but it turned out to be a gesture of great importance. When the meal was finished Frederick clicked his fingers and at once the footman brought champagne to the table.

"What have I done to deserve this?" asked Robert.

"I think you know, Robert. Please untie the scroll in front of you." Then turning to his butler, shouted: "You, what are you waiting for? Open the champagne."

"Yes, your Royal Highness." Robert read the text then stood enabling him to curtsey with panache.

"Thank you, your Royal Highness. It is indeed a great honour you bestow on me and on the Rochfort name."

"Nonsense, my friend, you deserve it and I might add there's more to follow. Here's to you, Baron Belfield, a title richly deserved, drink up."

Gaulstown

Robert could hardly restrain his arrogance on his return; the title meant a great deal. Robert was now a Baron in his own right and he knew that the logical next step would be Viscount Belfield. He summoned Lady Elizabeth, George and Arthur to the library, a more fitting stage to deliver his homily to himself he could not envisage. The news was greeted with muted enthusiasm – suppressing their true feelings had become second nature to all at Gaulstown.

"Congratulations, Robert, everything you promised has so far come to fruition," said George.

"Yes, I remember you making that very promise to both George and I in this very room. You promised to enhance the Rochfort name and you have delivered on your promise," added Arthur.

"You are quiet, Mother, are you not happy for me?"

"Forgive my silence, Robert, for I am overcome with emotion. How you have made this happen I dread to think. I fear Prince Frederick has yet to meet the real Robert Rochfort."

"What are you implying, Mother? Can we not put the past where it deserves to be, in the past?"

"Yes, Robert, let's do that, let's confine our experiences to history; but unfortunately we cannot erase them." She then raised a glass in a half-hearted salute saying, "Congratulations, Baron Belfield. Champagne anyone?"

Downstairs

"Baron, me hole, that scoundrel should be locked up not given a fuckin title."

"What have I told you, Ned Flanagan?"

"Well this time I don't care, Mrs Doolin, and at every opportunity I will shout it from the rooftop."

"Not too loudly mind," said James Clarke. "Be careful, Ned, use your ceann, your time will come."

"Ay! You're right, Mr Clarke, but–"

"No buts, Ned, no buts."

"What options do we have?" pleaded Mrs Doolin. "We are here to serve and serve we will, now less of the gossip, back to your chores, all of you, go."

Brackenstown

"Robert arrived at Brackenstown full of the joys of life. His status enhanced immeasurably now that he had been elevated to the Barony. His mission now was to convince Mary Molesworth that he was not only a Baron, but also perfect husband material. Robert was ushered to the parlour by Viscount Molesworth who made the introduction.

"May I introduce Baron Belfield, the right honourable Robert Rochfort."

"We have already met, Father."

"Yes, I am aware of that, Mary, but this is protocol, this makes the process official. I shall leave you two to renew your friendship."

Robert decided not to waste any more time.

"Mary, may I take this opportunity to say how beautiful you look – and before you say anything, I am aware of your feelings towards me and as you know your father is actively seeking a union between our two great families."

"I beg to interrupt, Baron."

"Please Mary, call me Robert."

"You are a Baron. I shall acknowledge you by your official title, my lord, born out of respect and not loathing, but I feel at this juncture honesty is absolutely required. I know my father is intent on joining our two families, so I assume he has conjured some fantastic romantic notion that I– why are you laughing?"

After regaining his composure Robert tried to explain.

"Please forgive me, Mary, quite the opposite. Your father was very forthright, the Viscount did enlighten me as to your feelings for me, he said that you did not find me at all attractive and extremely pompous; he certainly did not embellish your feelings for me, that's why I laugh, Mary. But I would like to get to know you better, Mary Molesworth, for I fell in love with you the first time I laid eyes on you all those years ago. You were sixteen, I was twenty-three and totally against my parents' plans for me to marry Elizabeth Tennison, but alas to no avail, rebellion was futile. Mary, my feelings for you are now laid bare, just say the word and I will inform your father that I have no interest in his proposal; that way you can pursue your own agenda, but before you make your decision please let me try to convince you that I am not the pompous ogre that you think I am. Unfortunately there is nothing I can do about my handsome face."

Mary could not contain her laughter saying, "What a surprise, you do have a sense of humour after all."

Robert now sensing a slight thaw in the outer layer decided to try his luck further.

"Mary, let me take you to my lodge on Belvedere – you can indulge your passion for fox hunting. I vividly recall your rather passionate rebuke at dinner, do you remember you chastised me for my awkward attempt to denigrate fox hunting?"

"You remember that so clearly – you are full of surprises, my lord."

"What do you say, Mary? One weekend, just one weekend, chaperoned of course."

"May I take some time to ponder your request, my lord, I mean Robert?"

"Take all the time you may require, Mary and if I may be so bold I recommend early September it is such a wonderful time to visit Belvedere, the beginning of Fall. You will witness both Belvedere and Lough Ennell at their most endearing."

"My lord, you propose a very convincing argument."

Chapter 25

Gaulstown two months later

Robert was determined to make the most of this opportunity and secure Mary's hand in marriage; nothing was left to chance. Robert had instructed Lady Elizabeth to visit the Dowager Countess in Drogheda, an obvious strategic move. The witch would not have the chance to ruin his proposal before he had the opportunity to seduce Mary with a combination of smoke and mirrors. Including Robert's much abused secret ingredients, a little pinch of fact and a larger pinch of fiction, all of it he hoped would reveal the intentional subliminal messages he wished to convey, like status, prestige and great wealth – what woman would not want a man like that to father her children?

Robert suspected Mary would never be able to call Gaulstown her home – he remembered on her first visit Mary referred only to Belvedere when reminiscing about her visit to Westmeath. That encouraged Robert to prepare a plan B. He instructed members of the household staff to spend time at the lodge in advance of the visit; the intention was to transform the hunting lodge on Belvedere into a place more befitting a female's nature with flowers, perfume and soft furnishings all plentiful. The strategically placed oil lamps were intended to enhance the mood. Mary in Robert's opinion was no different from any other woman – convince her that she is the chosen one, emphasize the many benefits of being married to such a powerful man and cloak in secrecy the dangers that lay just under the surface. 'If I play my cards right it should help Mary make her mind up,' he thought. After all she was a highly intelligent young woman, just the partner Robert needed to take his plan to the next level. Smoke and mirrors, he reminded himself, smoke and mirrors.

Downstairs

With the visit only days away, Mrs Doolin was summoned to the parlour to give her assessment of the preparations at the hunting lodge.

"Mrs Doolin, please take a seat. Have you completed the preparations on Belvedere?"

"Yes, your Lordship, everything is ready. Miss Molesworth can only be captivated by Belvedere's beauty."

"Excellent, Mrs Doolin, excellent."

The Carriage carrying the Molesworth family came to a halt on the loose gravel.

"Welcome, Viscount, ah! Lady Jane, it is lovely to see you again. Robert's timing was precise; he reached the carriage door just in time to take Mary's hand personally as she was last to vacate the carriage.

"May I?" offered Robert.

"Thank you, my Lord."

"Please, Mary, let's dispense with protocol."

"Yes, my lord, if you prefer."

"Come, refreshments are in order after your journey."

"Where is Lady Elizabeth? We are so looking forward to hearing all the gossip," enquired Lady Jane.

"I am so sorry, Mother was summoned to Drogheda only yesterday for the Dowager Countess is unwell, Lady Elizabeth extends her apologies and to reiterate her intention to visit you in Brackenstown as soon as conditions prevail."

"What a shame, some things we have no control over," replied the Viscount.

George and Arthur entered the parlour and after pleasantries were exchanged all sat down for drinks before dinner. Mary was excited and looking forward to her second visit to Belvedere.

"I so enjoyed my one and only visit to Belvedere; your father, Robert, was so kind, you must miss him terribly for his countenance, he was an example to all, a fine gentleman."

"I second those sentiments," said the Viscount, "he is a great loss to all of us, especially you, Robert, you must miss his guidance immensely?"

"Yes, I miss him dearly."

George did not comment, he just looked to the floor intending to hide his true feelings. Arthur looked directly at Robert with piercing eyes. It was hard to tell what he was thinking but one thing was for certain, he still blamed Robert for the Baron's death and the death of his wife Elizabeth.

Arthur had not seen Mary since the celebratory dinner at Gaulstown the evening of the Belvedere hunt. He had forgotten how much he enjoyed her company that night, just watching her laugh and be happy made him feel warm inside. Did he still harbour feelings for Mary? Robert suspected as much and was determined to find out how much of a threat Arthur might be. The next morning Mary accompanied Robert on the short carriage ride to the hunting lodge on Belvedere as arranged. When the carriage entered Belvedere through the large black iron gates, Mary was instantly consumed with a feeling of belonging, she had felt it on her first visit when the Baron smeared the blood of a fox on her cheeks, she could not explain it then nor could she explain it now, but it was a feeling she would never relinquish. That evening after dinner Robert invited Mary to sit on the veranda with him; he placed a woollen blanket over her legs to ward off the September evening chill.

"What a beautiful evening, Robert, see the reflection of the moon, the way it pretends to dance on the waves. Mesmerizing."

"Yes, Mary, your powers of observation truly fuse the lines between reality and art."

"Precisely, Robert, precisely." They both giggled as they sipped their champagne while gazing over Lough Ennell. On that clear moonlit night Mary was in love, in love with Belvedere; she was already planning her wedding. When the time came for the Molesworth family to leave Gaulstown and return to Dublin, everyone felt a union was a strong possibility.

Mary had had very little experience of life on the Gaulstown Estate; she had only ever visited on two previous occasions and each time she felt it to be a cold, lost place, certainly not a place she wanted to call home. No, in Mary's mind Belvedere would be her home one day; she felt something spiritual every time she entered through those large imposing gates. Mary was certain about her feelings for Belvedere – as for Robert they were adequate; she neither felt love nor hate, 'a good foundation for an aristocratic marriage' she thought. Lady Elizabeth had on many occasions dropped subtle warnings to Mary but she did not believe them or chose to ignore them, she could never be sure.

Mary Molesworth had a plan of her own and no one was going to deter her from it. After the last attempt by Lady Elizabeth to sway Mary away from a union with Robert, she had all but given up trying, all she could do now was wait to see what transpired. Robert suspected the witch was doing her best to prepare Mary for the inevitable proposal of marriage and trying to influence her decision, but he was confident in the knowledge that Mary was in love with her spiritual home Belvedere and no one was going to distract her from her dream. He decided it was time to ask the Viscount for his daughter's hand in marriage.

The Newspaper's headlines read: Mary Molesworth marries Robert Rochfort in the fairy chapel at Gaulstown Hall. The guest list was a list of who's who at the pinnacle of Irish society. Although invited, Prince Frederick declined on the basis that the political environment was not conducive to a royal visit at this time but he did send his Viceroy. The wedding was almost a carbon copy of his marriage to Elizabeth Tennison, except it continued for two days, enough time for Robert to test his younger brother's feelings towards his new bride – but after careful observation Robert found Arthur to be the perfect gentleman, he danced with Mary many times and behaved impeccably. He could not say the same for George, after observing his manner while in Mary's company. 'I shall have to monitor his behaviour,' he thought.

Over the next few months Robert availed of every opportunity to engage Mary in lovemaking; his intention was twofold: the fact that Mary looked younger than her age was something that appealed to Robert, for now he found her sexually stimulating; but his most important reason was to have a family – 'why else would I pursue such a dangerous agenda?' he thought. 'I need a son to carry on my individual bloodline – only then will I find peace in this turmoil we call life.'

The Baron once remarked 'a leopard does not change its spots' and true to Robert's nature he eventually succumbed to his dark side, although he did find lots of time to be in Mary's company. He was or seemed to be content and why would he not be, having the best of both worlds. Most of his time was spent carousing whorehouses in Dublin or London, long periods of absence from Gaulstown were becoming the norm again and certainly were not conducive to building a happy marriage, but on occasion when Robert did return they both went through the motions.

Robert's inspiration was still lust, not surprising as they were only married eleven months. But Mary's was rather more clinical, for she had secured a promise from Robert on that fateful moonlit night overlooking Lough Ennell. Robert, drunk on a mixture of brandy, champagne, lust, infatuation, maybe even love. Or a pinch of all of that. Whatever the reason that night Robert promised to build Mary a family home where the hunting lodge now stood. Nothing, not even Robert's womanizing or his overbearing arrogance, was going to stop her claiming her prize.

Gaulstown, months later

Mary was in her quarters when she heard a knock at the door. It felt late yet was only half past nine according to the Thomas Elliott table clock that stood on the mantelpiece. Taking the small candelabra from the side table, she opened the door and was both startled and surprised to find George standing there. He stared directly into Mary's eyes causing her to freeze momentarily.

"Are you going to invite me in?" slurred George.

"Certainly not. What are you doing, George? Could this not have waited until tomorrow? This is quite inappropriate. My husband–" then raising her voice slightly– "your brother is not in residence as you are aware."

George realized he had misjudged signs of friendship Mary may have extended in the past. "Forgive me, Mary, I meant no impropriety, I merely wanted to extend an invitation to sit and chat for a few moments. It must be quite lonely with Robert being away so frequently."

Mary, not entirely convinced of George's true intentions, decided to adopt a conciliatory response.

"Thank you, George, thank you for your thoughtful gesture. But please in future you should arrange a more suitable time before delivering such invitations."

"Yes of course, Mary, I apologize, I fear the demon alcohol may have played its part. Good night, Mary," as the door was firmly shut.

But unknown to all, secreted and unobserved behind a pillar some distance away was Catherine Murry. She had witnessed the encounter but not hearing the exact words exchanged left room for supposition and Catherine was already constructing her version. The next day Mary was quite perplexed – was George a true friend or was there another more sinister reason for his lack of respect for protocol? Still not able to determine his motives with any certainty, Mary decided to take the short carriage ride to Arthur's newly renovated home, Belfield House.

She was hoping he could shed some light on many aspects of life on the Gaulstown Estate and his interpretation of George's rather strange behaviour would be honest and fair. Mary trusted Arthur although she could not be sure why; it was a gut feeling and that was enough for Mary, it had never let her down.

"Mary, welcome to Belfield, I can only surmise the reason for your visit is to marvel at the skilled reconstruction you see before you."

"Partly, Arthur, but if I am to be totally honest I have some insecurities regarding life at Gaulstown."

"The parlour is this way, Mary. Tea?"

"That would be nice."

"Do I sense a degree of frustration, Mary, or am I barking at the moon?"

"Not frustration, Arthur, merely curiosity."

"Let's sit, make yourself comfortable and I shall endeavour to answer in the only way I know how."

Mary continued.

"George paid a visit to my quarters last night and I am mildly unsure of his true intentions."

After Mary had explained the events of last evening Arthur stood and walked to the large patio doors that led to the balcony and pointed to Gaulstown Hall, partly visible through the foliage now that autumn had received a visit from nature's equivalent of the grim reaper. Still pointing, Arthur continued. "Mary, it's of no use you searching for grounds to dislike that place. I could give you sufficient reason to dislike Gaulstown, but I am reasonably certain that George was there for no other reason but to try and alleviate your perceived sadness."

"Sadness?" replied Mary. "That was not the impression I was hoping to convey, but nevertheless if that is the prevailing breeze that blows through Gaulstown then so be it."

Arthur continued:

"George and I have talked in the past, or should I say discussed your pending marriage to Robert and if I am not mistaken Lady

Elizabeth also tried to advise you as to the fluctuations you may encounter if you accepted Robert's invitation of marriage. But we all agreed you had a strong constitution plus the fact you never took heed of the advice offered, our conclusion was to let you negotiate your own way through this very confusing maze that is Gaulstown."

"Thank you, Arthur, for your candour and you are correct. I have never taken advice from interested parties, for I always felt the hand of betrayal often lay too close to the cards until now. That is why I sit in Belfield this evening; I trust you, Arthur. Now can I continue my inquisition or have I outstayed my welcome?"

"You are always welcome to visit Belfield, Mary, for I feel we should confide in each other; it could be beneficial maybe even necessary – who knows what life may throw our way?"

"Yes, I agree," said Mary and as she stood she thanked Arthur once more for his honesty and promised to visit Belfield whenever the opportunity presented itself saying, "A problem shared is a problem halved," as she gently kissed Arthur on the cheek. Arthur stood close to Mary's buggy holding the oil lamp firmly at arm's length; his intention was to help Mary find the stirrup step. Mary mounted her buggy and lifting the reins she applied two sharp tugs meant to encourage her charge to move forward into the darkness.

As Mary drove through a bed of half rotten leaves that had given up their struggle against the inevitable encroachment of winter, she felt the bond she had established with Arthur would somehow prevail. Observing from one of the attic rooms was no other than Catherine Murry – she was beginning the process of adding two plus two, but as everyone at Gaulstown knew Catherine's ability to comprehend mathematics at any level was minuscule.

One month later

"Robert, I am with child."

Robert was shocked by the casual way Mary decided to inform him.

"Did I hear you correctly, Mary, you are with child?"

"Yes, Robert, you are not mistaken." That was the way Mary decided to break the news of her pregnancy to her husband, then added rather casually, "Have you commissioned an architect to design our home on Belvedere? You implied last week that you had made your decision."

Robert reacted with restrained joy for he knew it was presumptuous to celebrate – after all, it could be a girl. Seeing what he presumed to be disappointment in Mary's eyes, Robert tried to compensate.

"Mary, before I reply to your second question may I say how pleased I am to hear you are with child." Then taking Mary's hand he came closer and kissed her gently on the cheek while whispering, "I have not forgotten my promise to you and yes I have made my decision regarding who will design the project. I had intended to discuss my choice with you this very evening over dinner."

"Wonderful, I shall take Ebony for a canter this afternoon, fresh air helps one's appetite, I believe. I look forward to dinner – you know how important Belvedere is to me."

"Indeed, Mary, but should you be riding in your condition?"

"Oh Robert you can be such a fool at times, I will know when to take life at a more leisurely pace." That evening Robert broke with tradition by inviting Mary to take dinner with him in the library as it helped facilitate the many documents and sketches. The necessary drawings were spread on the large half-moon shaped table situated in the centre of the gable wall directly under a more recent oil painting of Robert by the renowned Irish Artist Charles Jervas, a portrait artist who had also painted Jonathan Swift's portrait. The table still provided enough space for two dinner settings, both Robert and Mary took turns inspecting various views of the house exterior frequently standing together discussing a detail, until at last Mary exclaimed:

"It's perfect, Robert, how long will construction take?"

"I thought you might ask. Four years, Mary, time to complete our family."

"Is it not possible in two years, the construction I mean?"

"Every effort will be made to hurry construction I have been assured."

"So be it," said Mary with a sigh. "Now tell me, where did you find the architect?"

"His name is Richard Castles, extremely sought after. I made him an offer he could not resist. Everyone has their price, Mary, even you, my dear."

"For the life of me," and looking directly into Robert's eyes she continued, "I don't know what you mean, Robert." Then smiling she said, "We understand each other perfectly."

Downstairs

Ned Flanagan sat with Mrs Doolin over a steaming cup of tea in the anteroom and informed her about a conversation he had overheard between two of the parlour maids and Catherine Murry. He assured Mrs Doolin the reason he was reporting this particular conversation was precautionary.

"I heard Catherine say she had seen the Baroness visit Belfield while Robert was in London and that she thought it improper for her to do so."

"My god, are you telling me that Catherine is spreading gossip about her? Well I must put a stop to that."

"I agree you better have a talk with that one, Mrs Doolin, nip it in the bud before it brings trouble on the lot of us."

Mrs Doolin sprang to her feet and scurried back to her kitchen intending to have words with Catherine. Entering the kitchen she shouted, "Where's Catherine?"

"Don't know" was the chorus.

"Theresa Staunton, where are you? There you are, go upstairs and fetch Catherine, tell her to come at once then look in on Lady Elizabeth; no one has set eyes on her today."

"Yes, Mrs Doolin, straight away."

The scream could only be described as piercing. Ned swore it was a Banshee.

"Where did that come from?" asked Mrs Doolin. "Sounds like it came from upstairs, go, Ned find out what that was, go. Where's Mr Clarke?" Just then Mr Clarke entered the kitchen.

"I am right here, Mrs Doolin."

"Thank god, Mr Clarke, have you any idea what that scream was?"

"Please, Mrs Doolin, you better sit down."

"Oh sweet Jesus you've gone very pale, Mr Clarke, what in god's name has caused the blood to drain from your face like that?"

"Lady Elizabeth is dead."

Gaulstown Hall once again plunged to the depths of despair, the third death in six years.

"Told yez this place was cursed" was the only explanation Ned had to offer.

"The doctor has been summoned," assured Mr Clarke.

Speculation was rife including one possibility that old Larry Cleary down at the village inn was promoting when he told anyone that bothered to listen. Pointing and spitting in the general direction of Josie Ryan, he stood wagging his finger.

"If this was happening in my family the authorities would be digging a little deeper. I'm certain about that but then I'm no Baron. I warned yez before about that scoundrel, like when Baron George met his strange end or Mistress Elizabeth's untimely passing. But would any of yez listen?"

"Ah! Sit down, ya cribbing ould fool, enough of your ould shite, no one is listening, no one."

Dr Sweeney signed the death certificate 'sudden cardiac arrest' that left George and Arthur with no reason to call for a second opinion, but they could not rule out foul play. As far as they were concerned if Robert was in residence then he had opportunity.

"He could have placed a pillow over her head in the middle of the night, you know how frail Mother has become over these last few years," cried George.

"This time I am inclined to agree with you, George, but we can only invite a second opinion with Robert's consent, and who is going to suggest that?"

Time passed and once again Gaulstown returned to some form of normality.

The birth of Robert's first child, a girl, was met with little celebration; they named her Jane. But ten months later Mary gave birth to a boy and this time the news was greeted with great fanfare. The celebrations went on for weeks. King George the 2nd was named godfather by proxy to the child they named George after Robert's grandfather or most likely the King himself. No doubt Robert's choice of godfather was facilitated by his good friend Prince Frederick – as far as Robert was concerned it was a public relations exercise meant to bestow even more status on the Rochfort name. 'The publicity from such an announcement should diminish any negative rumblings still associated with the Rochfort name' thought Robert. Three more sons were to follow. Richard, Robert and Arthur. The events of the previous few years were now largely forgotten, but not entirely.

Chapter 26

Life at Gaulstown began to tread a familiar furrow. Robert was back to his old tricks again, for him life at Gaulstown had become monotonous, he found the children tedious and boring, and at every opportunity he got as far away from Gaulstown as possible.

The Baroness spent most of her time with her very young children. She too grew increasingly frustrated, not with the daily chores because she had none and certainly not with the children, she loved everything about them, their simplicity, honesty and general abandonment amused her greatly. No, Mary's frustration was born from a lack of intellectual stimulation; that in part was the reason why Mary began to visit Belfield House on a more regular basis. Arthur, in the opinion of all at Gaulstown without exception, was considered an intellectual, well versed in the arts, politics and international topics of the day, the main reasons Mary so enjoyed Arthur's company. It did not take long for the gossip mongers to start spreading their poison, and over the next twelve months the rumours began to gain traction. George was first to mention Mary's frequent visits to Belfield House. Why was he so quick to believe the malicious contents contained in a couple of scribbled notes pushed under his door in the dead of night? Maybe his jealousy of Robert was clouding his vision for it never did diminish with time, but more likely it was a form of retribution for Mary's perceived rejection to his earlier offer of friendship. As it turned out it was none of those, Catherine Murry was secretly keeping George informed of Mary's every move, for she was still in love with George ever since the day she had seduced him, when he was fourteen and she was twenty-six. For two years Catherine engineered clandestine meetings at every opportunity, sometimes in the barn, sometimes in one of the unused attic rooms at the top of the house and even once in the greenhouse.

It ended when George turned sixteen and threatened to tell his mother; her secret had never been discovered and to this day Catherine still prayed for some form of divine intervention.

Why would George implicate Arthur? After all, Arthur never did give him any reason to be jealous; that is, until now, did he believe the scribblings of the anonymous writer that Mary was visiting Arthur on a regular basis for months? Did he honestly think they were having an affair or was he in love with the Baroness?

"What are you referring to, George?" enquired Robert.

"I am referring to your wife's frequent visits to Belfield."

"How frequent?"

"Once a week."

"Why would you inform me of this development, George? I fail to recognize the potential benefits for you or for Gaulstown. What's your evidence? Have you been spying on her?"

"Certainly not, Robert, but I do have my source."

"Care to name your source, George? You do realize how serious this is? It may be innuendo, George, it may be malice, but one never knows where such information might lead for I fear there is seldom fire without smoke."

"No, Robert, I would rather not name my source not until it becomes absolutely necessary."

Robert was seething, he could not believe Mary could be so reckless; as for George what was his motivation for exposing the alleged affair? Robert thought George was the one most likely to attempt to have an affair with Mary, not Arthur. Robert decided to take matters into his own hands. He summoned attention from below stairs, and on hearing the bell Mrs Doolin sent Ann Quinn to answer but Robert dismissed her saying, "Go find Catherine Murry, she is responsible for the supervision of the parlour." Catherine was very nervous – she had never had to answer directly to Robert and as she stood there, she could feel her left leg tremble uncontrollably but unseen under the long apron she always wore.

She assumed every conceivable sin venal or mortal she had ever committed was scratched on her forehead there for Robert to see, but of course that was all in her mind. Robert intended to use her as his spy in the household.

"I have reason to suspect my wife visits Belfield House at regular intervals. I need to know if that is true and if she does how often, on what days and at what times. Keep a log with every detail recorded. You can write, I presume?"

"Yes, my Lord."

"Keep the log in a secure place and tell no one. If you do, I shall use the power I possess to destroy you and your family." Raising his voice he shouted, "Is that understood?"

Catherine was struggling to stand let alone say the words, but she managed, "Yes, my lord."

Little did Robert know but he had just instructed the wolf to keep watch over one of his flock. When Catherine returned to the kitchen to make the obligatory report to Mrs Doolin, she had enough time to concoct a story saying the Baron was not happy with the way the fire had been set.

"Why did he not call for me, I wonder, still I'm glad you were the one he chose to chastise this time, god knows I've taken enough grief for you lot in my time. Ok back to your duties."

One month later Robert retrieved the log from his informant and to his surprise it did prove one thing: Mary was visiting Belfield on a regular basis. 'This does not look good,' he thought, 'I will have to confront this deceit and make certain Mary understands the implications of such behaviour.' That night Robert set his trap.

"Have you been to visit Arthur in his new home?"

"Yes, Robert, I have on occasion sought Arthur's wisdom on certain issues. I recently sought his advice regarding my interest in music – as you know the library is his domain and I wondered if he could source some literature on the life story of one of my favourite composers."

"What is the composer's name"?

"Domenico Scarlatti, an Italian composer, I adore all of his sonatas. Arthur was so helpful, he located a volume that included his 555 keyboard sonatas. Why do you ask?"

"Just curious, did you have occasion to visit at any other time?"

"Yes, when I was in search of reading material or a stimulating intellectual conversation. What is this, Robert, an inquisition?"

"Just conversation, my dear, just conversation." Robert was now ready to spring his trap.

"Do you intend to visit Arthur anytime soon, if so I may accompany you?"

"No, I have not decided yet, but you should visit when you find time. Arthur would like that."

Robert decided it was time to spring his trap.

"I do not want you to visit Belfield without a chaperone – is that understood?"

"Why, Robert, don't you trust me?"

"You should know by now I trust no one, have I made myself clear?"

"Yes, very clear."

Robert continued.

"I have to travel to London on official business. I leave tomorrow evening. Maybe when I return, we can visit together."

"London again," said Mary, "so soon, you may as well live there for you spend more time in London than you do in your ancestral home."

But when the time came Robert did not leave for London; instead, once outside the gates of Gaulstown he instructed his driver to take him to Belvedere House. He would stay the night in a makeshift bedroom on the ground floor as building work continued and tomorrow he would take the short carriage ride back to Gaulstown at 8pm, the precise time Mary supposedly called on Arthur every week. On the carriage ride over to Belfield Robert was in a thoughtful mood, 'maybe it is innocent, maybe it is for the intellectual stimulation that Arthur gives freely to everyone, maybe I am overreacting'. Robert's carriage entered Gaulstown estate under a blanket of stars.

The reflection of the moon flickered on the gold inscription high on the gates. "In Deo Speramus." How appropriate, thought Robert as his carriage wound its way along the avenue. When almost at the big house the carriage took a sharp left turn in the direction of Belfield House.

"I just saw the Baron's carriage on the avenue, Mrs Doolin, did he not leave for London yesterday?" enquired Ann Quinn.

"You must be mistaken, girl."

"No, Mrs Doolin, I'm not mistaken. It was the Baron alright, I seen his face clearly on me way back from the glass house."

Anxiously Mrs Doolin tried peering through the large kitchen window.

"Where's the carriage now, girl? I don't see it."

"No, Mrs Doolin, the Baron's carriage turned at Sullivan's corner and headed in the direction of Belfield."

"Oh blessed Jesus go find the Baroness. Tell her I must speak with her immediately. Go, girl; go like the wind, I pray she hasn't left yet."

The words "Ok, Mrs Doolin" sounded like an echo as the maid ran in the direction of the service stairwell.

"No, Ann, take the grand staircase, it's quicker."

Everyone on the Gaulstown estate knew about Mary's weekly visits to Belfield. The reason no one made an issue of it except for Catherine Murry was their understanding of the situation. The loneliness of Robert's first wife Elizabeth Tennison and where that led to, no one wanted a repeat of that. Mrs Doolin's intuition was screaming, if this gets out of hand it could be the end of life as we know it. I must warn her. "Has the Baroness left yet?" She raced as fast as her ageing body would facilitate, at the top of the stairs she held on tight to the handrail while she caught her breath again shouting, "Has the Baroness left yet?"

"The Baroness isn't here," shouted Ann from the direction of her living quarters.

"I fear this is just the beginning," added Mrs Doolin.

Belfield House

As Robert's carriage approached Belfield he gave the signal to stop, then sat for a moment. This was his first time to visit Belfield since its complete renovation. Robert felt a strange attraction to the scene before him, maybe it was the dull orange glow that seeped from the parlour window and came to rest on autumn's carpet of dead leaves strewn on the forest floor, or maybe he was softening his attitude towards Mary. What if she felt the same way every time she came here, that would explain a lot? No, thought Robert, that can't be the reason Mary loves Belvedere more than life itself, there must be another reason. Then something caught his eye, it was Mary's buggy partially hidden by foliage at the side entrance reminding Robert why he was there in the first place. Was Mary having an affair with his younger brother? That thought jolted Robert from his melancholy and once again the wood panelling between Robert and his driver felt the full force of his anger as the snake's head was unleashed with the command: "Proceed, Patrick, let's conclude our business here."

Robert raised the Blackthorn to a queer angle, attempting to enlist the moon's help as he wiped the gold handle with his silk handkerchief, checking for damage. Arthur was first to hear the carriage pull up outside the entrance.

"Who could that be?"

Just then Arthur's butler entered.

"Baron Robert's carriage is out front, Master Arthur."

"Wait, Sean do not open the door, not yet." Mary was now standing.

"It can't be," she said, "Robert left for London last evening."

"We should not keep him waiting. Sean, welcome the Baron and escort him directly," instructed Arthur.

"Yes, my Lord."

Arthur looked at Mary and she could see the fear in his eyes as he said, "Mary, we have committed no crime."

"I fear Robert might not interpret the scene with such leniency." Then Mary stopped in her tracks.

"May I present Baron Robert Rochfort."

"I was hoping the information I have received was without substance, but alas the evidence looks pretty damming."

"I don't know what you mean, Robert. Are you spying on me?"

Robert just laughed.

"Please, Robert, it's not what you think," said Arthur. "I know it may look strange but our relationship is purely platonic, let me explain."

Robert screamed.

"I told you not to visit Belfield without a chaperone and you promised to obey, but the instant I turned my back you broke your promise."

Crash, the sound of a sixteenth century Chinese porcelain vase splintering as it crashed to the floor, the tiny fragments filled the air then slowly began to settle; seconds had passed but it felt like an eternity. Two more blows from the snake's head followed in quick succession, smashing a pair of antique busts. All now lay scattered on the floor, the Chinese exuberance for colour quite distinguishable from the clinical formality of the Greek porcelain; ironically one was a bust of the Greek god of love, Eros. Robert's spittle carried the words.

"Do you take me for a fool? This liaison has been active for more than one year now. I have been reliably informed that every Tuesday evening at this time you, Mary, seek the company of my brother and I can only come to one conclusion."

"The wrong conclusion, please believe me, there is no impropriety; we merely talk, talk about everything. I have never been unfaithful,

Robert, please listen, I beg you."

"Enough of your lies, I shall deal with you later. As for you, Arthur, we will settle this one way or the other at dawn this approaching Sabbath." Now almost nose to nose, he added, "Can you think of a better day to meet your maker, Arthur, because I cannot?" And as he stormed from the house he screamed "choose your seconds". Arthur's mind was racing.

"Robert intends to kill me. What should I do, Mary?"

"I shall talk to him, maybe he will listen," as she grabbed her wrap and ran to her buggy. When Mary got back to Gaulstown Robert was nowhere to be found. Arthur was frantic, all he could think about was the upcoming duel. He did not know whether he should take flight or stay and fight – after all he had done nothing wrong; he knew that, Mary knew that; but in the eyes of the only one that mattered: they were both guilty.

Chapter 27

The Duel

S ix am late October. A cold, crisp sunny morning, the kind of morning to encourage the laziest soul from their slumber and embrace life, but today Arthur wished he could stay in his comfortable bed and not have to face what could be his last few hours on this earth. The cards have been shuffled, dealt and thrown to the wind; now they must fall where faith decrees and as the first shafts of sunlight began to appear through what remained of the season's foliage a single crow began to squawk. The large oak and ash that surrounded Belvedere House to the east were originally planted to protect the cabin from the unpredictable east wind that never failed to turn up when you least expect it. To the west on the opposite side of the lough, Lilliput looked serene, surrounded by hundreds of silver birch that stood like sentinels on guard duty and when the sun's rays eventually reached across the Lough the few surviving leaves seemed to dance.

Belvedere House was almost finished now except for furnishings. Robert had hoped Belvedere would be the family's home, but now that circumstances had changed so had his plans. 'Belvedere shall be my private residence except for invited guests,' he thought. 'It shall be a place where gentlemen can indulge their passions with impunity.'

How ironic, Belvedere House built with passion and love yet the first meaningful act to take place on its soil was born from jealousy and rage.

The two buggies carrying the brothers came to a halt twenty yards from each other, both men dismounted accompanied by their seconds. It was immediately obvious from Arthur's posture that he had no stomach for this fight, and it wasn't long before he started to plead his innocence to any wrongdoing.

"Please, Robert, you must believe me, Mary is no more than a very dear friend."

Raising his voice Robert replied, "A very dear friend, I believe you, Arthur." Then without warning he lunged forward and struck Arthur to the ground shouting, "It is my judgement you are more than a friend; I say you are an adulterer, now get up and fight with some dignity. Seconds, charge the pistols."

When Arthur heard Robert's request for pistols to be readied he totally fell apart, his mind now drifted back in time, in what seemed like a split second the entire scene at the paddling pool all those years ago came flooding back. Scrambling to his feet Arthur began to run in the direction of Belvedere House. Robert with the glare of the morning sun directly behind him took advantage. He instinctively grabbed one of the loaded flintlock pistols that were placed on a velvet cushion. Shouting "coward", he raised the weapon to eye level and fired in Arthur's direction as he fled. The flash of gunpowder scorched the skin on the back of Robert's hand, causing him to drop the weapon. In the melee Arthur had been grazed on the upper right arm – the bright red staining on his crisp white shirt sleeve was conformation enough – but he still managed to mount his buggy and take the reins. Half standing, half sitting, Arthur drove like the Devil in the direction of Gaulstown, intending to place as much distance between himself and Robert as he possibly could.

Arthur's buggy was observed bolting up the avenue and when the news reached Mary, she dropped everything and ran in the direction of Belfield House. She summoned the strength from somewhere to run faster and harder than she had ever ran before and with her lungs ready to explode she at last stumbled on the steps of Belfield. Struggling to her feet she followed the trail of blood from the entrance porch all the way to the imperial oak staircase that led to the upper floor. There she found Arthur in a very agitated state, blood still seeping from the wound then forming little droplets on the tips of his fingers. But he was still alive.

"Arthur, I am so sorry, this is all my fault, please let me attend to your wound."

"No, Mary, no time for that, it's only a flesh wound."

"What are you intending to do?"

Arthur, still packing and talking at the same time, stopped what he was doing, walked over to Mary, took her two hands in his and said:

"Mary, none of this is your fault, but I fear the consequences will far outweigh the veracity of any perceived wrongdoing by us."

Moving fast now he ran to the safe and proceeded to stuff its contents into his travel bag. Turning to Mary for the last time he began to cry. Mary ran to embrace Arthur, he took her in his arms as they both wept. When they finally released each other from that tender embrace, Arthur looked into Mary's eyes then drew her closer still. After exchanging tender smiles he kissed her full on the lips and to Mary's complete surprise she reciprocated. Realizing the danger they both faced, Arthur whispered, "We may never see each other again in this life, Mary, but do not despair for our spirits are now entwined for eternity." Reluctantly, Arthur slowly released Mary from his embrace.

Grabbing his bag he started to make his way down the grand staircase as quick as his trembling legs would allow. Mary was now leaning over the handrail shouting, "Arthur, where are you going to go?"

Halfway down the stairs he shouted his answer. "England, Mary, England."

That was the last time Arthur Rochfort would ever set foot on Gaulstown soil.

Chapter 28

Ringsend

C larence Tennison was following events at Gaulstown with great interest; he had not been in touch with anyone there for years. With all the accusations of blame now being openly discussed in public, the prevailing mood seemed to suggest Robert had numerous potential enemies. 'This may be the only opportunity that presents itself,' he thought, 'time to make good my promise to Elizabeth on her wedding day.' With renewed vigour Clarence spent the next days planning his revenge.

Downstairs

Shock had taken hold of the entire household and spread like wildfire to the village of Rochfortbridge. Back in Mrs Doolin's kitchen the entire domestic staff were instructed to gather around the large rectangular oak table; two more stood leaning on the wall close to the pantry. After what felt like a lifetime, Ned Flanagan was first to speak.

"I knew something like this would happen one day, I'm sure you all know what I think of Baron Robert."

"We don't need to hear it all again, Ned," insisted James Clarke, "not now."

"Sure, if I can't speak me mind then I might as well say nottin."

"Don't worry, Ned. No one here has forgotten the suffering you and your family have endured all these years."

"Thank you, Mrs Doolin."

"Well yez must be all wondering why you're here. Master George wants to reassure everyone after what happened this very morning on the shores of Lough Ennell, he will be down presently to put our minds at ease. I don't know how he's going to do that, especially after his brother just shot Arthur – pure jealousy, what else could it be? Sure the Baroness was only seeking friendship with Arthur, everyone knows Arthur is a complete gentleman and as for the Baroness she would never break her vows. Anyway ya have to listen to thunder I say, so no shenanigans when Master George appears, de yez hear me?"

A chorus of "Yes, Mrs Doolin" quickly followed.

The next few weeks passed at a snail's pace but there was nothing slow about the gossip mongers; mind you, they had plenty of reason to gossip. They wanted to know things like, was it true? Was the Baroness having an affair with Arthur? What's going to happen if the Rochfort family tear each other apart? They soon began to realize it was out of their hands and they did not have to wait long for the retribution to commence. Robert had returned to Gaulstown directly after he shot Arthur with the intention of finishing him off, but Arthur was on his way to Waterford and relative safety, not worth the chase. He decided there was no better time to lay down the new ground rules, more rules for the already congested List.

The Baroness should be securely locked in her quarters, only one maid to be assigned. One walk per day in the gardens at dusk. The Adulteress is always to be accompanied by her maid. The Adulteress will have no contact with her children except limited observation from the attic window in her new quarters. The Adulteress shall be moved to her new quarters with immediate effect, a single room at the top of the house. All rules must be obeyed without exception.

We walk along the enchanted way

Through bramble thistle and thorn
The cycle complete she urges retreat
As the bugler blows his horn
Searching for strength in sacred text
Seeking sustenance each day
We live in hope or die in vain
Along the enchanted way

Belvedere

Belvedere was now established as Robert's official home; he had abandoned Gaulstown, designating it a prison. Robert let it be known he intended to visit Gaulstown at least once a week, that way no one could predict with certainty when his carriage might appear on the avenue. No one ever did break the rules thus guaranteeing Mary's life would slowly descend to the depths of despair, or worse, madness. October was a defining month on many levels; equilibrium had well and truly deserted Gaulstown. A month to forget, once again the passing of time gave the impression of normality and ten months on from that faithful act on the shores of Lough Ennell, time had worked its magic: things looked almost normal at Gaulstown except for the fact everything was abnormal.

But for Robert, life was good, Belvedere was gaining quite a reputation as a party house; visitors came and went at all hours of the day and night in all manner of dress. Prostitutes were brought to Belvedere from established Dublin brothels to ensure its hard-earned reputation never waned. Some of the more adventurous guests would often sleep on the lawn just like tonight, a warm summer breeze carried the echo of laughter and merriment across the lough to the Lilliput shore. But this evening was a little more relevant, a little more special. Robert had arranged a very important reunion; it had been a long time coming and as the champagne flowed the three friends stood on the balcony of Belvedere House and raised their glasses, "To the Trinity". The conversation drifted from domestic affairs to the big questions of the day, then to more mundane matters. But no one brought up the terrible injustice of the Baroness' imprisonment in Gaulstown Hall except for a very drunk George when his jealousy found its way to his inebriated tongue when he slurred:

"Have you been to Gaulstown lately, Robert? I hear the Baroness has the place all to herself." Then turning to Richard and James, "Did you gentlemen know my brother has incarcerated his wife in Gaulstown for being unfaithful with Arthur – he had to flee to England to escape Robert's fury?"

"Yes," said James, "I have followed the situation" but Richard did not respond.

"The alcohol has loosened your tongue, George, be careful or you may lose it. Is that understood?"

George struggled to his feet and left. Robert apologised to his two friends on behalf of George, but Richard and James had no intention of getting involved in Robert's private life; instead James changed the subject to something they all enjoyed, sex. The next day Robert decided to visit Gaulstown unannounced. It was something George had said, that Mary had free range in what was supposed to be her prison – he would see for himself the conditions and make his own judgement. When he arrived he decided to walk in the gardens; he had forgotten how lovely it was at this time of year. To his horror he turned to walk in the direction of the glasshouse only to meet Mary coming towards him. He immediately turned on his heels and made a quick retreat but not before Mary screamed after Robert calling for forgiveness, but to no avail – the last word Robert heard before he mounted his carriage to leave was "mercy". Robert was furious that he had had to endure the humiliation of a face to face encounter with the adulteress and decided that would never happen again. He ordered the maid to carry a bell at all times and to intermittently sound its tones as a warning to all not to converse with the adulteress.

When George sobered up he regretted his impetuous reference to Mary's imprisonment and decided to apologise the next time he talked with his brother, then his mind turned to Belvedere House. After seeing it in all its glory he had decided it was time to commission the building of his own house on a small piece of Belvedere, approximately four hundred yards southwest of Belvedere House, a piece of land that was left to him in his father's will. George decided this was his opportunity to get one over on his status-driven older sibling, he decided to build a much larger house in full view of Belvedere. He did not consult Robert during the design process and for good reason as he intended to commission Richard Castles to prepare plans for the project, the same architect who had designed Belvedere House – another reason why George decided on a commencement date to coincide with Robert's next planned trip to London and after Robert received an appeal from Prince Frederick that trip was due to take place in a couple of months. 'Better get things moving,' he thought.

Robert had been invited to London at the request of Prince Frederick who wanted someone he could trust to manage his upcoming marriage to Augusta of Saxony-Gotha. George had been reliably informed that in all probability Robert would be ensconced in London for at least two years. Enough time to establish Rochfort House, the name George had chosen for his new home; he was determined it would not be known simply as the home of Baron Belfield's brother.

George had finally decided to vacate the shadow of his more influential brother and act like a senior member of the Rochfort family and exercise his right to construct a house of his choice on his corner of Belvedere, and when the time came for Robert to leave for London, his carriage had no sooner left Belvedere for Waterford, George not without some trepidation decided it was now or never and gave the go-ahead for the construction of Rochfort House to commence.

The reason Robert had decided to accept the invitation to involve himself in Prince Frederick's upcoming wedding was twofold. Robert had heard rumours of tension between King George and his son Frederick, not unusual in wealthy aristocratic households and less so in matters of Royal succession. But if for some reason things were going to deteriorate further between father and son then he better move fast if he wanted to secure his life's dream: the title, first Earl of Belvedere, and that thought sustained him on the long monotonous journey.

London

On arrival Robert was escorted to his accommodation at St James's Palace, where over the next two years he would have little time for social activities. The seriousness of the task before him was obvious, he only had to observe the frantic comings and goings of high-ranking members from the Royal household. But before he could concentrate on the proposed wedding Robert would have to convince Prince Frederick to secure in writing a declaration of intent from his father the King while they were still communicating, a promise to confer on Robert the title Earl of Belvedere at a date yet to be determined, a sort of indirect payment for services rendered. His reasoning was simple. Robert had his own spy inside the Royal Household as Frederick had said something in an earlier conversation that put Robert on his guard. He instinctively knew when a storm was about to blow and blow hard.

After securing the document of intent, Robert was quite happy to immerse himself in the execution of his duties in relation to the Royal Wedding. It did not take long for rumours of a rift between the King and heir to materialize, a rift that would eventually become a chasm, Frederick's continued belligerence encouraged the King to honour his son's legal requests much earlier than he intended but stipulated that in future Frederick's requests would not be granted. The trouble began when Augusta of Saxony-Gotha arrived in London to marry the Prince of Wales. Augusta and Frederick did not enjoy the luxury of a long courtship – in fact he had never set eyes on her. The only member of the Royal family ever to meet the Princess Augusta was Frederick's father King George the second on one of his return visits to Hanover and that was enough to seal a deal. Augusta was chosen because of the provisions laid out in the Act of settlement some years earlier – the act made it essential for members of the Royal family to marry Protestants if they wanted to retain their inheritance rights. When just a young woman, Augusta found herself in a foreign land, knowing virtually no one and not able to speak the language. Her parents had told her that there would be no need to learn English as they assumed that after twenty years of rule by German Princes everyone would by now be speaking German.

The first hint that things might not be all they seemed was when Frederick's sisters decided to make a fuss after the Prince of Wales tried to alter seating arrangements for family meals, giving his future bride precedence over them. Robert was aware of the tensions, but his remit was to make certain everything went according to plan and pre-empt any display of family disunity.

When the big day came Robert stood in the Chapel Royal in St James's Palace proud of his considerable achievement. It had cost him two years of his life, but in his opinion worth every second. Now he could turn his attention to Ireland and his beloved Belvedere, but today the wedding was his priority as he started to mingle, intending to make certain everything was perfect. Augusta was radiant as she stood by her husband; earlier rumours of her extreme beauty were somewhat misplaced but not entirely baseless. Augusta was pretty at best, her pale complexion combined with a slightly elongated face meant she had to work hard for any compliments directed her way. Robert was hearing a lot of stories about Frederick's many rows with the King, the Prince was unhappy with his uncertain political role and his lack of financial means leading to demands that the King increase his allowance. The King was so incensed he called his son incompetent, greedy and threatened to ban him from court; Robert felt quite pleased with himself for securing the Royal letter of intent when he did.

After the elation of the wedding success Robert was now looking forward to returning home but the news from Ireland was not good, one newspaper headline called it Bliain an marú, year of slaughter when both the potato and grain harvest had failed due to consecutive years of heavy frost in winter and too much rain in summer, resulting in famine. Riots broke out all over Ireland, in Dublin people stormed the grain storage silo at Drumcondra killing two police officers and in their rush to satisfy their extreme hunger proceeded to contaminate what was left of the grain. With the soaring cost of food people in towns all over the land vented their anger and frustrations on grain dealers, bakers and known storage places.

A band of hungry, weary citizens boarded a vessel in Dublin bay that was laden with oatmeal bound for England, they removed the rudder and sails making certain it did not leave. One of the hungry mob was heard to shout "The Sassenach will receive no more grain from this port, not while we Irish are dying in the streets". To restore order King George the 2nd issued Robert with the power to quell the riots with force if necessary.

Belvedere

When Robert returned to Belvedere he did so in his capacity as first Earl of Belvedere. Great fanfare ensued but the superficial display of bunting wasn't going to fool anyone – with people starving on the streets of Mullingar the situation was so serious local officials had no option but to reacquisition land for what became known as the Famine graveyard. But today no one cared as long as the food was plentiful, and the champagne was both flowing and free.

The cream of Irish society were only too happy to dismiss the growing inconvenience of hunger. Today was their chance to be associated with the Earl using the occasion for no other reason than self-advancement and the Earl used it for the same reason. As Robert walked out on to the balcony he was greeted with applause, he stood for a moment, then nodding his head in appreciation declared "Champagne everyone". The Earl then responded to a hand on his shoulder.

"Congratulations, your lordship."

"Yes, congratulations, Robert." On turning he was greeted by his two oldest friends.

"How are you, James and you, Richard? Welcome to Belvedere."

"I see you have invited the sharks tonight, Robert, not your usual guest list," laughed James.

"One cannot survive on tiddlers alone," added Richard, now Earl of Cavan.

"That, my friends, is precisely why you are here. Why should I suffer alone?"

"What magnificent suffering," laughed James.

"You have lost none of your charm, James, I have been informed you have received your next posting."

"I am to be posted to Scotland as soon as next week, you know the Jacobites are rebelling again and they sent for me."

"Congratulations on your promotion to Brigadier General."

"Thank you, Robert, some are suggesting I may have friends in high places!"

The three friends laughed as they touched glasses and whispered "To the Trinity". Robert looked happy and relaxed on the outside but inside he was livid. Tonight was his first glimpse of Rochfort House. Robert pretended not to see the monstrosity just four hundred yards to his left but now was not the time to wash the family linen in public, certainly not at his own homecoming party.

Chapter 29

The first Earl of Belvedere was now untouchable, his close ties to Royalty were a deterrent to any would-be highwayman or assassin, except for the most determined that is, or maybe the hungriest. The Earl's first attempt at restoring order was to instruct the troops based at the Royal Barracks on Aron Quays to intervene and quash the rioting with all available resources. Several rioters were killed, making the Earl a target for reprisals from the downtrodden masses, but that did not disturb Robert's mind – after all they were placed on this earth to serve their masters and not to inconvenience them by going hungry.

A couple of days later Robert walked onto the balcony at Belvedere; this time he was alone, shouting profanities to the four winds.

"I believe he called it Rochfort House, the audacity! George will regret building this monstrosity."

It took weeks before he calmed down enough to realize there was nothing he could do; his father had willed it to George, all legal and above board.

Robert realized the Rochfort name had taken a battering over the last few years and now was his chance to be in the news for all the right reasons – why destroy the illusion of harmony, he thought, I shall simply block out the view. Robert's solution was to build a wall, one high enough and wide enough to block the entire view of his subordinate brother's house, built to resemble a sham Gothic ruin and to that end it was stunning, designed by renowned Italian architect Barrodotte who supervised its construction.

The craftsmanship was second to none, so convincing was the design and construction some visitors to Belvedere believed it to be the remains of the original house, the result of a catastrophic fire perhaps. It did not take long for Ned Flanagan to call it the Jealous Wall, it was the first of many follies Robert went on to commission; he had by his deeds become one of the most hated figures in Ireland especially by the poor who recognized his actions for what they were, callous and cruel, especially after the full effects of the famine were laid bare. But now that Robert was an Earl with considerable influence over power there was very little anyone could do except wait for time work its magic.

Ironically Mary was now officially the Countess of Belvedere and yet she was just another prisoner waiting for her day in court. The Countess spent the next four years in solitary confinement. During that time she planned many escape scenarios – one of her attempts was so naive as to cast doubt on her mental state when she struck her maid with a piece of wood that was close at hand then running through the fields not knowing where she was going or what she was going to do when she got there, exhausted she was discovered sitting in a clearing with her head in her hands. She was taken back to her prison cell where she was chained to the wall until Robert was certain she had learned her lesson. If her mind was only a wee bit clearer she might have remembered where she hid some money and jewellery, but her decline had been so swift she could hardly remember what transpired yesterday, her only hope was that her sanity should reappear as quickly as it had deserted her.

After months of repetition Mary slowly began to claw back some of her sanity. She remembered where she had hidden some cash for a rainy day and while walking the halls she began to recognise some of the faces depicted in oil paintings that still hung on the walls in the section she was allowed to walk. Slowly things were beginning to come back to her and this time she would not be running through the fields. Her only companion was her personal maid and she was not allowed to speak to her. After weeks of pretending to be worse than she actually was, Mary was ready to try one last time and this time she was determined not to make any mistakes.

The fog clouding her mind had lifted slightly, enough clarity returned for her to realize no one was coming to help her; if she was to be extricated from her predicament she would have to do so on her own. This was one of those moments of clarity and she knew she had to act and act fast. Every Friday evening at 7pm a delivery wagon called at Gaulstown. Next Friday Mary would be ready and when Friday finally arrived she was escorted to the gardens for her daily exercise but today Mary was listening intently for the distinctive sound of the delivery carriage that brought provisions from Dublin, mostly food items that could not be sourced locally.

Ten minutes had passed when at last the carriage could be heard as it lurched up the avenue pulled by four large work horses creating a very distinctive noise. When it finally came to a stop, Mary set her plan into action – this would be her one and only chance to escape the nightmare of her captivity.

She fell to the ground pretending to faint and as she lay on the grass Catherine Murry dropped her bell and ran to secure help. When she was out of sight, Mary sneaked through the undergrowth along a well-used shortcut to the provisions store far away from prying eyes.

She had in her pocket enough cash and jewellery she had secreted behind a section of loose skirting board when she first learned of her pending fate all those years ago. All she had to do now was convince the driver to take her back to Dublin with him. He agreed after Mary said she was a member of Gaulstown domestic staff and had just received news that her father was on his death bed.

"Where will I drop you, ma'am?"

"Brackenstown," answered Mary, "and here's another two shillings if you take me there directly."

"Giddy up."

When the news reached Robert at Belvedere, he demanded the local police locate Mary and return her to Gaulstown. The driver of the provisions wagon, not knowing anything about the woman he had agreed to take as a passenger, dropped Mary outside the entrance gate to Brackenstown estate in Swords, County Dublin. After some time, Mary caught the attention of a young maid doing her chores, she called to her and was just about to enlist her help when she noticed her father Viscount Molesworth standing at the entrance.

Mary cried out from the other side of the gates pleading with her father to let her come home, but to no avail. The Viscount turned away from his daughter then instructed his confused footman who had very recently taken up employment at Brackenstown and was not fully aware of the history involved that led to the events now unfolding before his eyes.

"Take this woman back to Mullingar and make sure you hand her over to her husband, the right honourable Robert Rochfort, Earl of Belvedere at Gaulstown Hall," instructed the Viscount.

Mary's heart sank; this was not what she expected, her last ray of hope dashed and by her own father. She cried out:

"Father, why have you abandoned me; I am your daughter, for heaven's sake have pity?"

"I have no daughter," hollered the Viscount, his reasoning for this extraordinary rebuke apart from the fact he was devoid of compassion was embarrassment.

On the return journey, Mary's hands were tethered to the iron hold bar just over her right shoulder, uncomfortable to say the least. Mary's mind was now as empty as the carriage she rode in, every bump –and there were many – felt like every other bump until approaching Rochfortbridge Mary was handed one last chance when the young driver, not knowing the local lay of the land, asked his captive for final directions to Gaulstown.

In her desperation to escape her prison she directed the young inexperienced footman in the direction of Belvedere telling him "Gaulstown is that way" while pointing in the opposite direction. If she had known it was George who had started this cycle of events, she might have re-evaluated the trust she was about to extend to him this very night. A short time later Mary again offered the coach driver final directions.

"Driver, take the next right turn, we are almost there."

Immediately after passing through the large black gates Mary instructed the young driver, "keep left, driver, keep left". Suddenly Rochfort house came into view, named Rochfort House by George, a decision he now regretted and had recently tried to remedy that mistake by placing large notices in all the bigger print outlets. In the descriptive article George's new home was referred to as Tudenham House, the probable reason for the change in name was George's attempt to appease the Earl. Tudenham House was now firmly established as the home of George Rochfort. The driver was finally able to dispel most of his mounting anxiety when he laid eyes on the sheer size of Tudenham, breath-taking. Such a fine house, he thought, it's got to be the right one.

A large rectangular three-storey house over basement Tudenham House was in the words of Sir James Caldwell, sitting sheriff of Fermanagh, who wrote in his account of his visit, that Tudenham was the finest house in the district. A direct snub to Belvedere and the Earl, proof if it was necessary that most of Robert's peers on the surface proclaimed his many virtues, but in private they still had their misgivings.

George, awoken by his butler Ned Flanagan, hurriedly made his way to the entrance wondering why anyone would visit at this ungodly hour and when he observed Mary being untied from her shackles he muttered in a low voice, "I hope this is all a dream." But he soon realized that this dream was in grave danger of becoming a nightmare.

The young driver still holding Mary's wrist spoke quite firmly: "Are you the right honourable Robert Rochfort 1st Earl of Belvedere, is this Gaulstown Hall?"

George instinctively answered, "Yes, thank you, my good man, I shall take responsibility from here."

With that the young driver released his captive.

"Mary, what have you done? Come in, how did you escape? Does Robert know you are here?"

Mary left nothing out and was now begging George to protect her.

"Please, George, don't send me back to that place, have pity."

"Mary, your own father has rejected you, my own brother was shot because of you and your husband will probably kill me if I side with you. Robert hates me, you must know that, so it follows if I am to survive this purge then I must also reject you and return you to Gaulstown, tonight."

Mary had just enough time to drink some water before George ushered her from Tudenham instructing his driver to return the Countess to her prison at Gaulstown Hall. If he thought this good deed might in some way contribute to Robert's conversion, maybe even help decrease his brother's hostility toward him then he really was delusional. George was destined to fend off insults from his older and more powerful sibling for many years to come.

Two years later and any resemblance to the old Gaulstown had almost disappeared. After Robert vented his anger in response to Mary's many escape attempts, Gaulstown became a ghost house. The facade looked familiar but that is as close to the old Gaulstown it would ever be. Time may be a good healer but it's also a slow healer. Mary Molesworth, the first Countess of Belvedere, still walked the lonely paths on Gaulstown, her grey cold place as she once referred to it.

George was still manager of the estate but with little or no personal contact between him and his brother, most of their correspondence went through their lawyers. Any resemblance to the old Gaulstown had truly vanished. But for Robert life was moving at a more productive pace, and he declared Belvedere his official residence.

He split the Gaulstown household apart taking most with him to Belvedere and those remaining would continue in employment at Tudenham, unfortunately some would find themselves surplus to requirements. Robert instructed Aideen Doolin to choose the staff she knew to be reliable, honest but most importantly "loyal". She chose Mary Clarke and Theresa Staunton, kitchen maids. James Clarke, head butler; Patrick Clearly, driver with responsibilities for the general upkeep of the Belvedere estate; and finally Ann Quinn was now expected to combine her job as parlour maid with that of kitchen maid. Aideen tried her best to convince Ned Flanagan to join them at Belvedere for a new beginning. Ned's response was predictable.

"No, Mrs Doolin. I couldn't continue working for Robert not in Belvedere, it may be prettier than Gaulstown but in such tight confines I couldn't trust meself. No, Mrs Doolin, Master George has offered me the post of head butler at Tudenham House, it's only a few hundred yards away, sure we can meet for an ould chat whenever our responsibilities allow. It's a much bigger house, plenty of room to hide when things get complicated."

"That's the best news I've heard in a long time, Ned Flanagan."

"May I ask you a personal question, Mrs Doolin?"

"As long as it's not too personal, Ned."

"No, Mrs Doolin. It's a wee bit delicate."

"Out with it, Ned."

"Why don't you take Catherine, she is young and please forgive me, Mrs Doolin, but you will soon be entering your senior years. Maybe you should take more of a supervisory role."

"Stop right there, Ned Flanagan, while I have breath in my body I shall continue to do the job I was put on this earth to do. Now that you have raised Catherine's name I will let you into a little secret; but before I do, I will need you to swear on the holy bible, Ned Flanagan."

"Where is it, Mrs Doolin"?

"I don't know, Ned I can't find it, but keep your gob shut anyway. The Earl specifically instructed that Catherine was to stay at Gaulstown and continue her duties as maid to the Countess. He informed me that he had information confirming his suspicions about Catherine Murry; she is not to be trusted. From now on she is just as much a prisoner as the object of her jealousy all those years ago, remember Ned?"

"Thought you might say something like that, Mrs Doolin, sure I warned you about that one."

"Me and everyone else, Ned Flanagan, so maybe it's not such a secret after all, is it," as they both laughed.

"One more thing, Ned, now that we no longer serve the same master, you can call me Aideen."

"Ay. Ok, Mrs Doolin, I mean Aideen."

Chapter 30

Over the next few years Gaulstown fell into disrepair, with Robert refusing to pay for the upkeep. He went even further when he left just a skeleton staff to ensure Mary's misery continued unabated. The children were moved to Belfield House, this was to be their home for the entirety of their adolescence, a governess would oversee their education, a cook, two maids and a footman would help them navigate the years ahead. They all received strict instructions not to enter the grounds of Gaulstown let alone the main house.

After so many years in England scrounging from distant relatives, life became unbearable for Arthur and in the end with no money and very little chance to acquire any, he had but one choice, to return to Ireland and place himself at Robert's mercy. If Arthur thought Robert might have changed, he was sadly mistaken. Arthur was arrested the moment he set foot on Irish soil and charged with adultery, he was committed to Marshalsea debtor's prison in Dublin, and at the same time Mary was taken under escort from her prison at Gaulstown to the capital where she too was thrown into the same debtors' prison to await trial. Arthur had no contact with Mary in prison and had all but given up hope of ever seeing her again.

His instincts were correct: they would never meet again, not on this earth.

Mary was appointed a state lawyer, but she immediately suspected him of working for Robert. He consistently advised her to plead guilty, saying, "The court will be more lenient if you just admit the affair. Can you do that?"

"But we never had an affair," answered Mary, "we were simply good friends."

"That may be so, Countess, but if the powers that be – and I am sure you fully understand to whom I refer – if he must fight you in court then the sentence may be far worse; it could mean deportation to the colonies."

Mary just nodded in bewilderment for she knew the result was a foregone conclusion and with that in mind she decided to ignore the prepared confession in front of her. Mary was now under great mental as well as physical stress, but she somehow found the strength to say the words, "If I am to be found guilty no matter the strength of my argument, then I will not compound one mistake with another. I will not sign that confession."

The date was set for the trial and when it arrived Mary stood alone in the dock. Arthur was deemed too unwell to attend, he was fined twenty thousand pounds in his absence and his release was conditional on payment of the fine in full. When Mary realized Arthur was unable to pay the fine and would most probably die in that rat-infested sewer they call a prison she lost all hope. As she stood in the dock her life force was slowly draining from her body and when she heard the judge start to speak, she hung her head and clung to the wooden handrail with a vice like grip.

"How do you plead, guilty or not guilty?" asked the judge.

With all other avenues now firmly sealed, Mary felt her knees began to buckle as she sobbed "Guilty", hoping her plea would encourage Robert to take a more lenient approach and maybe grant her a divorce.

The Judge released Mary into the custody of her husband to do with as he sees fit, then brought the gavel down hard.

Under the weight of her predicament the Countess lost all her fight and was quickly losing her mind to some form of melancholy.

Gaulstown and all its decay would be her prison until the Earl decided otherwise. Mary was unaware of the public interest in her predicament – she assumed people would condemn her for her perceived lies, but nothing could have been further from the truth. A high proportion were sympathetic to her plight, for everyone still had their doubts when it came to the Earl. As the years passed people began to forget Gaulstown was ever a home; the large entrance gates were removed, redesigned and partly incorporated in one of Robert's favourite follies on Belvedere, the Gothic Arch. The avenue was now no more than a dirt track, the large pines that once lined the avenue were unceremoniously hacked down with venom, some of the villagers swore they witnessed the Earl chop them down with a sharp axe; either way cut down they were and used to build a new boathouse on the shores of Lough Ennell at Belvedere. Ivy covered most of Gaulstown's exterior now and the large glasshouse had disappeared from the skyline. The place looked abandoned, desolate except for the wildlife that made it their home mostly birds of prey, appropriate under the circumstances. But every now and again from behind the ivy-covered windows a pair of wide eyes would scan the view, waiting for her prince to appear.

Chapter 31

Belvedere

It was a starry night, the full moon's reflection bounced off the many puddles on this potholed track. The rain had stopped and Robert's carriage was almost at the gates of Belvedere when a masked man appeared from the bushes. He stood in the middle of the road just as the driver slowed down to take a right turn. He pointed his blunderbuss as the Earl's carriage came to a stop then moved briskly to the carriage door shouting as he went.

"Are you Robert Rochfort, Earl of Belvedere?" Then reaching for the handle he yanked the door open. A blinding flash lit up the night sky, bright enough for Thomas to see the large fragments of bone and tissue exploding from the back of the highwayman's skull.

Robert poked his head out, looked down at the body and said, "Picked the wrong man on the wrong night, my good fellow." Then pulling the door closed he gave two taps of the snake's head on the wooden panel with the instruction, "Drive on, Thomas, leave the wretch there, he's not going anywhere. You can inform the police in Mullingar tomorrow morning, but now I really must get some rest?"

"Yes, my lord."

The body was removed the next day and the police started their investigation into the attempted murder. Did the highwayman act alone? Was he hired by someone? Or was this political? The local police chief told reporters:

"At this time, we have lots of questions but no answers. Only when we identify the highwayman can we determine if he had any accomplices. He did not carry any papers on his person, nor did he have any distinguishable marks except for a small scar on his lower right leg. We have circulated his description; someone will come forward with information. Until then we need to know did someone take him there, we found no mode of transport. We are determined to bring the perpetrator or perpetrators to justice," adding, "we will get to the bottom of this assignation attempt."

After weeks of investigation the police had identified the gunman involved. They sealed off a section of dockland on the river Liffey near Ringsend, Dublin. When the search revealed no weapons on the premises, they began their search for documentary evidence and after breaking the lock on one of the desk drawers they found a small journal with entries that looked quite innocent except for one, the date was quite significant. The words 'got you!' followed by the first line of an address 27 Caple Street. Superintendent Oliver Fagan immediately connected the address to a high-profile unsolved murder case.

"Right," hollered Fagan, "let's find the owner of this establishment, a Mr Clarence Tennison according to these documents; it was his partner Sean Flynn that tried to assassinate the MP Robert Rochfort. What are you lot waiting for? Find this man and bring him in, go."

Clarence was nowhere to be found, his house on North Great George's Street looked abandoned, the drapes were closed and there was no response to the repeated attempts to gain entry.

"Break down the door."

Clarence had had just enough time to empty his bank accounts and ready Sweet Bess for a long journey.

"Not much point in waiting for the hangman's noose to tighten, I shall ply my trade from the Caribbean to the Americas under a new identity and wait for my next opportunity. I will never give up, one day I shall avenge my daughter's death and surprise shall be my secret weapon."

Two years passed, Robert was still lord of the manor, his visits to Gaulstown had ceased years earlier and Mary Molesworth was all but forgotten. She had not laid eyes on her children in almost fifteen years. Over that time the children had made numerous attempts to visit their mother, but the Earl was adamant and stood firm. The children were so afraid of their father they never once tried to visit without permission let alone try to free her, while Robert continued to live the life of a bachelor, travelling extensively around Europe in his capacity as King George's Viceroy, a position he did not seek but as it turned out it was a position he grew to relish. He so enjoyed meeting various heads of state and he never tired of hearing his name announced at official functions, the right honourable Robert Rochfort, Earl of Belvedere.

Downstairs Aideen Doolin was brewing a fresh pot of tea for herself and Ned when he glanced up from the pamphlet he was reading and said: "You know, Aideen, I was just thinking the other day, whatever happened to Mr Tennison, he just disappeared from the face of the earth."

"No idea, Ned, but it's a big world out there."

"Aye, that's a fact. If the police were looking for me and I had the money he has they wouldn't find me either. When is the Earl due back?"

"This coming Friday, Ned."

"How long for this time?"

"Six weeks."

"Better get used to brewing me own tea then."

Robert returned to Belvedere intending to enjoy what was left of summer. Beginning to feel his age, he instinctively knew when he needed to rest and recuperate. He intended to walk every track on Belvedere, something he had promised himself when he made it his home; these next six weeks would be his and his alone. He never once gave a thought for Mary or his brother Arthur; as far as he was concerned they could rot in hell and rotting in hell they were, a living hell. The Countess on her better days – and they were few and far between – would stand for hours looking through the natural spaces between the heavy ivy that now covered almost all of the Gaulstown façade; it had grown so vociferously over the years that it had collapsed part of the tower on the east wing, exposing the interior to the elements. But that did not concern Robert or anyone else as the entire house had been stripped of all valuables including fabrics, furniture, art works, even the Rochfort history in stained glass had been stripped and sold, reused in constructing new history for some other aristocratic family.

Mary would stand there for hours on end, some days her melancholy would lift a little and enough clarity would return to kindle a little hope but not enough to light a substantial flame. On occasion she imagined Arthur approaching on his charger intending to relieve her suffering, but alas Arthur was in his own hell, stuck in his rat-infested place of torment and misery waiting for his god to grant him mercy.

The shattering news that Arthur Rochfort had died in prison was greeted with great sorrow in the community. Aideen Doolin was sitting at the kitchen table when James Clarke delivered the sad news.

"Poor boy, he did not deserve to die in that place; he was the sensitive one, the only one with a heart. Oh I despair, Mr Clarke, what has happened to this family? I so long for the old days." As she wiped the soft tears she fought hard to contain and through her sobs she confided in Mr Clarke.

"Mr Clarke, I know this is an odd thing to say but I am not certain I can continue to stay in Robert's service."

"Mrs Doolin, don't talk like that, what would we do without you? May I be frank?"

"Yes of course, Mr Clarke."

"If you leave, what will become of us all? That's how much you are respected in this house, Mrs Doolin, this place will fall apart without your humble guidance."

"That's a wee bit of an exaggeration, Mr Clarke, but thank you for your generous words. Mind you, I have been thinking about things quite a lot lately. You see, my brother wants me to come live with him, he never married, just like me and now the years are creeping up on both of us. It just feels like the sensible thing to do."

"Your brother lives in the village, I believe, or do you have other family?"

"No, Mr Clarke, he's the only family I have."

"Of course, Mrs Doolin, you do what's best for you, sure we'll all have to face that decision sooner or later. Who would you recommend for the position of housekeeper?"

"Not much point looking outside Belvedere, Mr Clarke, sure Theresa has all the necessary qualities and she's been with me since she was a wee girl."

"I totally agree, Mrs Doolin, whatever you decide you will have my complete support."

"Thank you, Mr Clarke, I knew you would understand. The bell, Mr Clarke, someone at the front door."

"Yes, Mrs Doolin, I'm on my way."

"Superintendent Fagan."

"Good afternoon, is the Earl in residence?"

"Yes, Superintendent, please wait here, I will inform his lordship."

After a few moments. "The Earl will see you now, this way."

"Good afternoon, Superintendent Fagan, you have some news?"

"Yes, your lordship, we have received information regarding the fugitive Clarence Tennison. We have reason to believe he is back on Irish soil and if that is the reality then it is my duty to inform you and to encourage you to take extra caution with your personal safety."

"Thank you, Superintendent, do you know of his whereabouts, when was he last seen?"

"The only positive identification came from a neighbour who laid eyes on him and reported the matter to the police; that was two days ago. The neighbour is a very respected member of the medical profession; we are treating this with the utmost urgency."

"Please sit, can I offer you a brandy perhaps?"

"Thank you, your lordship."

"May I ask what you intend to do, Superintendent?"

"With so little information to lean on, I suspect we are both devoid of answers, for now that is. I have men trying to locate Mr Tennison and put him where he belongs, in prison for the murder of Terence O'Malley, a prominent Dublin journalist."

"Tennison did not discharge the weapon himself, it was his business partner, was it not, the same man that tried and failed to kill me?"

"Yes, your lordship, but we have come to the conclusion the pistol and instructions to neutralize both the journalist and you came directly from Tennison; therefore he is as guilty as if he squeezed the trigger himself."

"Yes, I fully agree, what security measures do you suggest we implement?"

"I suggest you take a bodyguard with you at all times until we locate Mr Tennison." Then raising himself from his seat, the superintendent thanked the Earl and took his leave. Robert considered the advice he had received from Superintendent Fagan but decided against using a bodyguard. It was the Earl's opinion that Clarence Tennison did not have the necessary resources to organize another assassination attempt.

'It's been years since he left Ireland in a hurry, how could he encourage anyone to help him' he thought and decided to proceed as normal. Nothing was going to interfere with his moonlit walks or his love for horse riding. The only precaution the Earl did take was to carry a loaded a pistol on his person.

[It is with great sadness we report the death of
Brigadier General James Hamilton.]

The devastating news of the death of James at the battle of

Culloden was met with widespread sorrow and regret. The article went on to praise the Brigadier's leadership in the face of the enemy. Brigadier General James Hamilton under the command of the Duke of Cumberland led British forces into battle.

> *Great courage and exemplary leadership was shown, resulting in the bloody defeat of the Jacobite army. Between 1500 and 2000 Jacobites were killed or wounded in the brief encounter; the battle lasted no more than one hour. The British victory at Culloden halted the Jacobite intent to overthrow the House of Hanover and restore the House of Stuart to the British throne… But for the cunning strategic planning of Cumberland and his determination not to let the Jacobites take the high ground, combined with the bravery of Brigadier Hamilton in executing his orders with gusto resulted in a great victory for the crown forces.*

On receiving the news of James' untimely death Robert felt compelled to honour his friend's memory. The 2nd Earl of Cavan, Richard Lambert, was already on his way to Belvedere to discuss what form the celebration of their friend's life should take, for he and he alone knew how James felt in relation to the act of settlement and James' personal preference to serve the Catholic House of Stuart rather than the Protestant House of Hanover. Richard remembered that discussion with great clarity, especially his commitment to honour the oath of allegiance he had made to his Hanoverian King and true to his word James had put his personal misgivings to one side and carried out his duty with distinction.

"His lordship, the Earl of Cavan."

"Welcome, Richard, welcome. The Jacobites have taken the Trinity's most extrovert member."

"Yes, Robert, this is indeed a very sad time for the remaining members of the Trinity and of course the Hamilton family. I propose conveying our sympathy in a more public way; after all, James gave his life in defence of the Realm."

"That, my good friend, is precisely why we meet today." The Earl then instructed James Clarke to bring a bottle of brandy to the balcony and the two men sat in prolonged silence, no doubt encouraged by the proliferation of nature's bounty that surrounded this jewel that was Belvedere. It was a warm summer's evening and the smell of the juniper floating on the soft breeze was intoxicating; every now and again the Owlets that had taken up residency in the stables would call out to their mother and in return she would answer offering reassurance.

After some time, Richard was first to break silence. "Shall I pour?"

"Please do," answered Robert, then pointing to the oil lantern hanging from trellis above their heads, "Observe, Richard, the moth flies to the lantern flame oblivious to its potential danger, just like Icarus who flew to close to the sun in his pursuit of freedom. It reminds me somewhat of James sitting on his charger just before battle commenced. I wonder in that precise moment did he too have some inner force driving him to his own destruction."

"Possibly, Robert, for we know James was a man of many qualities and just as many flaws but his honesty was by far his best quality. You were witness to that element of his nature on many occasions–" as they raised their glasses in a toast

"To James." And as the full moon cast its brilliance on the still waters of the lough they both fell silent once more.

Sometime later Richard suggested, "We should consider organizing a memorial service at St Patrick's Cathedral, it would not only be appropriate but absolutely deserving. What say you, Robert?"

"Formerly Christ Church Cathedral, what an inspired suggestion, Richard. Jonathan Swift is not only dean of St Patrick's but is also an old family friend. I remember Dean Swift's visits to Gaulstown with great clarity all those years ago and I am certain he would be honoured to pay homage to one of our fallen heroes."

"Shall I contact Dean Swift?" offered Richard.

"I would not expect you to undertake the responsibilities on your own, but please by all means contact Dean Swift to arrange a meeting to discuss our proposal. James, more brandy?"

"Yes, my lord."

If Robert thought this was going to be a formality, then he was mistaken. With the passage of time Robert could be forgiven if his selective memory had faded somewhat, but for some the sudden deaths in quick succession of Robert's father, then one year later his first wife Elizabeth Tennison, followed two years later by his mother who at the time was very much against Robert's marriage to Mary Molesworth, and the subsequent imprisonment of the Countess raised questions about his integrity.

Jonathan Swift, a devout Christian, was one of many who were not entirely convinced of Robert's innocence, but on reflection Jonathan Swift decided the intention was to honour a brave soldier and not the wicked Earl of Belvedere, and so agreed to Richard's proposal. When all the formalities were over and the remaining members of the Trinity had laid their friend to rest, Robert returned to Belvedere and continued his recuperation while the Earl of Cavan had issues of his own to attend to – life as an Earl was not what he had hoped it to be, certainly not the bed of roses he was expecting, but at least he had a wife that loved him and children he adored and loved. Apart from the heavy workload that weighed him down at times he could always depend on the laughter of his children to make him realise how lucky he was. But for Robert there was no necessity for such frivolous nonsense; he did not care one way or the other if his children were laughing or crying, and now that they were adults he cared even less.

When Robert's children were younger they had often visited Belvedere, they had found it the perfect environment to indulge their childhood fantasies and as the years passed their pursuits changed from games like hide and seek one minute, then fighting off the pirates trying to land their boats on the shores of Lough Ennell the next, shouting and screaming as they slashed at the wind with their wooden swords.

But as the boys got older and more used to the abject indifference of their father and the unseen unfelt love from their imprisoned mother, they became accustomed to life without parental affection. From childish games they progressed to more energetic pursuits like fox hunting or climbing. Belvedere had some of the tallest oak and ash in Westmeath, so attempting to climb any one of them was exhilarating to George Augustus, the eldest; fishing was a close second. But his fishing expeditions on Lough Ennell were strictly supervised and that was a source of great frustration for him as he loved to chase the one brown trout that the whole of Westmeath had heard about, but no one had actually laid eyes on. The phantom brown that became widely known as a Bouchaill Saille, the fat boy. But now years later the three young men began to take more interest in their mother's plight – it was twenty seven years since their father had given the order to incarcerate their mother in Gaulstown Hall and twelve years since anyone had seen as much as a glimpse of the Countess; her personal maid Catherine Murry made quite sure the rules were followed to the letter. It was almost one year since the Earl had contact with any of his children, they had discussed at length their mother's plight many times, each in turn promised to confront their father and demand her torment be ended, but when push came to shove their brave talk could not be backed up with action; courage was hard to find. Eventually after many attempts to raise the level of courage needed, something changed. Together they decided to confront their father and plead for their mother's release.

Chapter 32

"Father, this is the first time we have dared to ask you to show mercy; it's been so long now we fear for mother's sanity. Is it not time to display a little compassion?"

"I have shown nothing but compassion; remember, I have the power, I could have had the adulteress transported to the colonies – was that not a display of compassion?"

"Yes, Father and we are all grateful for that."

"May I speak, Father?" asked Richard.

"Yes, you may."

"With the greatest respect I am 22 years of age and not a child anymore; you, Father, at my age were about to inherit both Gaulstown and Belvedere estates resulting from the untimely death of Grandpapa. Is it not time you recognized the fact that we are men?"

"That's what I like to see and you, Arthur, have you anything to add?"

"Yes, Father I have. We demand you release Mother from her captivity and reinstate her freedom. She has been locked up in that filthy cockroach-infested room with no human contact for twenty-seven years now. The last time I saw Mother's face was fourteen years ago and that glimpse through distorted glass will haunt me forever. For all our sakes, Father, do the right thing and show some pity."

The Earl paused for a moment.

"Let me begin by saying I feel proud and happy to see you boys have the spirit to issue a demand of such magnitude and yes, I will yield to your demand and release the adulteress."

The three siblings looked at each other with expressions of shock, amazement and alarm.

'This is too easy,' thought George.

Robert then stood and poured himself a large brandy before saying, "With a caveat."

'I knew it was too simple,' thought Richard.

"The adulteress shall be released from the confines of her room and allowed to wander the halls of Gaulstown until the end of her days; is that quite clear?"

"But, Father–"

"Enough. The adulteress got what she deserved. Remember she had carnal relations with your uncle, my brother, he paid the price for his betrayal and I intend to see the adulteress suffer the same fate."

"All of that is disputed," shouted Arthur. "What proof do you possess?"

Raising his voice, the Earl spoke with conviction.

"Proof, what more proof do you require? The adulteress admitted the affair. You are just like your uncles, they too had abundance of nerve but totally devoid of courage. Now get out and do not attempt to contact the adulteress while I have breath in my body. Go."

Downstairs

James Clarke had witnessed the encounter and could hardly wait to inform Mrs Doolin.

"It's been a long time since the boys were here in Belvedere."

"I know, Mrs Doolin, but wait till I tell you what happened."

"Surely not more upheaval, Mr Clarke."

"Regrettably things did not go well for the boys, Mrs Doolin."

And after James relayed the events Aideen felt faint and had to sit for a few moments to gather her thoughts.

"Oh my god, we have been here before many times, I am certain the Earl has lost his mind, the poor Countess and her unfortunate children."

Placing a chair close to Mrs Doolin, James said, "Would you like to sit down, Mrs Doolin, are you sure you are all right? You look very distressed."

"The way the master continues to mistreat the Countess and his family does not appeal to me. I have made my mind up, Mr Clarke, I shall leave the Earl's employment at the end of this month. Please, Mr Clarke, fetch Theresa; we need to discuss her future role as Housekeeper – that's if she wants it, there's no guarantee, Mr Clarke, no guarantee."

Chapter 33

Robert's rest period was well and truly over. He had received a letter from the King requesting his help in dealing with a very delicate matter, or so he thought, but the truth was everyone knew about the difficult relationship that was allowed to persist between the King and his disobedient son and heir, they were constantly at each other's throats and the reason was financial. The Prince had exhausted every avenue available to him in his pursuit of a much larger allowance than the King was prepared to extend to his ungrateful son, and after clearing all his liabilities some years earlier the King had no intention of repeating that mistake. When Frederick realised the King was not going to extend further credit, he coerced some affluent friends of his into paying most of his gambling debts, then embarked on a revenge strategy that he hoped would endear him to those same wealthy friends. His first act of rebellion came when Frederick opposed the unpopular Gin act that was intended to control the flourishing Gin trade and then had the nerve to apply to Parliament for an increase to his public allowance, but when the King had a private word in the ear of those that mattered his request was denied. This drove a deeper wedge between the King and his son leading to the King's request that Frederick's friend and confidant, the Earl of Belvedere, should come to London and use whatever influence he might hold over the Prince of Wales to try and alleviate the problem.

When Ned Flanagan observed the Earl's carriage leave Belvedere for London he immediately made his way along the fairy path that crisscrossed the entire estate. Poking his head around Mrs Doolin's kitchen door, Ned delivered his usual line: "Any chance of an ould cup a tea?"

"Hello Ned, come in," invited Mr Clarke. "Mrs Doolin is having a wee lie down. I don't think she has recovered from the events of yesterday."

"Why, what happened yesterday, Mr Clarke?"

"Sit down, Ned, the brew is ready."

"What in god's name has that devil been up to this time? If he has upset Aideen I will go to the gallows with me head held high."

"Aideen, is it now?"

"I meant Mrs Doolin."

"It's not that serious, Ned, to command such a drastic course of action as a visit to the gallows but it did upset Mrs Doolin."

After James went through the whole sad saga again, he recognized a substantial change in Ned's demeanour.

"Are you alright, Ned?"

"Yes, Mr Clarke, my mind has just been cleared of any lingering doubts that I still harboured."

"What do you mean, Ned?"

"Tis nottin, Mr Clarke."

Just then Mrs Doolin appeared in the doorway.

"Mrs Doolin, there ya are, come sit down and I'll pour ya a nice cup a sweet tea. James told me all about the events of yesterday and your intention to leave the Earl's employment."

With that James Clarke took his leave saying, "It's alright for you two but I have chores to attend to, we will talk more about this when I return."

"Thank you, Mr Clarke, you have been very understanding," said Mrs Doolin.

"I'll swing for that bastard yet," said Ned.

"Ned Flanagan, what have I told you before about that tongue of yours."

"Sorry, Mrs Doolin, I mean Aideen, I meant no disrespect to you."

"I know that, Ned Flanagan, sure I know that only too well. It looks like I have reached the point in my life where I think there is no point to my life, if you know what I mean. Ah don't mind me, Ned, sure in the end we all see the things we love perish in front of our very eyes; life can be cruel."

Ned stood with tears trickling down his cheeks and when he spoke his voice was trembling ever so slightly as he proclaimed, "It doesn't have to be this way, Aideen."

Noticing a marked change in Ned's voice, Aideen looked up to see Ned fumbling with his worn jacket sleeve as he tried to wipe his tears away.

"Ned Flanagan, whatever is the matter?"

"Marry me, Aideen for I have always loved you. I have a nice bit a money put by, sure we'll be grand and we can live in me little cottage in the village, me only regret is not askin ya sooner."

Aideen Doolin stood with tears welling up in her eyes then slowly reached for the embrace she so longed for all these years and through sobs of her own whispered, "Ya big eegit, Ned Flanagan, of course I'll marry ya, I have waited so long to hear you say those words."

Gaulstown

Mary Molesworth was now free, free to wander the ghostly halls of Gaulstown alone for the rest of her natural life. Mary's personal maid Catherine Murry was serving a similar sentence.

Years earlier while hiding in one of the alcoves close to Mary's living quarters she had witnessed George's clumsy attempt to gain entry to Mary's living quarters under the pretext of keeping her company while the Earl was in London on business. Ironically it was Catherine's love for George that helped drive her intense jealousy of the Countess and now she too would serve her sentence alongside the object of her jealousy.

Catherine was allowed one day off every month and she as a creature of habit never ventured beyond the confines of the village. She always spent it with her mother, mostly baking bread during the day and in the evening she would accompany her mother to O'Hara's snug, making sure to sit well away from the other women in this female-only section of the inn. On the other side of the partition the men of the village were quite content to drink as much porter and smoke as much tobacco as they could or until their money ran out. Lizzie Murry started the conversation with the same question every month.

"What the hell is going on up there in that big empty house, Catherine?"

"I'm not able to talk about that, Mammy, I told you a hundred times, now leave me alone and talk about sometin else."

"Like what, sure there's nottin else going on around here, Jesus look around ya, the only gossip you'll get from that shower is, me poor back me scabby leg or I need to see the doctor with me nerves. I've enough a that shite, come on, Catherine, how is the Countess doin? You should know, you're with her day and night. Come to think of it, who's looking after her today?"

"No one, Mammy, I told ya it's not allowed, she has to fend for herself till I get back in the morning."

"Get another jug a Porter, Catherine, you're the one with the wages."

Two hours later and after a few jugs of porter, Lizzie continued.

"I was talking to John Doolin yesterday."

"Mrs Doolin's brother?" enquired Catherine.

"Ay and wait till I tell ya. You know the butler that works for George Rochfort over there at Tudenham, Ned Flanagan, you remember him? Well he only went and asked the Doolin one to marry him."

"No I didn't know that, but I'm not surprised; sure them two were always going to end up married but I don't know what you're cribbing about, I thought you'd be delighted."

"Why would ya think that?"

"Well it leaves the coast clear for you to put your size twelves under Doolin's bed!"

Both mother and daughter burst into laughter, bringing strange looks from some of the other customers and a sharp rebuke from Nancy Keenan, the local bike.

"Are you two laughing at me?"

"Ah shut your mouth, ya smelly bitch."

And just as Nancy was sharpening her claws, the landlord poked his head through the serving hatch.

"I'm warning you, Keenan, sit down and behave yourself."

"But those two were laughing at me, Mr O'Hara."

"No we weren't, Finnian, don't mind that one," said Lizzie.

"Either way, cease your bad language the three of yez or else."

When everyone settled down Lizzie tried one more time to get some gossip about the Countess saying, "I heard she's gone completely mad. Is it true?"

"Promise me you won't say a word to a soul, Mammy, promise."

"I promise," answered Lizzie.

"I don't think the Countess is mad but she is very confused, she sleeps most of the day, maybe that's because the drapes have to be kept closed at all times now or maybe the darkness is some sort of comfort for her, I don't know; she just likes the dark, either way it's some kind of melancholy."

"What's the difference between melancholy and madness?"

"I don't know but she walks the hallways at night carrying her lantern, then stops here and there to stare at the empty spaces where oil paintings of Robert's ancestors once hung and talks a lot of gibberish."

"Maybe it's some kind a foreign language."

"Maybe."

"Does she know who you are?" enquired Lizzie emboldened with porter.

"Not sure, she never looks directly at me, don't think she even remembers her children's names but that's what Clare thought that time she nearly escaped."

"She did escape and where did she go – first to her ould fella up there in Dublin and he told her to feck off, sure that would be enough ta start some form of melancholy."

"I know all that, Mammy, don't start again."

"You just don't want to talk about the next bit, when she begged George to take her in and hide her."

"Don't bring him into it or I'm off."

"The truth hurts," she slurred as the drink took hold, "remember I know all about you and that George."

"That's it, I'm going home."

"Ah don't be like that, sure I'm only joking, go on get another jug a porter." And after a long period of silence: "Does she even know she has children?"

"Don't know, sometimes I think she does, the other day I heard her sobbing saying something about her babies."

Chapter 34

London

The Earl spent weeks mediating between the King and Prince Frederick but to no avail, it all ended with the King banishing the Prince from court, not one of Robert's most successful mediation attempts. The Earl made his apologies to the King and returned to Ireland.

Waterford Ireland

As the Earl disembarked at Waterford harbour a pistol was discharged and amid the confusion one of the passengers that happened to be disembarking close by was shot and seriously wounded. For a few seconds no one was quite sure who the intended victim was nor the identity of the attacker, until a loud voice hollered from the end of the gangway.

"Prepare to die, Robert Rochfort." It was obvious the Earl of Belvedere was the intended victim, Clarence Tennison older, slimmer, his time sailing the high seas of the Caribbean had indeed been good to him but now Clarence was on borrowed time and if he was to avenge his daughter's death then this might be the only opportunity he would ever get. This looked very much like the end of the road for Robert Rochfort as Clarence moved swiftly along the gangway then stopped, pointed his pistol directly at the Earl's heart, no more than two feet away as he bellowed:

"I will spare your life if you confess to having a hand in the untimely death of my dearest daughter Elizabeth, you know you are guilty, admit it here before the good people of Waterford or prepare to die."

The Earl was visibly shaking and in a stumbling voice he managed to say:

"I loved Elizabeth – how could you think–"

Suddenly a shot rang out and Clarence fell to his knees at the feet of his intended victim. Death was instantaneous. Luckily for the Earl a police constable was only yards away when the first shot rang out and it had taken this time to source and load his weapon. When the news reached Belfield House there was confusion, some said the Earl was killed, others said he was wounded.

"What should we do?" said Arthur. George was first to offer advice.

"Let us wait for confirmation as to the Earl's fate, to act now could bring great misfortune to each and every one of us."

"I do not intend to wait a moment longer," said Jane, the almost forgotten eldest member of this dysfunctional family. But then she was a girl which meant her input was of no relevance.

"Jane, you are my sister and I love you dearly but you must not let your feelings take you to a place of no return. Please do not be impetuous, sister, if you enter Gaulstown at this time with the intention of freeing Mother and it transpires the Earl is alive then you may also suffer the same fate or worse."

"So many times I have dreamt of plunging a knife into his rotten black heart and rushing to free our beloved mother to hold her in my arms and beg her forgiveness for not having the strength or courage to act sooner."

"Jane, please wait just a couple of hours, we may have a definitive answer by then," pleaded Arthur.

"If in two hours' time there is no new information will my brothers help me to free our mother from her unspeakable torment?"

The boys all answered at once. "Yes."

Just then a lone messenger came riding up the avenue at a great gallop shouting:

"The Earl is unharmed, the Earl is alive." The words no one wanted to hear.

When news reached Prince Frederick he decided to visit his friend in Belvedere; the horrendous effects of the famine had by now been largely forgotten if not entirely and he had the perfect cover story. He was after all the Chancellor of the University of Dublin Trinity College, he had every right to arrange a surprise visit under the auspices of an inspection. Robert and the prince had kept in regular contact after Robert's aborted attempt to reconcile King George and his disruptive son, but this was a chance for the two men to catch up and discuss their favourite pastime.

"Time to sample some of the famous Irish hospitality," laughed Frederick.

Trinity College Dublin some months later

Great excitement surrounded the visit of Prince Frederick, every aristocratic vein was stretched to breaking, some say bribes were exchanged to secure an introduction to the future King. Soon after Frederick had completed his visit to Trinity he was escorted to his accommodation at Dublin Castle where Robert was waiting to welcome his old friend. Both men greeted each other with much affection and retired to discuss current affairs among other things.

"We will take champagne in the throne room," commanded Frederick; "you look well for a man that cheated death by inches I believe."

"Not quite, your Highness, considering he killed a fellow passenger who happened to be standing at least three feet away does not amount to cheating death, more like incompetence on the assailant's behalf!"

"Let us rejoice in his lack of skill, shall we?" as they raised their glasses. "What time can we expect Richard?"

"Richard will meet with us tomorrow at Belvedere, your Highness."

"I am so looking forward to seeing with my own eyes this paradise I have heard so much about."

"That, your Highness, is first on the agenda for the coming day, tonight is a celebration of your visit. I have taken the liberty of inviting some friends and some not so friendly but without exception we all pretend to sit on the same side of the isle."

The next morning Prince Frederick and the Earl of Belvedere climbed onboard a nondescript carriage, they thought the least amount of people that knew about the visit to Belvedere the better; it would afford the Prince some uninterrupted leisure time. Robert had invited a select group of influential friends, knowing that whatever happened behind closed doors would never be discussed under any circumstances. He had sought the help of some of the most prominent Dublin madams, requesting at least one dozen highly motivated young women and men to immerse themselves in the art of the Kama Sutra for their pleasure; this promised to be two days the Prince would not forget. Standing on the balcony at Belvedere Frederick exhaled.

"You were quite right to say this was a little piece of paradise. From what I witness Belvedere has a magic of its own. Where is your brother? Will he be joining us for the entertainment?"

"No, your Highness, we have not spoken for some time; all our business is processed through lawyers."

"Just like my father and I. Hard to find forgiveness and compromise, don't you think, Robert?"

"Never sought it, your Highness, it's of no consequence to me now. Come, Frederick, let me introduce you to six of the most influential men in Ireland."

"Only six?"

"Yes, your Highness, the rest of the entertainment has much more to offer."

They both turned laughing as they entered what they knew was going to be a night where men of power and influence relinquished their moral restraints and indulged their fantasies.

Chapter 35

When rumours of the future King's visit had begun to surface, they were quickly dismissed as false, but Robert was pleased with all the public speculation and innuendo. It afforded the Earl a reputation he did not deserve, that of a gay bachelor, while the opposite was in fact the truth. The public knew what he really was, a cruel manipulative dictator. Robert continued to believe his way was the only way things would be done and for the next few years continued to reject pleas for leniency and demands to release his wife from her torturous bondage; all pleas were dismissed without exception.

The Earl was now unofficially semi-retired and intentionally so; he decided it was time to fulfil his promise to himself and enjoy Belvedere with all its winding trails and hidden secrets, especially the period of transformation from day to night. It was on one of those faithful nights Robert picked up his cane and went for his nightly walk in the grounds. The full moon cast its light far and wide, Lilliput on the far shore was visible under its generous illumination, its reflection seemed to dance on the surface of the lough then break on Ennell's shore.

Beautiful, he thought and decided to walk to the shore using the generous light provided to guide him. At the same time fate was about to play a pivotal role. On the far side of the lough a small larch fishing boat was slowly moving through the shadows, brushing aside the reeds with stealth before its passenger hauled himself from the shallow water and settled his oars. Then the darkly clad stranger calmly began to row in the direction of Belvedere. He too was dependent on light from the moon to guide him on his quest for revenge. After some time the Earl sat on a rock, both to rest and enjoy his tranquil surroundings. Looking to the distant Lilliput shore he did not see the dark clad stranger emerge from the shadows and when he did it was too late, a severe blow from a blunt object rained down on his skull with such force the assailant thought he heard an echo bounce on the still waters of Lough Ennell. The Earl was barely alive trying desperately to focus, struggling to recognize the face that was now just six inches away from his.

"Don't you recognize me; can you not see the likeness?"

Then removing his hood the stranger moved away just a little, allowing a shaft of moonlight to caress his face. Late thirties, early forties, rugged beyond his years, the result of his occupation no doubt and when he spoke he did so with a soft colonial accent.

"Please forgive my unannounced visit, your lordship. I can see by your vacant expression you still have no idea who I am. You don't recognize your own son." Then leaning in closer he whispered in the Earl's ear, "You heard me correctly. I am the bastard son you banished to the colonies, the result of your evil seed; therefore logic surely must follow logic. I now find myself in the enviable position of judge and jury but best of all executioner. It is my divine right to avenge the rape of my mother Sarah Flanagan when she was no more than a child. If it pleases his lordship I shall continue to dispense justice. How do you plead? Guilty or not guilty? What's the matter, have you lost your tongue? Have you anything to say before I carry out the sentence?"

Robert stared blankly at the night sky.

Slowly the young man stood upright, then looked down at the man he had come to despise and with no mercy he struck the fatal blow. After some time Sarah Flanagan's son began to cover his tracks, he deposited some of the blood and hair that got lodged on the baton he had just used to kill the Earl of Belvedere, his father, smearing just enough on the same rock Robert had just sat on was meant to suggest a heavy glancing blow. His death will be the result of a fall, I have no doubt, he thought. This adopted son of an Australian sheep farmer was not going to go to jail for what he saw as his duty to exact revenge. Making sure not to leave any evidence, the dark clad assassin walked carefree back into the shadows and with a ripple or two the little larch boat gently made its way to the opposite shore where an accomplice was waiting to ferry him to safety.

At 11pm Theresa Staunton was informed by her chambermaid that the Earl's supper had not been touched.

"He went for his evening walk about eight pm. Has no one seen him after that time? Ann, will you please talk to every member of the household and determine if anyone has laid eyes on the Earl?"

After some time and with no sign of the Earl, the household were instructed to search the entire estate.

When a lone messenger delivered the news of the Earl's death his children dropped everything and ran in the direction of Gaulstown Hall, just a mere four hundred yards away, with one objective, to free their mother from her long ordeal and beg her forgiveness. But what they found was a haggard old woman staring blankly, seemingly not recognizing her children until Mary slowly moved closer to her only daughter Jane.

She stood with a curious look in her eyes maybe a hint of a smile as she searched the young woman's familiar face wondering why she felt overcome with love. Mary gently reached out and softly stroked Jane's face with her wrinkled hand then said something that caused quite a commotion.

"He's dead, isn't he?"

"Yes, Mother, you are now free." Hugs and tears were in abundance.

At 2am neighbours began to knock on each other's doors.

"Did you hear the news?"

"The Earl is dead."

"Jesus, Mary and Joseph what in the name of god happened?"

"He had a heart attack."

"No, he was murdered."

"No, he was attacked by a pack of wild dogs" was another favourite. By 4am the villagers had all settled down but sleep was hard to find. Ned Flanagan was making a cup of sweet tea for his one true love when there was another knock at the door.

'Oh, for god's sake can yez not wait till morning to find out what happened to the ould bastard,' thought Ned as he made his way to the front door.

"Who could that be?" he shouted.

"Answer it," instructed Aideen Flanagan as she chuckled to herself thinking how happy she felt at this moment.

"What can I do for you, gentlemen?" enquired Ned.

"Can we come inside, Ned?" enquired the youngest of the gentlemen.

"Do I know yez?"

When the young man removed his hood under the light of the full moon Ned was overcome with emotion as he stuttered, "Our Sarah's boy" and as the tears began to flow the two men engaged in a long embrace.

"Who is it, Ned Flanagan?" enquired Aideen.

"Come in, it will soon be light, we don't want anyone to see yez."

With the door closed Ned ushered the young man and his companion into the kitchen. Aideen Flanagan walked into the kitchen yawning and tying the ribbon on her nightgown when she realised.

"Oh my god," she cried, "you're the spit of your mammy," as she welcomed the young man with a loving embrace. He introduced himself as Edward, the son of Sarah Flanagan and James Keegan, an Australian sheep farmer, then introduced his good friend and travelling companion Kevin Purcell.

"Your sister, my mother, died last year, Ned; my only regret is she did not live to witness what transpired here tonight. I don't have a lot of time, you will understand when the full extent of my actions this evening become apparent, the less you know the safer you both are. I had to meet you, Ned, for Mother never stopped talking about you, her favourite brother, and Bridie my grandmother – is she still alive for I need to convey a letter?"

"No, Edward she died of a broken heart a long time ago."

"That's not what I was hoping to hear, we will not see each other again in this life, Ned, but I hope we can all be together in the next. Now we must go. It was lovely to meet you, Aideen, god bless you both."

Belvedere was cordoned off while the authorities tried to determine the cause of death, the rumour mill was in full swing with the cause changing by the minute, from a fatal heart attack to a marauding pack of dogs and all in between. One witness claimed he had seen the silhouette of a small boat cross the lake in the early hours. It was too soon for the police to make a definitive statement, sources at Gaulstown were speculating that this was indeed a tragic accident, meanwhile most who knew of the Earl were pleased to hear of his demise and were anxious to witness the release of the Countess from her prison. A press release two days after the discovery of the Earl's body stated that the authorities were working on the assumption that this was indeed a tragic accident, declaring the case closed. Mary Molesworth spent the next few weeks regaining both her strength and what was left of her sanity.

"What do you propose we do with Gaulstown, Mother?"

In a weak voice she said, "Burn it and its contents to the ground. Let there be no trace of that abomination."

Mary's request was carried out with gusto. She was now free to implement her only wish, to join a convent in northern France, take a vow of silence and wait for her day of judgment. Mary asked to see Belvedere one last time before her self-imposed exile, for it was Belvedere she fell in love with all those years ago, not the wicked Earl. Only fitting she should say goodbye to her one and only true love.

O wicked Earl with your heart of stone
Your follies all built with rage
You tried to ruin our Paradise
With the guile of a Shakespearean Sage
I will search for the key that will set me free
To find my true love once more
So, we can walk hand in hand
On sweet Lough Ennell's shore
O I long to be on Lough Ennell's shore
At the dawning of the day
to watch the mist rise from your ancient isles
To the arch on Belvedere
Where under lock and key you kept a place for me
In the shadow of your jealous wall
You banished me from Belvedere
To your prison at Gaulstown Hall
O Belvedere sweet Belvedere
Our spirits are entwined
You are the cosmic setting
To blend subconscious minds
I will send all my love on the wings of a dove
To my true love once more
So, we can walk hand in hand
On sweet Lough Ennell's shore
Now children's laughter will echo once more
and music shall fill the air
Where love not hate will reverberate
On sweet Lough Ennell's shore.

End

www.ingramcontent.com/pod-product-compliance
Lightning Source LLC
Chambersburg PA
CBHW020359030726
47496CB00007B/2216